RUNNING
GIRLS

ALSO BY MATT BROLLY

Detective Louise Blackwell series:

The Crossing
The Descent
The Gorge
The Mark
The Pier

DCI Lambert series:

Dead Eyed
Dead Lucky
Dead Embers
Dead Time
Dead Water (prequel)

Lynch and Rose series:

The Controller

Standalone titles:

Zero

THE
RUNNING
GIRLS

MATT
BROLLY

THOMAS & MERCER

Published by Thomas & Mercer, Seattle

www.apub.com

Amazon, the Amazon logo, and Thomas & Mercer are trademarks of Amazon.com, Inc., or its affiliates.

ISBN-13: 9781662506161
eISBN: 9781662506178

Cover design by Lisa Horton

Cover image: ©Evannovostro / Shutterstock;
©MR. BUDDEE WIANGNGORN / Shutterstock;
©Mara Fribus / Shutterstock; ©Leonardo Alpuin / Arcangel

Printed in the United States of America

To the memory of my friend, Matt Wulff

Prologue

He couldn't remember how many times he'd been here or how many thousands of people he'd seen running along the seawall over the years. Until yesterday, no one had come close to that first one, but there she was—and here she was again, twenty-four hours later. How had he not seen her in the past? As he'd hoped, she was a creature of habit, once more gliding along the sidewalk as if she were floating above it, her gait so reminiscent of the first that she could have been her reincarnation.

The gait—the very word itself a siren call—was always the first thing he noticed. The subtle differences were undetectable to most—the length and speed of the steps, the pelvic sway, the elongation of the lower leg—but he discerned each and every variant with a voyeur's obsessiveness.

And he'd waited so long.

What appeared to be a regular running motion was disrupted every nine or ten steps, when her left leg would drag.

The similarity to the first truly was uncanny.

He'd spent so many months watching the first. Her disruption had also occurred on average every nine steps. Neither woman had a limp as such, but something on their left side had made them weaker. With the first, her deviation was the result of a dislocated ankle. A childhood injury she'd all but outgrown—a detail she'd revealed to him during those delicious few hours they had together. Heat prickled his skin at the memory. It was so long ago now but it was impossible to forget. There'd been accusation in her look, yes, but much worse was the bewilderment. That, he couldn't shake. The suggestion being that what he'd told her was nonsensical, that his obsession, and subsequent actions, were somehow laced with insanity. That look was burned onto his memory.

But now here was another opportunity.

Why the young woman ran the way she did, he didn't know. Maybe it was coincidence, or maybe she'd suffered a similar injury to the first. It didn't matter. She was inches away now. He could reach out and touch her tanned skin, interrupt that delicious gait in mid flow. Yet, although it had been so long since the last one, now wasn't the time. Slowing his own gait, the hint of the woman's woody perfume catching on the breeze, he watched her move away along the seawall.

Behind him, the island city continued as if nothing of note had ever occurred on its shore. It was summer and Galveston's white-gray sand was full of tourists. Things were about to change, and the discovery of the woman couldn't have come at a better time. With her perfume fading, the air carried a hint of salt and the taste of something danker, indefinable. He was attuned to the island's signals and wondered if the beach dwellers shared his instincts.

Back along the promenade, the outline of the woman dissolved. She had become one of many shuffling figures, but even from here he could make out her steps. She appeared to glide where others stumbled, the affliction of her left leg more a balletic charm than a hindrance.

He'd been here before, and he knew what was coming.

SUMMER

Chapter One

As the Greyhound pulled into the Houston bus terminal, Frank Randall experienced a surge of anxiety. He'd never really liked the city, and after so much time away the thought of so many people in one place was unnerving.

The trip here had been bad enough. He was used to crowds—fifteen years in a Texas state prison, and six months in a Huntsville halfway house, would do that to a person—so being cooped up for four hours in the company of strangers should have been a breeze. He'd been warned there would be a time of adjustment, but watching the various people board the dirty-blue vehicle had almost made him long for the inside.

He'd passed the miles in silence, the young woman sitting next to him not acknowledging his presence—her focus on the shiny gleam of her cell phone's screen, her ears plugged with white earphones. As the Texas wasteland scrolled by his window, Randall had searched for clues as to how the world had changed. They'd had television and access to the Internet inside, so the new styling of the motor vehicles, and the haircuts of those riding inside them, didn't faze him. Even the fascination with screens wasn't a surprise. He'd read articles about the new obsession with cell phones and tablets. He'd even developed a little obsession of his own, signing up to every educational class he could inside, the majority of which were conducted via online learning.

What use is that learning now, he thought, as he struggled down the stairs of the bus, his right foot catching on the metal lip, jarring his leg—broken inside—and almost sending him tumbling.

The driver made no move to help, his only response an accusatory glare as he pointed to the pile of bags at the foot of the bus, as if he knew where Randall had been these last sixteen years and the reason for his incarceration. Randall hobbled over to the luggage, his leg and back muscles tight. He was about to grab his duffel bag when the young woman who'd sat next to him pushed through to retrieve a pink monstrosity of a suitcase.

"Excuse me, ma'am," said Randall, but she was already gone, the suitcase following behind her on wheels.

Like Randall, the bus depot was stuck in time. The fumes of stale diesel and cigarette smoke kindled a memory. He'd made the journey to the city a few times with Annie. Unlike him, she'd liked the hustle of the place. The last time they'd visited they'd spent the night, catching an Astros game before spending a few hours in some trendy bars that had made him feel lost. Annie's appetite for life had always surpassed his and he'd often wondered how she'd hacked their life together.

Maybe it had been the gulf. As much as she loved the bright lights, nothing could compete with her love of the murky waters off Galveston.

More likely, she'd put up with me for so long because of the time I spent away on the refineries, he thought with a rueful smile as he recalled the passion with which she would always greet him when he returned from his time away.

Randall then crashed, as that happy recollection was dashed by the memory of the last time he'd seen Annie.

That catastrophic argument that had resulted in Annie striking him, before she'd taken Herbie on a walk she never returned from.

It was another hour before the Galveston Greyhound was due to leave. Randall battled through the hurrying crowd, feeling frail and invisible as he dragged his leg to the counter of a Starbucks and ordered a black coffee. The order-taker—his name badge declared he was a barista, but Randall couldn't get on with such terms—barely looked old enough for high school. When he asked Randall for his name, Randall's first response was to clam up, as if it was some sort of a test.

"So we know who to call for," said the boy, with a weariness that suggested it wasn't the first time he'd said those words to a befuddled old guy.

"Frank." Randall whispered the name, as if everyone was listening; as if someone would stop and say, "Aren't you the man who murdered his wife?"

Randall could still taste the coffee two hours later. Dank and earthy, it coated his mouth as if it had infected his saliva. The Greyhound to Galveston was less crowded and he'd managed to bag a seat on his own. Everyone was busy on their screens but Randall was entranced by the landscape. They were still on the endless gray track of the interstate, but the gulf was close. He felt it in his blood, imagined the smell of salt in the air beyond the confines of the bus.

When he caught his first glimpse of the water, as the bus approached the causeway into Galveston, Randall was surprised by his visceral response. He was a BOI—Born on the Island—and it was the only real home he'd ever known. He found himself crying for the first time since that night when the guard had locked his cell door shut. He tried to suck in the sobs, his body shaking as he forced the tears back. He rested his forehead on the cold, flat windowpane, his focus on the rippling waves, as he imagined the feeling of the warm water on his body, the sense the gulf always gave him of being part of something larger than himself.

People swarmed the shore, scuttling along the promenade and populating the beach. Randall wondered if any of them would know him. His social circle had been so small as to be nearly invisible sixteen years ago. Now, surely, only a handful of people would remember him, though he imagined the number who knew *of* him would be much greater.

He was on his feet the second the bus stopped. In another minute, he closed his eyes as his boot landed on the gray slab of concrete of the depot, the smell of salt-tinged air unleashing a thousand memories, each of which, one way or another, contained Annie.

Annie in a light, billowing yellow dress standing outside the pleasure pier as if she owned the whole town; Annie, naked, stepping into the warm gulf waters as he watched, mouth hanging open, tripping over his clothes to join her; Annie in her wedding dress, smiling as he leaned in to kiss her; Annie, scowling before turning away with Herbie, her red hair flowing behind her as she rounded the corner, never to return.

Would it always be this way, he wondered as he picked up his bag from the hot concrete. It didn't matter. It was a risk returning, but there was nowhere else to go. Seeing the house would bring back more memories, but he'd rather be trapped with the ghost of his wife than alone in a town where she'd never lived.

Randall ignored the line of taxis. What better way to reacquaint himself with his hometown than a three-hour hike home? His right knee cursed him but he dragged himself out into the bustling crowds, through the historic town center toward the port, the smell of the water, and the detritus odor of algae, combining poorly with the hint of ammonia in the city drains. He kept his eyes toward the ground like he'd learned in prison, but still felt alien gazes focused on him. He tried to picture what he'd looked like sixteen years ago when the patrol car had hauled him in. His hair was longer but thinner now, his eyes shadows of what they'd been. He was trimmer, but his skin felt loose and papery on him. What would Annie think of him now? He'd always been punching above his weight with her by at least two or three divisions, and it was hard to fathom why she would have stayed with him during this last transition into old age.

The heat and exhaustion finally got the better of him two miles along Seawall Boulevard. The thought of another two-hour hike to come was enough to pull him into a small bar and order a diet soda. He smiled as he made eye contact with the young barwoman. Like Annie, she had red hair, and her smile in return was enough to knock him off balance.

"I don't suppose you could order me a cab?" he managed at last.

"Where you going, hon?" said the woman, surprising him with a hint of Louisiana in her voice.

"Near Jenkins Road. A bit off the tracks, but there's a road."

From her jeans pocket, the woman retrieved a cell phone and arranged for the cab. Randall told her to keep the change from the ten-dollar bill he placed on the counter and left to wait for his ride outside.

Fifteen minutes later, a silver car glided soundlessly to where he stood. The driver buzzed down his window. The man looked to be about Randall's age, though he carried it much better. Healthy tan, teeth an impossible white. "You Randall?" he said. "Jenkins Road?"

Randall nodded. "Close by it," he said, opening the back seat of the cab.

"Holiday?" said the driver, the car making a barely perceptible humming sound as it glided away.

"I have a place there."

"How long you lived out there?"

Randall glanced out of the window, unsure how to answer the question. "All my life," he said eventually.

Twenty minutes later the driver dropped him at the foot of a dirt track that led to his old house. "Sorry, can't risk taking her any further."

Randall thanked the driver and watched him ease the car away before beginning the short hike. The vines and bushes surrounding the track were denser than he recalled but he supposed lots could change in sixteen years. Chattering cicadas accompanied him as he made his way across the baked earth, the noise from the insects incessant as if they were welcoming him home. Randall's boots slipped beneath him for no good reason, and every few steps he had to adjust his stride as a dull ache hit his knee.

As Randall rounded the corner to the house, he half expected Herbie to come bounding toward him. He pictured the dog, a golden retriever/Labrador cross, straining on his leash as Randall was pushed into the back seat of the patrol car, the dog's eyes wide and pleading as the second of his owners was taken away from him.

The windows of the house were boarded up, and as Randall placed his hands on the soft wood he shivered involuntarily, his blood running cold. The lock on the door had been changed, the old set of keys he'd been handed back on discharge worthless. Randall dropped his bag and slid to the ground. The late afternoon sun was still high, and although his body was coated in sweat, he couldn't rid himself of the coldness.

He sat that way for some time, even though Annie wouldn't have wanted him to mope. She'd have told him to get to his feet, to start fixing his situation before dark crawled up on him.

"Best do as she says," he muttered, hauling himself up. Heat returned to his body as he searched the back of the house, his effort rewarded when he uncovered a set of rusted tools in his old shed.

As he pried loose the first of the boards from the front window, the musty smell of the trapped air leaking toward him, he heard the distant noise of an approaching vehicle. He stopped, the sound of his heart thumping in his ears. The cicadas stopped chattering as the engine roared, then faded into nothing.

Randall continued working on the boards but he was aware of something heading his way. It was the same feeling he used to get when Annie and Herbie returned from their walks. A change in the air, in the quality of the few sounds that reached them out here, before he could hear the dog trampling everything in his path to see him again.

He'd managed to free the final board, glimpsing inside of his former home, by the time he heard the footsteps behind him. He eased around, expecting the worst, as he'd done on a daily basis for the last sixteen years.

Three men stood maybe ten yards away. They all appeared older than him, but that didn't make them any less of a threat. Randall recognized one of them. The man was twenty years his senior, but still had that iron-backed rigidity Randall had always respected and feared.

"Frank," said the man, nodding his head half an inch.

Randall blew out a deep sigh and lowered his eyes. "Warren."

"I heard they'd let you out. Didn't think we'd see you down here again."

"No, sir," said Frank.

Warren Campbell was Annie's father. He'd been the chief of police at the time of Randall's arrest. Randall appreciated why Warren was here; knew firsthand that his sense of justice went beyond that of the courts. Randall opened, then shut, his mouth. He could plead and explain, tell Warren what he'd told him all those years ago, but he would have had better luck talking to the cicadas. Warren, like everyone else, needed someone to blame. Otherwise, Annie's life and death made no sense.

Randall understood that and, although he wanted to run, he held his ground as the three men moved toward him.

Chapter Two

Sometimes Laurie felt as if she had only two body shapes: plump and muscular athlete. David had hinted on more than one occasion over the last year that she was overdoing it, and glancing down now at her short, stocky legs, bulging as she pumped the pedals of her road bike, she was inclined to agree with him. There wasn't an inch of fat on them, but they still looked bulkier than before. Whirling beneath her saddle as if independent from the rest of her body, Laurie let them guide her along the seawall, her speed creating its own breeze, which drifted through her shoulder-length auburn hair and cooled the hot jets of sweat coating her skin.

The exercise bug had started as a means to shed the baby weight and had soon developed into an obsession. She'd signed up for a triathlon in Houston, but that goal wasn't what motivated her. Exercising made her forget, if only for a time.

She almost declined the call. She had her earphones in, the tempo of the music driving her onward, helping her to not remember, and the interruption of the call was an annoyance. But curiosity got the better of her and she answered.

Little in this town escaped Laurie's attention. When the informant who'd called her told her that Frank Randall had been seen at the bus terminal, all thoughts about continuing her ride disappeared. Fortunately, she was only half a mile away from her apartment.

She hurried back and dumped the bike inside. Changing into her tennis shoes, she retrieved her firearm from the safe and headed to her truck.

Her first thought had been to call David, but he was away on work and telling him now would only make him worry. Her husband had lived for sixteen years without Frank Randall in his life, and could survive another couple of weeks without having to know that his father had returned.

Laurie's more pressing concern now was David's grandfather, Warren Campbell. Campbell was the ex-chief of police. If Laurie knew Randall was back, she could be sure as hell that Warren had found out too.

As she headed out to Randall's old place, Laurie tried Warren's number, cursing as it went straight to voicemail. She'd always got on well with her now grandfather-in-law, had even taken his surname since David had disowned his father's surname. She'd been a rookie detective when Warren was chief. He'd been well respected and liked by her colleagues. On the few occasions they'd talked, he'd always been supportive and encouraging, and it had been a sad day when he'd retired.

However, she often wondered if Frank Randall would have ever left his home alive if Warren had found him the day Annie died. She could picture the scene as if it were yesterday. She'd only been on detective duty for two months and it was her first big case working alongside her mentor, Jim Burnell.

Randall had reported his wife missing when their dog, Herbie, had returned alone after leaving for a walk with Annie three hours earlier. Randall claimed he'd spent the next two hours with Herbie trying to find his wife before calling it in. When Laurie arrived at the scene, Warren was already there. He'd been talking to Randall, who'd looked shell-shocked. Warren was up in his face, the conversation only going one way, as if somehow Warren already knew what Randall had done. Only Burnell's intervention stopped Warren doing something he may have later regretted.

Annie's body was discovered three days later. Although half ravaged by the local wildlife, there was enough of her left to enable an identification. Laurie winced as the memory of Annie's twisted body played before her. She'd been found on her side, one knee higher than the other, one hand on her hip, the other extended before her. One of the CSI commented that, had she been lifted from her prone position, it would have looked as if she was running. Annie had died from a savage incision to her neck that had severed her carotid artery. The autopsy would reveal that her legs had suffered multiple breaks and fractures, the patellae on both legs cruelly dislocated, both ankles snapped into unnatural positions. It was not known if the injuries had occurred before or after her death.

Randall pleaded innocent but, although the murder weapon was never found, the evidence soon mounted against him. The DNA evidence found on Annie was damning, if partly explainable due to the marriage, but what sank him was the skin samples found under Annie's nails, which matched the wound Randall had on his face at the time. As the case developed, people came forward claiming they'd seen the Randalls arguing on numerous occasions, with one important witness describing seeing the couple arguing near the Camino Real area on the day she died. Eventually, Randall changed his plea to guilty. His lawyer somehow managed to plea bargain, and although he was convicted of homicide, Randall used the defense of *sudden passion* to mitigate the charges against him and was sentenced to a maximum of twenty years.

Laurie met David during the preparation of the case against his father, but their relationship didn't start until a year later. By that

14

point, Warren had changed. Since then, Laurie had seen a similar change in too many parents who'd lost their children. Usually, they looked older, as if the life had literally been sucked out of them. It had been different with Warren. He'd had that hounded look too, but something in him had also hardened during that period. He'd remained a strong and loyal grandparent to David, and had been there for both of them during their recent troubles, but something had been lost in him the day his daughter's body was found, and now she was worried he was going to try and get it back, her fear intensifying as she spotted Warren's truck blocking the turn into Randall's old house.

Laurie parked up next to the truck, her legs heavy from cycling, her shorts and T-shirt still sodden from perspiration. The track up to Randall's house was only just recognizable beneath the vines and barnyard grass, which appeared to have been left unchecked since Randall had been taken away. She'd been able to drive up the track during the investigation but a hundred yards in now and the weeds had swallowed her up. The hush, broken only by the sound of the insects, was unnerving, as if the land was holding its breath.

She found herself drawing her firearm. Now would be the right time to call in the situation, but, right or wrong, she wanted to try and contain it herself.

She saw Warren first as she reached the end of the track. Despite his advanced years, he loomed above his two companions, his back iron-straight. She recognized the two men flanking him, Warren's old deputies, also retired. Between them they totaled nearly two hundred years, but she knew that wouldn't stop them from giving Randall a beating. Or worse.

Laurie placed her hand against a solitary oak tree, distracted by the sight of a gnarly vein snaking up the back of her hand and bisecting a thick ridge of muscle on her forearm. Behind the men, the house where David had lived as a child was in serious disrepair, which wasn't surprising considering it had stood sixteen years abandoned.

Randall stood before it now, in front of a hole in the house that had once held a window. Prison and age had shriveled him. He stood hunched, a weary acceptance in his eyes. Laurie caught a glimpse of David in his facial figures, and it appalled her to think Randall would have been baby Milly's grandfather, had she survived her birth.

Angling herself so the oak's low-hanging branches hid her, Laurie sucked in a breath as Warren stepped toward Randall and gut-punched him. Randall collapsed around his fist, then sank slowly to his knees in the dirt.

Laurie thought about David, the trauma inflicted on him by his father's act, and wondered what he would do now, if he were in her position. Would he intervene or would he join in with his grandfather? She feared she knew the answer, and guiltily felt pleased that he was away on work.

Randall didn't try to fight back. Warren's deputies stood guard as the old chief hauled Randall to his feet, only to knock him down again with a vicious blow to the face.

Laurie wasn't one for vigilante justice. She was straight when it came to matters of the law, and that made her feel like the worst kind of hypocrite as she remained silent even as Warren kicked his former son-in-law in the groin. Again, Randall sagged to the earth.

How long could she let this last? How far would Warren go?

One of the deputies went to pull Randall to his feet, but Warren stopped him. She heard him tell Randall to stand, his voice deep and resonant in the thin air. Randall was like a rag doll. He scrambled feebly in the dirt for a time, as if his bones had stopped supporting his body, before at last struggling to his feet. Laurie was less than fifty yards away but she could see his body shake. A line of puke mingled with blood on his shirt. Surely he couldn't take much more of this.

Warren began moving to and fro, as if he was winding himself up to do something unspeakable. That was, finally, enough for Laurie. She stepped out from the shade of the tree, a fierce blast of heat hitting her as she rushed along the dead ground toward the abandoned house. "Warren, that's enough," she called out, just as the old chief pulled Randall in close.

At first, she thought Warren was whispering something in the man's ear, but Randall's scream soon dispelled that notion. Only then did Warren turn to face her, as Randall fell to the ground with blood pouring from the flap of gristle where Warren had bitten his ear.

Warren wiped blood from his mouth and the absence Laurie saw in his eyes was the most terrifying thing she'd seen in a long time. Drawing close to them, she glanced at the former deputies, who both at least had the good sense to look apologetic.

"Laurie?" said Warren, some measure of life returning to his eyes.

"That's enough now, Warren."

Warren began nodding like one of those toy dogs you saw on the dashboard of cars. Laurie went to him and gripped her grandfather-in-law by the shoulders. He'd aged a decade in the last minute. His face was a crisscross pattern of deep grooves, his skin tanned and pitted with patches of white like an abstract painting. "Warren, you with us now?"

Warren glanced at his deputies, who hung their heads like chastised dogs. "I'm sorry, Laurie. You shouldn't have had to see that."

Randall was slumped against the house, watching the conversation as if his life depended on it.

"You get home now, Warren," Laurie said. "OK?"

Warren appeared set to argue, then, to her surprise, nodded.

"All three of you get going now," she said, "and there'll be no need to talk anymore about it."

Randall remained quiet as the deputies helped Warren down the path, as though he were the one who'd taken a beating. Laurie watched him stumble, his legs giving way every now and then, and wondered what she was going to say to Randall. After all, he was David's father, was now her father-in-law, though the only time she'd ever interacted with him was during his arrest and incarceration.

"You're Laurie?" said Randall, as Warren and his minions disappeared. "David's wife?"

Laurie forced herself to turn to him, to take in the damage. Randall's right eye was already swollen, his wounded ear pouring blood, but he didn't act as if he was in discomfort. His cracked lips were formed into a smile. "I'd heard that David got married. I'm so pleased for you both."

Laurie felt the sigh build up deep in her stomach. Randall looked like a harmless old man. The flesh on his arms was loose, pale skin hanging from his bones like flaps of a tent. He'd had sixteen years to consider what he'd done, but Laurie couldn't succumb to sentimentality. Weak and frail as he was, the man had killed his wife; had murdered her husband's mother. She would help him with his wounds but anything else would be a betrayal.

"Why did you come back?" she asked, peering through the hole where the window had once been. The interior was surprisingly well maintained, with original furniture and a number of dust-coated photo frames that Laurie refused to focus on.

"Where else would I go? This is my home."

Laurie stepped past him and through the opening, her leg catching on the rotten frame and tearing the skin above her knee. She moved toward the kitchen area, ignoring the sound of scuttling activity on the floor. With little hope, she tried one of the faucets, the pipes groaning to life but producing nothing except a blast of fetid air and a few brown drops.

The cupboards were bare beyond a few cans of tinned food and Laurie eased her way back to the opening, fighting the desire to leave, to be away from the man who had caused so much hurt for David.

Randall hadn't moved. The blood had dried on his swollen face.

"I have some water and a first aid kit in the car," she said. "Are you OK waiting here?"

"Nowhere else to be."

Laurie hesitated. "Maybe we should get you to hospital," she said, glancing at his gnarled ear.

Randall looked genuinely perplexed. "What, this?" he said, after some thought. "This is nothing. Compared to . . ." he began to say, his words faltering as Laurie turned and made her way back to the truck.

By the time she returned to the house, Randall had moved. Laurie dropped the canister of water and first aid kit, her hand hovering by her gun. She'd been pleased to see that Warren's truck had gone but her paranoid side made her wonder if he'd parked further on and made a different way back to Randall.

"Mr. Randall," she called, the sound of her voice reverberating in the open patch of ground. As her voice faded, it was replaced by the sound of the gulf's waves carrying in the breeze. Where usually she found the sound comforting, in the desolation of the surroundings they somehow became threatening.

She gave a start as Randall shoved his swollen head through the opening. "Just throwing together something to eat," he said, as Laurie moved her hand away from her holster.

The door creaked open as she approached the house, Randall standing at the threshold like a welcoming friend. "I've made some soup. Just instant stuff, but still," he said, as Laurie stepped through the door.

"Now, how did you manage that?" she said, gesturing at the lone light bulb dangling from the ceiling.

"I had the juice switched back on before I came back. I guess David or someone has looked in on the place now and then? I'm surprised as you are that it's all working. I even have running water."

Laurie couldn't recall David ever talking about maintaining the place but didn't comment. "You're planning to stay then?"

"Nowhere else to go."

Outside, the sky was darkening, the sound of the surf louder, as if it was encroaching. "May I?" said Laurie, putting on some latex gloves from the first aid kit.

Randall nodded, wincing as Laurie checked the swelling on his face, the tear on his ear. He felt insubstantial to her, so light and frail a breeze might carry him away. "Nothing appears to be broken, but you should get that ear seen to. How do you feel?"

"I'm fine," said Randall, smiling.

"Any dizziness?"

"I'm fine, thank you for your concern."

Laurie took a last look around the house. It was hard to imagine David living here as a child. Harder still to accept the old man standing in the kitchen area was his father. Curiosity got the best of her and she picked up a framed photograph from the dust-filmed sideboard. She wiped the glass, and an image of David as a teenager, standing next to his parents, emerged behind the dust. He looked so happy, his smiling face an almost perfect younger version of the smiling man standing next to him.

"He was about fifteen then," said Randall, returning from the stove. "That's the little beach up the way. He used to go swimming there every day. Does he still swim?"

"Yes, he loves swimming. We both do," said Laurie, forgetting herself. "I have to get going," she said, placing the picture back.

"You'll tell him you saw me?"

Laurie saw such pain and hope in the old man's eyes that she had to look away. "I'll tell him."

"OK then. Well, it was lovely to meet you properly after all this time," said Randall, walking her to the door.

Laurie turned to face her father-in-law. Instinct made her want to return the compliment but she faltered. "You look after yourself," she said, turning and heading back through the clearing toward her truck.

FALL

Chapter Three

Laurie edged closer and closer to the shore, her limbs acting under their own volition. She'd been running for seventy minutes now and hadn't planned to stay out so long. When she'd left the apartment, she'd had no destination in mind. She'd simply wanted to escape the silence, to enter a different type of solitude: one of her own choosing. David had grunted in response as she'd said goodbye, not lifting his head above the sports section of the newspaper. Outside, she had started running and hadn't stopped. Now she found herself down on the sand, not completely sure how she'd reached this spot.

Such was her level of fitness her body worked on autopilot. She plowed through the damp sand with no thought, her heartbeat faster than resting but steady. Even the music in her earphones didn't really register. She was in a void and at that moment she felt as if she could run forever.

The argument had started last night. They'd both had a glass of wine and she'd tried to initiate something between them. She'd placed her hand on David's thigh as she'd leaned in for a kiss, only for his whole body to stiffen as if a spider had run across his chest.

"Jesus, David, do I repulse you that much?"

At least he'd had the good grace to be embarrassed. "Don't be stupid," he'd said, but his heart hadn't been in it.

"How am I being stupid? You flinched when I touched you. Actually flinched."

"I'm just not in the mood."

"Not in the mood? I wanted to kiss you, not fuck you."

David met her eyes. It had been over a year since they'd last had sex. The first few months had slipped by unnoticed, both of them too engulfed in grief for it to even be a consideration, and soon, unwittingly, it became a thing. It wasn't just the sex. Laurie missed the intimacy. Before, they would spend every evening on the sofa watching junk TV, limbs entwined. They would take walks to the shore, hand in hand. Now they sat in separate armchairs and rarely went out together. She couldn't remember the last time they'd even kissed beyond a perfunctory goodbye peck on the cheek.

Milly had died fourteen months ago. She'd been stillborn, Laurie having to endure an induced labor with the knowledge that her baby had died. She'd experienced so many horrors in her working life, but nothing had prepared her for that. And although David had tried as hard as he could to be supportive, something had cracked inside him.

Not that she'd remained the strong one. She'd joined the abyss David entered that day and she still wasn't clear of it. Neither of them had been great at talking about it. Although David had suggested counseling a number of times, Laurie would have preferred it if he'd ranted and raved. He had every right to feel the world was against him. His father had murdered his mother and now his little baby had died before she'd taken her first breath. It was the insular behavior she found hardest to deal with, mainly because it so much mirrored her own. David carried Milly's death like an invisible burden within him, as if it was his and his alone. She didn't begrudge him his grief, but she couldn't help resent his refusal to share it with her. Last night's argument wasn't the first and Laurie feared the same result every time she opened her mouth.

A group of young men drinking from brown paper bags appraised her as she ran up the beach toward the promenade. Laurie came close to stopping, to ask the sneering idiots what they thought gave them the right to look at her that way, but her legs kept pumping.

She should have felt good about her appearance. Every ounce of baby fat had disappeared and her body was a hard slab of muscle, but still she hated her reflection. Even now, David always made her feel good about herself and wouldn't accept her negative self-appraisal, but she couldn't see what he saw. Whereas he claimed to see perfection, she saw the same short, stocky schoolgirl she'd seen throughout her teenage years, only now with added bulges of muscle that made her feel even less feminine. She worried that her body's new shape was a factor in David's lack of interest in her.

Reaching the east jetty, she turned for home. The wind had picked up and whistled through her ears as she upped her pace for the final stretch. She loved these moments, her heart racing as her body began to fatigue. She wondered how long she could keep going at this pace before her heart snapped, and although she was so breathless she couldn't speak, she pulled up outside her apartment block with a smile on her face.

In the apartment, David was on his laptop, a fresh coffee on the table in front of him. "Good run?" he asked.

Laurie nodded, still breathless.

"Grab a shower and I'll fix you some lunch," said David.

She appreciated the gesture and although it was his subtle way of apologizing, it was also his way of ending the discussion. If Laurie brought up the argument, she would be the bad guy. "I'm not hungry," she said, heading toward the bathroom.

She heard the front door shut as she was drying. She hated prolonging the quarrel, but she couldn't let him off this time. How long did he think they could go on like this?

Some day off, she thought, as she prepared herself a sandwich. Sitting on the chair vacated by her husband, she tried to recall a time she'd felt less lonely and came up blank. She would have preferred to have been at work at that moment and was already looking forward to going back tomorrow.

David had left the laptop on and Laurie glanced at the local news site to see if she'd missed anything exciting that day. With a stab of regret, she took a quick look at his browsing history. David had been looking at articles about his mother's death. He'd been in his twenties back then, and Laurie wished she'd known him before that time. He'd always been a kind, sweet and funny soul, but she would have loved to see him when everything had been normal in his world.

She clicked on the link to *The Galveston Star* from years ago. The headline read: "Mutilated Body Found on Beach." Below was a picture of the ambulance that had taken Annie Randall from the place her body had been discovered.

Laurie had been a junior detective then, recently transferred in from Houston PD. After viewing the twisted remains of Annie Randall, she'd then accompanied Frank Randall to the hospital, where she'd endured watching him identify the bloody remains of his wife. She'd been surprised when the arrest finally came. It hadn't crossed her mind that Randall could be responsible for his wife's death. It had been a hard lesson to learn. A lesson that became harder three days later when she finally tracked down David at the offshore refinery where he'd been working.

It was a peculiarity that they never discussed: their first shared words had been when Laurie told David his mother had died, and that his father had been arrested on suspicion of murder. One of her first interactions with her now husband was to console him as he broke down in tears. Not an ideal start for a relationship, she supposed, though she had to concede she'd love to see something

28

even distantly approaching that level of emotion from him now. She would do anything to see tears in his doleful blue eyes, for him to fall to his knees and nestle into her as he'd done back then. Now he was a shell. He was hurting, but he was either unwilling or unable to share that hurt with her. And, yes, she resented him for it. He made her feel like she was to blame, both for his sadness and for what had happened to Milly.

It couldn't go on. She snapped the laptop shut, deciding she would end this impasse today, one way or another.

◆ ◆ ◆

Two hours later, and David still hadn't returned. As Laurie changed, she noticed another vein, this time on the back of a calf muscle. She pushed at it, recoiling at its springy texture, and quickly covered it up with a pair of jeans.

She called David's cell phone but it went straight to voicemail. Where the hell was he? Laurie paced the apartment, unwittingly putting extra pressure on the leg where she'd spotted the enlarged vein. Should she go after him? Like so many things in their marriage, they hadn't talked about the return of his father two months ago. When she'd told him Frank Randall was back, David had shrugged as if the information was nothing out of the ordinary. As far as she knew, he'd yet to pay his father a visit.

However much he would protest to the contrary, Frank's return weighed heavy on David, and Frank returning to David's old family home must have rekindled so many old memories.

The apartment felt like a prison. Laurie pulled on her coat and left, determined to find David and sort things out. She tried their local bar first, the bar they'd visited on their first date, eighteen months after the sentencing hearing that sent Frank to prison. The bartender told her David had left twenty minutes before, which meant she'd either missed him on the way there or he'd headed to another bar to continue his drinking. Her guess was the latter. His drinking wasn't yet at the problem stage, but it had been trending steadily in that direction for some time now.

The wind had picked up further and Laurie pulled her jacket closer as she moved up the block. She already feared the look David would give her if she tracked him down. She pictured the surprise and disappointment and it was almost enough to make her turn back. When had things gotten so bad that the thought of seeing her husband made her cower so?

Instinctively, she placed her hand on her stomach. Where once it had curved, for a time full of life, it was now a flat plate of lifeless muscle. The thought made Laurie blink back tears, her anger at David intensifying.

She walked toward the Strand where she'd run into David all those years ago and he'd surprised her by asking her for a date. She could recall that night with perfect clarity. The smell of sea salt in the air, the day's residual heat softening the sidewalk and lending a sense of hope to their encounter. He'd been different then. Not only from the man he'd now become, but from the man she'd encountered during the Randall investigation.

David had initially refused to believe it when his father had decided to change his plea to guilty. Laurie had taken him to see Randall in the county jail where he'd been held prior to the sentencing. Although she hadn't witnessed the meeting, she'd been told by the prison guard the pair had argued vociferously and after that day, David had refused to speak about Randall any further. To this day, she didn't know what had been said between them. If Randall had confessed to him, David had never told. She hadn't blamed him for that. David had lost one parent and was about to lose a second. Who would want that? Who would want to admit that their father was capable of such a horrific crime?

As part of her liaison role as a junior detective, she'd stayed in contact with David for three months after the verdict. During that time, she'd seen acceptance gradually wash over him. He'd grown up so much in that short time, faced up to things that would have destroyed most people. He'd struggled and although he'd refused her repeated suggestion of counseling, she'd felt after the last appointment with her that he'd been close to putting things behind him.

And on that night in the old quarter, he'd been full of hope and promise. He'd just been offered a new six-month rolling contract and his life was again full of possibility. Laurie had worried that seeing her would only remind him of his father's conviction, but if anything the shared experience somehow brought them closer.

Being here now threatened to tarnish that memory. She was so angry with him, not just for today but for the whole of the last year. She stuck her head through the door of every bar in the Strand, part of her pleased every time he wasn't there, and was about to head home when she saw him at the counter of a coffee shop. A surprising relief washed over her, as if he'd been missing for months, her heart rattling in her chest at the sight of him even though she'd seen him a couple of hours ago.

That relief soon dissipated as Laurie watched him carry over two drinks to a table where a woman Laurie had never met before sat waiting.

Chapter Four

The sound of the gulf. It was the first thing that reoriented him every morning; that took away the dread that he was still in a prison cell. His ears clung to that distant noise as he lay half-conscious, bypassing the screeching of the grackles and the ever-growing howl of the wind. It launched Frank Randall's morning routine—forcing his eyes open, maneuvering his weary bones out of bed, dropping him to perform the twelve meager push-ups the dwindling muscles on his upper body would allow him.

On this morning, like every morning since he'd been back, he opened the front door of the house and let bright sunshine flood the interior, the rich, earthy aroma of the grassland carrying in the morning air. As he did every morning, Randall thought about Annie and how she would have loved this peaceful moment, while still being eager to get out to explore their surroundings, to get her daily fix of the shoreline.

Brewing coffee on the stove, Randall considered his plans for the day. He'd spent the last couple of months fixing the place up until it resembled something close to the home he'd once shared with Annie and David.

He drank the coffee outside. The wind was strong but its currents warm. He smiled as he sipped the bitter drink, thinking he was now more alone than he'd ever been in prison. The last person he'd spoken to was his daughter-in-law, Laurie, who'd paid him another visit last week. Aside from her occasional appearances, and his exchanges with the delivery driver who brought him groceries every couple of weeks, he had little to no human interaction. The few people he did see on the shore steered clear of him, as if the stink of prison coated his body.

When he asked Laurie about David, her face would falter and she'd quickly change the subject. She was a lovely woman and he wasn't sure why she checked in on him. She let on that it was because of David, but Randall was pretty sure she kept her little visits secret from her husband.

He'd come to accept that David would never come to visit him and had made peace with the fact. He welcomed the little snippets Laurie offered him, but knew she was withholding information. Something had happened between Laurie and his son, and Randall sensed she wanted to tell him. He saw the pain in his daughter-in-law's features and wished he could help. Wished he was allowed to try.

A few weeks ago he'd given Laurie a letter for David, but every time he mentioned it she would just shake her head. He'd never tried that when he'd been in prison. David had made his position very clear after the sentencing.

Randall would never forget that look from his son as his sentence was read out. David had been sitting in the gallery, next to Warren. Randall had already known by then that he'd lost everything, but the sound of the judge announcing his guilt had still dizzied him, had changed something within him, as if the same DNA that had helped assure his conviction had been reorganized in his cells. David had exchanged a look with him before shaking his head and looking away. Randall had realized at that moment that not only had he lost his wife forever, he'd lost the whole of his family.

That he'd been all but forced to plead guilty by his lawyer made no difference. Randall told David his reasons for pleading guilty the last time they'd met, in a stinking interview room in the county jail. If the case had gone to trial and he'd lost on a not-guilty plea then he risked life imprisonment, or even the death penalty. Due to his previous good record, his lawyer had managed to arrange a plea bargain agreement that would see his sentence lessened. But for that he had to admit to killing Annie, and that was something David was unwilling to accept.

Finishing his coffee, he decided to postpone once again the painting of the fence. The delay would give him something to look forward to. It was still early morning, so if he set off now, he could reach the shore and make it back before lunch. He packed a water bottle and, after glancing at the sky, pulled on a rain slicker before shuffling off toward the beach.

At one time he used to run to the beach and back again. Even after running along the water for the length of the beach, he would be back within an hour. Now, his age and fragile knee meant it would take twice as long just to reach sight of the water. Not that he cared. If it wasn't for this, he'd be finding other ways of delaying painting the fence. If recent days were anything to go by, that would probably involve slouching around the little house trying his best to fight the thousand memories the place held for him.

Gray clouds accompanied him as he made his way down the dirt track, which he'd cleared over the last few weeks. Sweat dripped down his face, the slicker suffocating his skin, but still he felt the cold in his leg. The stabbing pain in his knee had reached his bones. He stooped and considered returning, dismayed to see the house still in view. When had he become so decrepit? Age had crept up on him in prison, his youth stolen from him along with his liberty.

He cursed under his breath and dragged his leg onward, determined to at least leave sight of his house. It was another hour before he crossed the main road and walked on the wooden panels protecting the dunes. He stumbled at the summit, sliding ten yards down the sand before his right foot caught in a rabbit hole and pitched him face-first into the powder. Laughing, he rolled over and sat up. Sand, small patches of grass, and, above, the pastel-gray cloud surrounded him. He knew he shouldn't remain sitting for long—it would make it all that harder to get back up—but for now, he was content to sit and admire the patterns the wind made in the sand. As the wind drifted over him, carrying loose sand that stung his dry skin and caught in his mouth, he half expected to see Herbie come bouncing over the lip of the dune toward him.

Even though the dog had been dead these last sixteen years—Laurie had told him he'd died not long after Randall was imprisoned—he was still disappointed when he didn't appear. *Maybe that is what I need*, he thought, as he got to his feet and continued walking. A dog would alleviate his loneliness and give him a reason to get up every day. Maybe the next time Laurie called round, he would ask her about helping him get one.

He couldn't tell how long it had been since he'd set off. Although prison life had been regimented, the days, months, and years had soon become meaningless. It had all been reduced to simply lost time, and Randall had the same disrespect for the blurring passage of time now he was on the outside. His life was now centered solely on his grocery deliveries—the only thing he had to be present for. He didn't wear a watch, and his estimate of the time of day was based on the level of light, something that was currently hard to read, with the low-hanging clouds.

His knee screamed in pain as he approached the shoreline, but the view was worth it. Strange how the mere sight of the rolling waves could so instantly infuse in him such a sense of peace. It was the one thing he'd had in common with Annie from the beginning; probably the thing that had kept them together all those years.

In too much pain to continue, he dropped to the sand once more, his bones rattling as he landed. Beneath the gray skyline, the outlines of the oil refineries in the shadowy distance gave the whole scene an alien aspect. It was truly like nowhere else on Earth and the ache of loss he'd endured in prison—both for Annie and for this place—returned to him. He'd lost his wife, his family, and, for the last sixteen years, his home. There was little else they could take from him.

He closed his eyes, and for a second he escaped his body. He was running along the shoreline once more, his heart pounding as he scythed through the sand, knowing that Annie was waiting at home for him.

When he opened his eyes, he thought about the area where Annie's body was discovered, on the approach to Camino Real. He could pinpoint the exact spot. Thickets of trees and wild grass decorated a two-hundred-yard stretch of land next to a channel of water. Blood raced through Randall's veins at the memory. He hated the way nature had continued unabated by his wife's death; the world should have stopped turning at that very moment. He touched his face, remembering where Annie had struck him that day. The outburst of violence was as much of a shock these sixteen years later as it had been then. Her actions had been so out of character that he'd stood there, dumbstruck, as a rage he'd never seen before glared out at him from her green eyes, the letter she'd found held tightly in her hand. The swelling in his face had never fully gone down; he could still feel the slight curve around his eye. It felt fitting that the injury that had effectively led to his imprisonment had never completely healed.

As his frail body settled deeper into the sand, he thought about how he would give up everything just to revisit that moment with Annie. To hold her after she confronted him with the letter and struck him. To rectify the situation, instead of allowing her to walk away.

"Now why the hell are you sitting in the sand like some kind of lizard? Don't you know there's a storm coming?"

A shiver ran down Randall's spine at the sound of that voice. He summoned only an incomplete memory before turning around to face its source, wondering how he'd forgotten the face of the man staring down at him with his hand outstretched.

Chapter Five

The image of the man's face was blurred by the glare of the sun from behind him, the glow surrounding his features making him look like an angel.

"What are you doing here, Maurice?" Randall asked.

"If the mountain will not come to Mohammed . . ."

Maurice was Randall's elder brother by four years. As they shook hands, Randall scanned his memories for the last time he'd seen him. However long it had been, the years had been as unkind to Maurice as they had to him. In Maurice, he saw a slightly bulkier version of himself. His eyes even carried the same haunted look, as if they expected something to happen at any second, the skin surrounding them an array of interwoven, haphazard lines and grooves.

Letting go of his brother's hand, Randall was struck by an unknown fear. Although they were out in the open, he felt trapped, cornered. The sky felt low, as if the clouds were falling toward him.

He stared up at his brother. "How did you find me?" he asked.

"Where else would you be?" Maurice's eyes scrunched together in concentration, as if he were trying to read Randall's thoughts.

Maurice was a preacher, or had been. Randall had no way of knowing if that was still true. He couldn't, for the life of him, remember the last time his brother had entered his thoughts.

Certainly not since his release. Even in those indeterminable days in his cell, he couldn't recall once thinking about the man who was staring back at him now as if he were trying to unravel a particularly tricky puzzle.

"I need to go home," said Randall, the sense of entrapment yet to dissipate.

"Here, let me help you," said Maurice, taking him by the elbow after seeing him falter.

The pain in his knee had flared to life, and he grimaced as Maurice hauled him to his feet.

The sky and land could sometimes play tricks on you, and Randall found himself back outside his house as if no time had passed at all.

"After all that happened," said Maurice, as Randall unlocked the door, "I can't understand why you would want to return here."

"It's my home."

Inside, Maurice lifted a family picture from the mantelpiece. Wiping dust from the glass, he said, "Does it help you face up to what you did?"

Randall didn't much care for the way his brother stared at the picture of Annie and David. "It's my home, right or wrong. It's where I belong."

"You've done your penance, Frank. There's no need for you to be living here with these ghosts of what you once were."

"What would you have me do?" said Randall, heating coffee for them both at the stove.

"That's why I'm here. I want you to come live with me."

◆　◆　◆

Randall wound down the window of Maurice's truck, as the vehicle shook and jarred its way down the path. The sense of claustrophobia had returned, his chest tight as he sucked in the air from outside. He looked behind him to see his duffel bag in the back seat of the car. A fragment of memory came back to him from earlier. Him falling faint, and Maurice handing him some water as he loomed over him. They'd talked but Randall couldn't recall much about their conversation, though at some point he must have agreed to this journey.

The sky was a rolling canvas of gray and white as they drove along Seawall Boulevard. Randall hadn't returned here since that first day back on the island. He welcomed his relative solitude in his house, but it was good to see people now and again. As the landscape scrolled by, he snuck glimpses of families strolling across the promenade, lovers hand in hand, a group of young men unloading their jeeps so they could fish on the jetty, and was reminded how he had become an outsider in his own town.

"Remind me where we're going, Maurice," he said, as they stopped at a crossing.

"My home," said Maurice, his eyes not moving away from the pedestrians walking in front of the windshield. "My church."

Again, Randall was struck by how little he knew about his brother. He recalled he was a preacher, but had no idea where he lived, or even what denomination he was. They had never been a particularly religious family growing up. Their father had been a quiet man who worked offshore for most of the year. Randall recalled going with his mother to a church as a very young boy, though he wasn't sure he could trust his memories. They were always picture-perfect snapshots. Beautiful, cloudless summer days where everyone was smiling, the men in their pressed suits, the women in their glorious flower-patterned dresses. Without fail, his memories from those formative times were tinged with happiness, even though that had all changed when his mother left.

He didn't ask for any more details. As Maurice headed over the causeway, Randall's energy began to fade and the pull of sleep became too much to deny. He closed his eyes and when he awoke an unknown time later, he was disoriented. "Where are we going?" he said, feeling ridiculous for asking such a question.

If Maurice was surprised, he hid it well. His crinkled face kept staring ahead, unblinking gray eyes fixed on the endless highway. "You're coming to stay with me for a few days, brother."

Randall had given up drinking long before his stay in prison, but the way he felt now reminded him of the fugue of inebriation. His reality was distorted. A little too real to be dreamlike, but distorted nonetheless. "I can't stay long," he told his brother. "I have my delivery soon."

Maurice nodded and kept driving.

The sky was darkening as they arrived at a small town on the outskirts of Dickinson, Maurice driving his truck up the pathway leading to a wood-paneled church.

"You live in a church?" said Randall, forgetting for a second that his brother was a preacher.

"I might as well. My place is at the back. Welcome to St. Saviour's."

Randall opened the truck door and swung his damaged knee down from it with a grimace. He missed his little place more than he'd have imagined he ever could, and searched for the memory telling him how long he'd agreed to stay here.

Maurice carried his bag to the small house to the rear of the church.

"You're still a preacher."

"Pastor Randall. Kind of catchy, ain't it?"

It didn't sound right to Randall's ears. Randall had been his only name for all those years on the inside, and it sounded wrong on another man, even if it was his brother.

As Maurice led him inside to the spare bedroom and invited him to freshen up, he recalled a time as children when Maurice had given him a beating for sneaking into his room one summer evening and going through his things.

"You need to do any stretching for that leg of yours?" said Maurice, standing in the doorway as if guarding an exit.

"It'll be fine," he said, sucking in the pain as he sat on the soft bed.

"Yep," said Maurice, shutting the door behind him.

Randall fought the urge to try the door, reminding himself that he was no longer in prison, but a guest in his brother's house. Still, it was hard staying in the room. There was a peculiar, unnerving silence, Randall straining his ears to hear anything beyond the hum from the bare light bulb above the bed.

Had they visited here once before? Him and Annie? It seemed like the kind of thing they may have once done, but he'd be damned if he could remember. *How I wish she was here now*, he thought, picturing her smile, her long red hair swept behind her shoulders, before a second picture came to mind. Annie's body close to the stagnant water, the strange way her body had been positioned almost as if she were running, the cruel breaks that had been made to her legs.

"Dinner's ready."

The sound of Maurice's voice jolted Randall. He couldn't tell if he'd fallen asleep or not, his mind still in its fugue-like state as he pushed himself off the mattress. He swore he could hear the sound of his knee creaking as he made his way along the wooden floorboards of the hallway to an ostentatious dining room, where

Maurice was already sitting behind a table large enough to accommodate ten or twelve people.

"You live alone here?" he asked, taking the nearest seat to his brother.

"I have to entertain," said Maurice, with a smirk. "Bible study class, church association meetings, that sort of thing."

Randall lifted his flatware and was about to start eating when Maurice stopped him.

"May we say grace?"

"Sorry, sure," said Randall, heat reaching his face. Like so many things in his present life, grace was now an old concept. Although he and Annie had rarely visited church, saying grace was one thing she'd insisted on. "It's good to give thanks," she'd say. "Even if we don't know who exactly we're thanking."

Maurice grabbed his hand and prayed, his palm surprisingly soft and smooth. "Please begin," he said, after he'd finished his words of thanks.

Randall nodded, and picked up the flatware again. The last time he'd eaten a meal with anyone else had been in prison and he felt just as uncomfortable now as he had back then. The room was too big, too empty for the two of them. A giant crucifix hung on the wall behind Maurice like a warning, Jesus's eyes glaring down on Randall as he ate, full of either accusation or pity.

"Why did you bring me here?" he said, after an interminable period of silence where each was forced to listen to the other chew his food.

"I'm your brother, Frank."

"I know."

"I want to help you."

"How, exactly?"

"I want to offer you salvation."

Maurice had beaten him on a regular basis until the day Randall turned sixteen. The beatings had never been particularly brutal, but were enough for him to live in a constant state of fear. Why he'd stopped when Randall had turned sixteen, Randall didn't know. Maybe it was because he was getting stronger, or maybe it was because their father had stopped the belt on Maurice at around the same age. Maurice had left for college not long after, and when he'd returned, he'd found God in a big way.

"I don't understand, Maurice."

"Why didn't you ever let me come see you in prison?" said Maurice, taking Randall by surprise.

Randall dropped his knife, his eyes glancing up at the accusing Jesus as he tried to recall any such request. "I didn't see anyone in prison," he said.

"I tried and I tried but always the same response. Why do you think that was?"

"Stop talking in riddles, Mo," said Randall, a familiar weariness coming over him.

"You've paid your debt to society, brother, but not to God. I can help you. Repent of your sins and it doesn't have to be too late for you."

Randall crossed the flatware on his plate. For the life of him, he still couldn't remember Maurice ever making contact with him at the prison, but one memory had returned, strong and unwavering. He and Annie had indeed visited this place once before, and although he couldn't recall sitting in this ridiculously decadent dining area, he did remember one thing.

Annie had hated Maurice after that stay, and had never once told Randall why.

Chapter Six

The irony was not lost on Laurie. Here she was, a senior detective in the major cases division, yet she had no idea why her husband had been meeting in secret with a woman she didn't know. Three days had passed since Laurie had found David at the coffee shop, and she still hadn't confronted him about it. She realized now, she'd immediately rushed to a number of conclusions and by the time he'd arrived home late that night she'd convinced herself he was having an affair. He'd gone to bed as if nothing had happened and that had been almost harder to accept than the perceived deceit itself. How could he be so relaxed about what he'd done, what he was doing? He could have at least acted guilty, or tiptoed around her. That he could carry on as if everything was normal had made her question everything about him and their relationship.

Her certainty that David was having an affair had faded the following day, but still she didn't confront him about his meeting with the woman. Part of her feared what he would have to say, and she still felt a little guilty for having spied on him at the coffee shop in the first place. Chances were high it was all innocuous, but why hadn't he mentioned it to her? He was about to leave for three weeks to work over in Texas City and still nothing had been settled.

They both hated these partings, or so she'd thought. She allowed David to envelop her in one of his bear hugs and for a few seconds it felt inconceivable that he would ever betray her. As she grabbed him back, involuntarily taking in the smell of his deodorant through his sweater, she came close to asking him about that night but didn't want to reignite the argument from three days ago.

They eased apart, and as she watched him leave the apartment she wondered when it had become acceptable for them to keep secrets from one another.

◆　◆　◆

Work was always a distraction and today was no different. Lieutenant Filmore ordered her into his office as soon as she arrived.

Filmore was a short, squat man, his balding head dotted with patches of uneven hair. He had been her direct boss for over ten years now and they had a strong relationship. Filmore had an easygoing way about him, and rarely played the boss card.

"Missing girl case for you," he said, handing her a printout. "Probably nothing, but wanted to send my finest."

"But they weren't available so you settled for me?"

"Something like that," said Filmore, with a grin.

Ten minutes later she was driving toward Offatts Bayou with her partner.

"Haven't even had a coffee yet," Remi groused, as they sped along Seawall Boulevard.

"Should have got to work earlier," she said, smiling as he scowled, thankful she'd grabbed a cup before leaving that morning.

She'd been working with Remi Armstrong for the last three years, since his promotion to detective. Like her, he was an IBC—Islander by Choice—having moved here with his family as a teen from the Midwest. He was hardworking and diligent, and despite his youth Laurie trusted him implicitly.

"So," she asked him, "what do we have?"

"Eighteen-year-old girl, Grace Harrington. High school varsity athlete. Went out running last night and never returned."

"And we're finding out about this now?"

"Dad is away in Houston on business. Mom was out for the evening. Got home late and didn't check the girl's room. Became worried this morning when she wasn't up and ready for school. Called her friends, reached out to her social media groups, and no one has heard from her."

"Boyfriend?"

"Girlfriend. Tilly Moorfield. They'd had a little falling-out last night before Grace went for her run."

"Here we are," said Laurie, pulling down a private driveway to a Mediterranean-style property overlooking Offatts Bayou.

Remi whistled. "I didn't know people actually lived in these places."

"What, you think they were for show?"

"Something like that. Holiday homes maybe. Not the kind of place you look for on a detective's salary, now is it?"

"Amen to that."

There was already a police presence at the house. Two uniformed officers introduced them to Grace's mother, Sandra Harrington.

Sandra was a tall, slender woman in her fifties. She was wearing tennis shorts and a sports jacket, as if she'd been about to go for a run or to the gym. She guided them to an expansive, wood-paneled sitting room. "Call me Sandra. I know what this looks like. An eighteen-year-old girl not coming back for the night, big deal, right? But you don't know Grace. She would never stay out, especially on a school night. And if she did, she would have been with Tilly."

"Tilly Moorfield," Laurie said. "Grace's girlfriend?"

"Yes."

47

"Where is Tilly?"

"She's on her way over. They'd got into a bit of a fight, but Tilly is beside herself with worry."

"And Mr. Harrington?"

Laurie spent her life reading faces—David had more than once told her she could be a pro poker player—and the change in Sandra's features at the mention of her husband was subtle, but noticeable. The word *distaste* came to Laurie's mind as Sandra squinted and said, "He's on business in Houston. He'll be here soon."

"OK, let's go through this stage by stage, Sandra," said Laurie, catching a look from Remi that meant, *Why the hell isn't the father back by now?*

"I'll go and check on the teams," said Remi.

Laurie nodded, the understanding implicit that he was going to check on Mr. Harrington's current location, and turned back to Sandra. "Were you here when Grace went out for her run?"

"Yes. I left at the same time. It was easier that way, as I could make sure the alarm was set."

"You set an alarm?"

"Can't be too careful," said Sandra, her brow furrowing in concentration. "Why do you ask?"

"You had to disarm the alarm when you came back?"

"Yes."

"Did that not make you think that Grace hadn't returned?"

"Oh, I see. No, Grace sets the alarm when she goes to bed and is alone in the house. It's triggered by movement downstairs. I presumed she'd set it before going up." She swallowed with some difficulty and said in a choked voice, "I should have checked in on her."

"Would you usually do that?"

"No."

"Then, please, you can't blame yourself for that. OK?" Laurie let the woman compose herself before continuing. "Grace's run. Does she always follow the same route?"

"I don't think so, but she nearly always heads toward the West End. She likes to run along the seawall, like all the others."

"How long does she run for?"

"Depends. Can be thirty minutes, sometimes an hour plus."

"She's a varsity athlete?"

"Yes. Middle distance."

"Eight hundred and fifteen hundred?"

"Yes."

"She must record her training times. Does she have a device?"

Sandra glanced down at her slender wrist. "She has one of these," she said, pointing to the smartwatch on her wrist.

"Great. That links to a laptop, I imagine?"

Sandra's face lit up as if Laurie had just solved the case. "In her bedroom."

Laurie followed the worried mother through the house. It was quite a hike. The high ceilings and wide rooms made Laurie and David's apartment feel pitifully small and poky in comparison. In many ways, the place was the type of dream house Laurie had always wanted. She pictured herself here with David, an unnamed child playing in the garden, and was immediately struck by guilt, as if she were betraying Milly's memory.

"Here," said Sandra at last, leading her into Grace's bedroom. The room was nearly the same size as Laurie's apartment. Posters and picture frames adorned the walls, but the room wasn't what Laurie had expected. It was impeccably neat and organized. In one corner was a laundry basket, half filled with clothes. On the desk, the only visible thing was a MacBook laptop.

"She likes her order," said Sandra, as if Laurie had been waiting for an explanation.

Laurie pulled on some gloves. "Do you happen to know the password?"

"Grace hates it but we insist on it. I never look, you understand, but anyway . . ." Sandra said, her thoughts drifting away.

Sandra wrote the password down and Laurie entered it and was a little surprised when it worked, half expecting that Grace had been paying lip service to her mother. Within minutes she'd located the app that recorded the runs and clicked on the entry for last night. She stole a glance at Sandra as she radioed in her results to Remi. Sandra was staring blankly at the screen, trying to make sense of the route planner that showed Grace leaving the house, running toward the seawall, past the pleasure beach and back east up 25th Street where, at the corner of Sealy Avenue, the route had seemingly ended.

Chapter Seven

A light breeze had picked up and Laurie felt a little underdressed in her thin cotton jacket as she pulled up on the corner of 25th Street and Sealy Avenue, where Grace's route had abruptly stopped last night. Both the girl's watch and her phone were offline, their latest known location somewhere within a fifty-yard radius of where Laurie was standing beneath the shadow of a palm tree.

The app managing Grace's route had been paused when she'd reached this spot, having run the five and a half miles in under forty minutes. Laurie used the same app to measure her runs and would occasionally pause workouts if she had to stretch or stop for another reason. As she looked around at the patch of grass with its cluster of palm trees, and the gray buildings on the other side of the road, a number of scenarios came to mind: Grace stopping to speak to someone she knew, then someone she didn't know. An image of Grace pulling up in pain, another of her stopping to stretch, another to check her watch, which had run out of power. Each was as plausible as the next. The truth she'd shared with Remi on the way over was that chances were high Grace had bumped into a friend, had turned off her phone and watch to avoid detection, and was probably somewhere sleeping off a hangover.

"No CCTV cameras in this vicinity?" she asked Remi.

"No. If we follow Grace's route, the last cameras were the traffic cams back at the seawall. We're trying to get access to them now."

Laurie had studied the girl's training routes on the way over, and never before had Grace taken this turn inland. It was this anomaly that was maintaining Laurie's interest. If Grace hadn't gone up 25th Street, then Laurie wouldn't have escalated the case. As it was, she was invested enough to begin a full investigation and called Lieutenant Filmore with her decision before heading back to the Harrington household.

A young woman Laurie recognized from a photograph on Grace's laptop greeted her at the front door. "You must be Tilly?" she said.

An oversized hoodie went to the girl's knees, her bare legs giving the impression she had nothing on beneath. She was shorter than Grace, her squat, tough body shape reminding Laurie of the way she'd looked after Milly's birth.

Tilly frowned, tilting her head. "How do you know that?"

"Detective Laurie Campbell. Can I come in?"

Tilly opened the door for her, silent as if still in a state of shock. From another room came the sound of people arguing. "Glen is back," said the girl, sheepish as she led Laurie through the lobby area.

"Mr. Harrington?" said Laurie.

Tilly sucked in her cheeks as the noise level rose. "Just got back from Houston. He's worried, obviously."

Laurie wasted no time heading to the kitchen area, where the Harringtons were in heated debate. The last words she heard before both fell into silence were from Sandra: "Maybe if you didn't spend every single minute of your life away from your family, you would know a bit more about what was going on," she said, her face reddening as she saw Laurie arrive, Tilly on her heels.

"Detective Campbell, I didn't know you were back. This is my husband, Glen Harrington."

"Mr. Harrington, Laurie Campbell."

Mr. Harrington smiled, the gesture well practiced. He was a handsome man, six-two, short brown hair, and green eyes. He was a little too good-looking for Laurie's taste, too picture perfect, and the way he smiled instinctively put her on the defensive. "You can call me Glen. Where are we, Detective?"

Laurie ushered the pair to the kitchen table. "Tilly, please join us as well," she said, Glen's smile fading as his hand drifted toward, but didn't quite touch, his wife's.

Laurie explained what she had discovered about Grace's running pattern, and how the signal for the run had stopped at Sealy Avenue.

"You don't let her run there in the dark?" said Glen, turning to Sandra.

"I wasn't aware she went that way, no," said Sandra, struggling to keep her temper. "Tilly," she said, softening her tone, "did you know Grace took that route?"

"No, I . . . no, I had no idea," said Tilly, glancing at Laurie with wide eyes.

"According to her records," Laurie said, "it's the first time Grace ever went that way. At least, in the last six months. Can you think of any reason she would change routes?"

Glen Harrington planted his elbows on the kitchen table. "I was under the impression that she changed her routes on a daily basis."

"And how in the hell would you know that?" said Sandra, scratching her nose as if she'd smelled something distasteful.

Laurie wasn't surprised by the tension between the couple. Their daughter was missing and that brought with it a unique type of stress. But the Harringtons' body language suggested that the disharmony was present long before today. When Glen had moved toward Sandra's hand, Laurie had noted a stiffness in the wife's body and neither of them seemed to be willing to offer much support to the other. *In every dream home, a nightmare*, she thought. "Grace's tracking device suggests she did take different routes—different distances, inclines etc.—but her route never went up 25th Street. Chances are she just fancied a change, but is there anything you can think of that would make her run that way? Any friends in the area, perhaps?"

"Tilly?" said Glen.

Tilly had her feet up on the chair, the oversized hoodie riding down over her knees to her shins. She looked back at the three of them, wide-eyed. She looked so young that Laurie found it hard to believe she could be in a serious relationship with Grace, whatever a serious relationship for an eighteen-year-old looked like. She seemed out of place, and at that moment much younger than the glamourous figure of Grace that Laurie had seen in photographs. "We had an argument," said Tilly, her eyes watering. "It was so stupid. I'd seen her talking to Mia Washington in the cafeteria. I overreacted, and Grace accused me of being possessive."

"Mia Washington?" said Laurie, noticing the strained look on the Harringtons' faces as Tilly began to cry.

"Grace's ex," said Sandra, as Glen winced.

"And Mia lives in that area?"

"Around there, yes," said Sandra, "but I've already called her mother."

"You called her mom?" said Tilly. "Why?"

"Not now, Tilly," said Sandra.

Laurie looked from Tilly to Sandra, wondering at the strange dynamic between the missing girl's mother and girlfriend. "I think everyone needs to cool down," she said. "First things first. You talked to Mia's mother today, Sandra?"

"That's right. She said Mia hasn't seen Grace."

"Did you speak to Mia herself?"

"No, but Jane assured me."

"OK, I will speak to Mia. And I appreciate this is difficult for you, Tilly, but when did Grace date Mia?"

"They split up six months ago. They were together for about a year," said Tilly, oscillating between sadness and fury.

Laurie glanced at the parents, who nodded in confirmation. "And the split? Acrimonious?" said Laurie, as if talking about a divorce rather than a high school romance.

"Mia can be a little bitch," said Tilly, showing a different side of herself. "She spread some horrible rumors about Grace when they split."

"Rumors?"

"You know, sexual stuff," said Tilly, this time causing both parents to wince.

"I see. But they were still friends? You saw them speaking together?"

"That's why I couldn't understand it. Why would Grace ever want to talk to her again after what Mia had done?"

"Did you ask what they talked about? Did they appear to be getting along?"

The fury had overtaken the sadness in Tilly. "Mia brushed a strand of Grace's hair from her face, if that helps?"

Laurie took the address from Sandra and instructed the trio to await her return. In her car, she updated Remi. "I feel like I'm in that movie, *Mean Girls.*"

"Never heard of it."

"Well, you're not that long out of high school yourself, I suppose."

"Very funny. What did you think of Mr. Harrington?"

"They are a very attractive family, I'll say that much."

"Very high net value family too. During the week, Mr. Harrington spends his time in a penthouse apartment in downtown Houston."

"Does he now?" Laurie instructed Remi to begin the arduous job of speaking to the students and staff of the high school. "Check in with Filmore. See what resources he can give us. I'm hoping I'm going to find this girl shacked up in her ex's closet or something, but if not, we're going to need to move fast."

◆ ◆ ◆

The Washington household, although well maintained, was a few rungs down the food chain from the Harringtons' mansion. As Laurie pulled up outside the apartment building on Rosenberg Street, it made her wonder how the two girls had ended up at the same school. There were a couple of elite private schools in the area, and from what Remi had told her the Harringtons could have easily afforded to send their only child to one of those. She made a mental note to make a subtle enquiry to the Harringtons about it at some point, before walking inside the building and along the corridor to the ground-floor apartment.

The young woman who answered the door was tall and slender, with cascading brunette hair. It took Laurie a few seconds to determine it wasn't Grace Harrington standing before her.

"Detective Laurie Campbell," she said. "Are you Mia Washington?"

"Yes, ma'am. Is this about Grace? My mom said Sandra called earlier."

"That's right. May I come in?"

"Mia, who is it?" came a voice as Laurie stepped inside the apartment. The place had a much homier feel than the Harringtons'. Family pictures lined the hallway, an absence Laurie had noticed at the Harringtons', as the smell of cooking tomatoes drifted from the kitchen area.

"It's the police, Mom."

Seconds later, Mrs. Washington appeared. Like her daughter, she was tall and slender, the pair an almost carbon copy of Grace and her mother. Laurie imagined the four of them playing doubles tennis in a country club, Tilly Moorfield a bespectacled onlooker, and chided herself for making assumptions on appearances alone.

"Excuse me if I don't shake hands, I'm in the middle of making dinner. I'm Jane Washington. You're here about Grace. Still hasn't turned up?"

"Detective Laurie Campbell. No, I'm afraid not. May I ask you some questions?"

"Of course, please come through."

Mrs. Washington led her through to the open-plan kitchen, a miniature replica of the one at the Harringtons'. As she contended with the large pot on the stove, Mia walked over to the kitchen counter, where she was preparing a batch of cookies for baking. The sight of mother and daughter working harmoniously struck Laurie as being a little too idyllic. She struggled to picture Grace and Sandra Harrington together like this, which was perhaps a bit unfair, as she'd never even met the missing girl before.

Mia handed her mother a tray of cookies before sitting down on one of the tall kitchen chairs. "You don't think she's really missing, do you?" she said, in the same innocent way a child would ask the question.

"She hasn't been seen since yesterday evening, Mia. When was the last time you saw her?"

"Yesterday in school."

"You spoke to her?"

Mrs. Washington paused, staring at her daughter.

"What has that little Tilly been saying now?" said Mia.

"Mia, don't be rude," said Mrs. Washington.

"You spoke to her?" Laurie repeated.

Mia glanced at her mother before answering. Her head was nodding slightly, and Laurie suspected she was deciding how best to answer the question. "Yes, I spoke to her in the cafeteria," she said, after a few seconds' deliberation.

"That's news to me," said Mrs. Washington.

"I don't tell you everything, you know," said Mia.

"What did you talk about?" Laurie cut in. The last thing she wanted was to get involved in another domestic argument.

Mia sighed. "You know we used to date, right?"

Laurie nodded, silently urging the girl to continue.

"Well, it ended kind of badly, but we've been on speaking terms these last few weeks. We were in the lunch line together and we started talking. I can't remember what about."

Mrs. Washington had returned to her cooking, every now and then shooting a look at her daughter.

"Anything else happen between you?" said Laurie.

Mia smiled. "Look, I didn't mean anything by it. Grace had a strand of hair stuck on her face and I moved it. Next thing I know, Grace has sat down and is having a fight with Tilly."

Laurie rubbed her forehead. The last thing she'd expected that morning was to be umpiring some high school love triangle. "So Grace and Tilly had a fight," she said. "What happened next?"

"Grace stormed off one way, Tilly went crying to the restrooms."

"And you?"

"Me?" said Mia, as if the question didn't seem relevant. "I continued eating. No way did I want to get involved in that mess."

"Do you have any idea where Grace could be?" asked Laurie, studying Mia's reactions.

"No, of course not. Like I said, we've started talking again, which is a miracle in itself, but we're far from being close."

"Anything you can think of that would explain Grace not coming home last night? Has she been involved in drinking, or drugs, partying of any kind?"

"Who, Grace? You're kidding, right?"

"Not her sort of thing?"

"Grace is as straitlaced as they come. All she cares about is running. It's so boring."

"She was running in this area yesterday evening, toward your house," said Laurie.

Mia's eyes widened slightly, but beyond that there was little to her reaction. "She used to run here all the time. Nothing new in that."

"Are you sure about that? The app on Grace's phone suggested she hasn't run in this area for the last six months."

"What can I tell you? I think she got a new phone. Maybe when she switched, it reset or something? All I can say is that when we were together, she was running round here all the time."

◆　◆　◆

The rest of the day felt like a bust. Laurie returned to the Harrington household and with the help of Sandra recovered Grace's old phone, where the running app confirmed Mia's testimony. Printouts from the app were now pinned on a wall of the incident room. Zigzagging pathways from the previous year, where Grace had made daily pilgrimages past Mia's house, had stopped the day they ended their relationship.

Tilly was sheepish about the incident at school but confirmed Mia's side of the story. For Lieutenant Filmore, it was enough to explain why Grace had been in the area last night. That she had made the change of route on the day Mia touched her hair in the school cafeteria was explanation enough for Laurie too, but it didn't help locate the girl.

Remi and the team had spent the day interviewing kids from the high school. The consensus on Grace was positive enough. She was popular, though not in a cheerleader-type way. She was dedicated to her schoolwork and running. Most of the boys had a crush on her, and several of the girls, too. She was a very attractive young woman and Laurie knew that often brought with it unwelcome attention. Nothing was made of her sexual orientation, which was something that wouldn't have been the case at Laurie's much more conservative high school. All the students were questioned over parties and get-togethers last night, but seemingly nothing beyond the weekly meeting of the chess club at a local diner had occurred.

One minute Grace was running along 25th Street. The next it appeared she was plucked out of thin air. And at present, Laurie had no idea how or why.

Chapter Eight

How Laurie ended up outside the house in the Strand was a mystery even to herself. Filmore had insisted she leave the station at 9.30 p.m. after she'd spent the evening scanning all available camera footage for a sight of Grace Harrington. They now had a video of the young woman running along the seawall toward the pier and heading up 25th Street, where she faded out of sight as she moved toward Sealy Avenue.

Too restless to do anything else, Laurie had changed into her running gear, desperate for a slice of time solely for herself. Soon she'd reached the Zen-like state where her body took over and she became merely a passenger. But as she trawled the island's streets, she soon found herself near Offatts Bayou, following the route Grace had taken the previous evening. After reaching Sealy Avenue, she'd continued running, stopping a few minutes later, breathless.

As her pulse dwindled to her resting rate, she glanced at the old Victorian house with its white-paneled wooden front and knew exactly where she'd arrived. The subconscious was a mysterious thing. Her counselor had explained as much to her in those weekly meetings after Milly's death, and here was the proof. She'd spent the day focusing so intently on Grace Harrington and her distraught family that she'd barely thought about David and the woman until now, yet here she was standing outside the woman's house like some deranged bunny boiler.

She shouldn't even have looked the woman up, but it hadn't been that hard to track her down. David had befriended her on Facebook, and Laurie discovered the woman was Rebecca Whitehead, Head of HR at the oil company where David worked as an engineer. The extra clicks she'd taken on the database to find the woman's address had been a mistake, and she'd shut the search down with shaking hands as soon as the address had appeared on the screen. But her subconscious hadn't forgotten, guiding her to this affluent area as efficiently as the satnav system in her car.

What she'd hoped to find here was anyone's guess. Had she really expected to see David through the gap in the downstairs curtains? He was supposed to be in Texas City, but what if he'd come here instead? What if that was what he always did when he claimed to be working in Texas City?

Laurie pretended to stretch as a couple with a black Labrador crossed the street to within feet of where she was standing. She was being ludicrous, acting in a way she detested seeing in others: without thought and full of emotion rather than reason. Of course David hadn't been coming here instead of working. The money he brought in from his work was good, but it was also a necessity. Her salary alone would never be enough to maintain their lifestyle. That didn't mean she was wrong to wonder if he was having an affair—the name Rebecca Whitehead had never once been brought up in conversation before—but it did make it wrong for her to be here now.

She started running again, heading toward the sound of the gulf, her limbs working in perfect unison as she fled the scene of her crime. Her thoughts turned to Grace Harrington as she tried to ignore the fluttering sensation in the pit of her stomach. She imagined the sleepless nights the girl's parents would soon be experiencing, and it made her feel all the more guilty for wasting this last hour running to Rebecca Whitehead's house.

The tide was high as she ran along the seawall, with its perilous drops. *How easy it would be to slip off the edge into the shifting sand,* she thought, and run those last few yards to the waiting gulf waters.

She began running faster as the fluttering feeling resumed. Laurie understood the cause of the sensation. It was her body reminding her of when it was pregnant, the feeling akin to the kicking she'd experienced when Milly was growing inside her. And while she hated the cruel reminder, she conceded it was something she deserved. Despite what David, her family, and her counselor had told her, she needed to be reminded of her failings; of how she'd failed Milly.

If she could have closed her eyes, she would have. The scenery blurred past her as she moved her body at a speed she would have once thought impossible. There was a tension in the air that reminded her of the seconds of peace before a storm would unleash itself. It made her think that she was too attuned to everything—to the weather, to the sound of the waves, to the pain and worry of Grace's parents, even to David's possible need for infidelity. She'd failed him and couldn't really blame him for seeking solace elsewhere. As she sprinted the last hundred yards to her apartment building, she wondered if this was all for the best. Being together was a constant reminder of Milly. What if every time David looked at her, he recalled those terrible moments at the hospital? Who in their right mind would want to be reminded of that? Laurie was content to carry the weight of that burden every time she looked in the mirror, but she couldn't expect David to have to do the same.

It was late but she couldn't face the empty apartment alone. She rushed in and changed tops, grabbing a banana and her car keys before the emptiness threatened to engulf her. Heat oozed from her body as she sat behind the wheel of the car. Her fresh top was already damp from perspiration, her jogging bottoms wet and clingy like a second skin. She started the engine and began to drive, again allowing her subconscious to guide her.

Once again, she sensed the tension as she found herself back on Seawall Boulevard. It was probably all in her imagination, but the inside of the car felt pressurized, as if there was a great weight pushing down on it. She shifted in her seat as the shoreline blurred by, finding herself driving along Stewart Road toward the small property where Frank Randall lived.

Just as she'd arrived earlier outside Rebecca Whitehead's house without any forethought, Laurie couldn't recall the decision-making process that had led her back to her father-in-law's house. She'd visited him on a number of occasions since his return, neither of them ever discussing his conviction. She'd done so out of a sense of duty. They didn't know each other, but he was David's father, and would have been Milly's grandfather. She'd been surprised at how easily she was able to put his sins to the side of her thoughts. When she saw him, she didn't think about the savage killer he'd once been. All she saw was a weak and vulnerable old man who didn't have a single person in the world looking after him.

She parked and walked the narrow road, which was now much clearer than before. For the second time that evening, she was loitering outside someone else's property, the focus of her attention once more connected to David. A light was on in the old house, a beacon in the darkness that made the modest structure look like a place out of time.

The distance between the access road and the front door played tricks on her as she walked toward the building. All at once, sounds of wildlife and the roaring gulf reached her ears as if for a few seconds time had stood still. Her shoulders slumped as she hit the hard wood of the front door, the fatigue from her earlier run beginning to register.

The door creaked open, Frank Randall sticking his head out from behind the screen. "Hello?"

"Frank, it's me, Laurie. I'm so sorry to visit so late."

"Oh, thank goodness. Please, come in," he said, holding the door open.

Tension eased from Laurie's body as she stepped through the entrance. The place always had that effect on her. She didn't know if it was the connection to David, or the photographs that lined the walls and mantelpiece, but there was a homey feeling to being here that was a welcome relief from both the tension at work and the uneasiness of her apartment.

"Please, take a seat. I'll make us some tea."

Laurie only drank tea with Frank. She'd never asked him where he got them from, but he used spiced tea leaves that carried a hint of burnt orange. She collapsed into the armchair, sinking into the loose springs, and had to will herself to stay awake. Beyond a thorough cleaning, the place had changed little since Frank had moved back in. The dust had been wiped from the photos, and she smiled at the pictures of David in his various incarnations from baby to the young man who had attended Frank's sentencing.

"Thank you," she said, sitting up to take the hot mug from her father-in-law.

"You're here late," said Frank. "Not that it isn't lovely to see you," he added, a little panic in his voice as the cup shook in his hand.

"Just passing," she said, conscious of her sweat-soaked clothes. "Thought I'd check in on you. How have you been?"

"I've been well." His eyes darted to the battered duffel bag she'd seen him with on the day he was attacked by Warren and his former deputies.

Laurie took a sip of the tea, hints of cinnamon reaching her palate through the burnt orange. "Planning a trip?"

Randall squirmed in his seat, his eyes struggling to focus on her. "Just came back."

"Oh?"

"My brother. He's a preacher, over Dickinson way. Came by to see me and took me to see his church."

"I didn't know you had a brother. David never mentioned an uncle."

"Maurice. David never met him. At least, I don't think he did. Annie never took to Maurice. I'd forgotten. I never took to him too much myself. He used to bully me as a kid, and when I got old enough to defend myself, he became all Christian. Didn't approve of the way I lived my life. I didn't much care, but I did take Annie to meet him, and then something happened."

Laurie placed her cup down. "What?"

"I don't know for sure. Annie wasn't someone you could push for an answer. She would either tell you something or she wouldn't. There was no changing her mind. All she told me was she thought Maurice wasn't quite right and she didn't want to see him again. And that was enough for me."

They spent the next few minutes chatting aimlessly, Laurie's mind working overtime. Finishing her tea, she said goodnight to Frank, noting the faraway look in his eye as she headed off. The first thing she did when she reached the car was to check for a preacher in the Dickinson area by the name of Maurice Randall. She couldn't quite believe that David had never mentioned an uncle to her, nor could she recall the man being present for Frank's sentencing. She hadn't asked Frank if Maurice had any children, and wondered now if there was a whole side to David's family she didn't know about.

A hit indeed came in for a pastor by the name of Maurice Randall in a small town outside Dickinson. She zoomed in on the grainy image on her phone of Maurice's smiley face. She wasn't sure when the photo had been taken, but he looked ancient: an even more weathered version of Frank.

What the hell are you doing? It was past midnight and here she was, sitting outside her father-in-law's house—*A convicted murderer, don't forget that, Laurie*—when a few miles away a mother and father would be trying to sleep, sick with worry that they would never see their daughter again.

Laurie threw the phone onto the passenger seat and drove off. She tried not to think about it, but as she made her way back across the sleeping island, all she could think about was Maurice Randall and why David had never once mentioned him.

Chapter Nine

Guilt still played on Laurie's mind as she arrived at the station the following morning. Exercise usually kept her focused, but although she felt alert in her body, her mind was a whirlwind of thoughts encompassing the missing girl, Grace Harrington, David and his mysterious meeting with Rebecca Whitehead, and Frank Randall and the revelation about his brother, Maurice. She wanted to snap out of it and focus entirely on the Harrington case, but her mind kept taunting her with images of Rebecca Whitehead and the grizzled face of Maurice Randall. Personal issues aside, there were a number of other outstanding investigations demanding her attention, which she could have spent every waking hour working on and never clear.

It was 6 a.m. and the skeleton night shift were still in the bullpen. She accepted a few nods of acknowledgment from the tired officers before pouring some coffee and taking a seat at her vacant desk. The updates from the Grace Harrington investigation were minimal. She'd been missing for over twenty-four hours now, which was a crucial milestone. The hope still had to be that she would turn up shortly, her tail between her legs, telling woes about an act of rebellion that had backfired. Laurie had seen cases pan out that way so many times before that it was still a legitimate expectation. However, the number of people reported missing in the

States in any given year was staggering, with official cases exceeding half a million. A high percentage returned, but sometimes people were never seen again. Laurie wouldn't be mentioning it to the Harrington family later, but within twenty-four hours a missing person could effectively be anywhere in the world.

That's the kind of optimism we need. She heaved a sigh and looked around the depleted bullpen slowly filling up with the day shift. Blocking everything else besides the Harrington case from her daily calendar, she decided to upload the details of the Annie Randall investigation from sixteen years ago. Last night's revelation about Maurice Randall had started her thinking, and she couldn't shake the need to find out more about the man. Guilt had been her go-to emotion for so long now that accessing the case felt like just another millstone to hang around her neck. She tried to justify her actions by telling herself that she would be dedicating the next twelve to sixteen hours to Grace Harrington, but as she loaded the old case file onto her screen she nonetheless looked furtively about her, a gnawing feeling eating away in her stomach.

She only had access to the case files as she'd worked on the investigation in the past, albeit in a reduced capacity, but a note would be made on the system that she'd accessed them and she would have to give some justification for doing so if asked.

Scanning through the old images from that time triggered a visceral reaction, and she fought to contain her shaking hands as she scrolled past images of David and Frank during the hours following the discovery of Annie Randall's body. They both looked like different people from those she'd seen in the smiling family portrait in Frank's house. Here, they carried Annie's death, for different reasons, in their features. It would be easy to read too much into it, but she was sure she could see the guilt, and maybe something approaching confusion, in the eyes of Frank Randall as he was snapped at the crime scene, staring, as if in shock, as Annie's remains were taken away.

As for the image of Annie at the scene, that would forever be branded into Laurie's mind. She'd witnessed the crime scene firsthand, but that didn't lessen the horror of seeing it again. It was hard to fathom that the near-skeletal remains with the cruelly broken legs would have been her mother-in-law. Laurie had often thought about what their relationship would have been like. Annie had been a beautiful woman, and David had been happy to share both the photographs and the happy memories of his childhood with her. Tragedy could often distort the truth, but David's memories of his mother were so consistent and heartening that Laurie was sure they would have got along.

Hearing Remi arrive, Laurie scrolled to another page. It was a list of family members from that time, and there he was, Maurice Randall, brother of Frank. A statement had been taken from him, but he hadn't been present at the sentencing, which explained why Laurie hadn't remembered him.

"Do you live here?" said Remi, taking a seat opposite.

Laurie clicked the file shut. "No, I just like to get to work on time."

"Ouch. I turn up for work *early*, trying to make an impression . . ."

"Stop muttering, and get me another coffee."

"Yes sir, ma'am," said Remi, dutifully grabbing her coffee cup.

When he returned, they set about planning the day's activities. Remi agreed the Harrington case had to be the priority. He would continue quizzing the high school students, many of whom they'd yet to reach, and would make further inroads into the local residents and the CCTV images along the route Grace had taken.

"I'd like to dig a little deeper into the family dynamics," said Laurie. "Glen and Sandra's relationship appears strained, probably from Mr. Harrington working away so often."

"With that in mind," said Remi, "I was going to suggest I pay a visit to Houston. Quiz Mr. Harrington's colleagues. Maybe find out if anyone else has been staying in that downtown apartment of his."

"You old cynic."

"Easy on the 'old', there."

The suggestion that Glen Harrington was having an affair put her in mind of standing outside Rebecca Whitehead's house last night. She shook off the image, which portrayed her as a wide-eyed, sweaty, jealous mess looking through the windows of the Victorian house in desperation. She wasn't sure what relevance Glen Harrington having an affair might have to his daughter's disappearance, but there could never be enough information when it came to family. The sad truth was that missing person cases often involved family members. And at this stage they had to consider the worst. Abduction, abuse, even homicide had to be considerations, and the Harringtons' second home would need to be investigated.

"You're right about the Houston trip," said Laurie. "Get Abbey and Rodriquez to do the high school work. We can see how willing Glen Harrington is to give up the keys to his other home."

The breeze had picked up as they left the station. Galveston was usually quite temperate, even during the winter months, but was infamous for its terrible storms, many of which resulted in catastrophic damage. She hadn't really been listening that morning, but had heard something about a storm brewing near Cuba that could potentially reach the Texas coast. Such threats were commonplace, but still, she couldn't help but wonder if the quickening breeze was portentous.

They took separate cars, as Remi would be heading to Houston afterward, and arrived at the Harrington house at the same time.

"No beach today," said Remi, rubbing his arms from the cold breeze as they waited for the door to be answered.

After a couple of minutes, the door was opened by Tilly Moorfield. She was in her pajamas, having seemingly stayed the night. "Detective Campbell," said the girl, peering out from behind her large glasses.

"Hi, Tilly. You've met Remi, Detective Armstrong, right?" said Laurie, wondering why Tilly was here again. She'd noted the odd way Sandra and Tilly interacted, and if she hadn't known differently, she would have presumed the pair were mother and daughter.

"Yes, please come in," said Tilly, as if it were her house she was inviting them into.

Both Glen and Sandra were heading down the polished wood staircase. Sandra wore a white T-shirt and baggy jogging bottoms that hid the shape of her long legs, her husband in jeans and a Harvard sweatshirt.

"Manage to get any sleep?" asked Laurie as Sandra ushered them through to the kitchen, where a fresh pot of coffee was waiting.

"I don't think so," said Sandra, pouring two coffees for Laurie and Remi without asking.

Glen Harrington poured himself a drink, not looking at his wife. "What news do you have for us?" he said.

"Nothing just yet, but I can assure you we're doing everything we can," said Laurie. "As we said yesterday, if you can think of anywhere Grace may have gone. Friends or family members, even if not local to Galveston?"

"We gave you the list yesterday," said Glen, as his wife collapsed onto a kitchen chair with a grunt.

Laurie knew only too well how grief could take a physical toll. It wasn't until months after Milly's death that the pain of aching muscles, the sense of her internal organs being bruised and battered, began to fade. What troubled her now was that the Harringtons already carried those signs in their slumped body language, as if they were already grieving. Only Tilly remained alert. "Can you think of anywhere she would have gone?" Laurie asked the girl.

There was defiance in Tilly's eyes, a sense of fight that at the moment was missing from Grace's parents. "She wasn't unhappy, you know. Yes, we had an argument, but that doesn't mean she was so unhappy she wanted to get away from here."

"We appreciate that, Tilly," Remi said, "but it would still be good to eliminate every possibility."

"I don't think you appreciate it though. You're acting like she has run away, but I think it's worse than that." Tilly lowered her eyes, catching the concerned glances from the parents.

"We're not rushing to conclusions of any sort," Laurie said. "I need you all to understand that. Our aim is to locate Grace as quickly as we can, and to that end we need you all to think." She took a sip of her coffee, and then another, waiting for one of them to speak.

"You should check on that bitch again," said Tilly, running from the kitchen in tears.

"Christ, amateur dramatics time again," said Glen. "That's all we need."

"She's worried, Glen," said Sandra.

"Can't she be worried somewhere else?"

Sandra shook her head in dismay. "I'll speak to her, and together we'll figure out if there is anywhere else Grace could have gone."

"Thank you, Sandra," said Laurie. "There was one place we'd like to check out. Your apartment in Houston."

Laurie waited for the responses, but neither parent said anything.

"Could be a natural place for her to go if she wanted to get away from things," said Remi.

Glen sighed. "Why the hell would she go to Houston? She doesn't know anyone there."

"Maybe that's the point," said Laurie. "She may have wanted some alone time."

"Well, I doubt she'd get that there, would she, Glen?" said Sandra.

"Really? You're going to do this now?"

"Just give them the keys, Glen. I'm sure you'll have a couple of hours to get whoever is staying there out of the place before they arrive."

Chapter Ten

Laurie was back with the Harringtons when Remi called later that afternoon. She'd spent the morning organizing the overtime team Filmore had signed off on, and then returned to the house both to support and further question the family.

"I need to take this outside," said Laurie as her phone rang, passing Glen Harrington, who was glued to his laptop and didn't look up.

Sandra and Tilly went on making lunch. Despite the difference in appearances, Laurie thought again how easy it was to picture Sandra and the girl as mother and daughter. They had a comfortable way with each other, their exchanges—relaxed and informal, despite the huge stress they were both under—reminding her of Jane Washington and her daughter the day before. Tilly lived with her father, and Laurie wondered if the Harringtons' was an escape for her, a place of relative luxury she could slip away to when needed.

Turning her back to the biting wind—the temperature had dropped a few degrees from that morning—she answered the cell phone. "Tell me you have something good."

"Not so far," said Remi. "Getting access was easy enough, but no sign of Grace in the apartment."

"And the other woman?"

Sometime after Sandra's outburst in the morning, Laurie had taken her aside to find out if there was anything she should know.

Sandra told her that earlier in the year, Glen had been having an affair and had been using the apartment for his infidelity. Glen had assured her it was all over, but she had her doubts.

"No sign that anyone other than Mr. Harrington spends time here. No second toothbrush. I'll do a bit more searching, see if I can turn up some more subtle evidence."

Finding Grace at the apartment had always been a long shot, but with the day fading away, Laurie could have done with some good news. "Neighbors, doorman?"

"Blanks from both. The porter recognized the photograph of Glen Harrington, but he only works weekends so didn't know him by name. I've distributed photographs of Grace, and I'm about to trawl through the apartment building's video footage to see if there are any signs of her, or anything else relevant."

"OK, keep me posted," said Laurie, hanging up.

Wanting to give the Harrington household a break, she took a short walk around the block until she was by the water at Offatts Bayou, watching the boats and the traffic heading over the causeway. She couldn't shake the feeling that Remi was probably wasting his time in Houston. It was feasible that Grace had access to a passkey or had somehow managed to get herself in the building, but it felt increasingly unlikely. What was more likely was Remi catching a sight of Glen Harrington with his mistress in the video feeds from the last few days, and this would in part explain the man's reluctance to hand over the keys earlier that morning.

The discord between Sandra and Glen seemed to be growing, and from what Sandra had told her, this wasn't entirely due to Grace going missing. As Laurie rounded the corner back to the house, it was impossible not to draw a parallel between the Harringtons' relationship and her own. While David meeting with Rebecca Whitehead could easily prove to be innocuous, both relationships were being defined by what had happened, or was happening, to a daughter.

Laurie reached for her stomach. It was a rare moment, but so focused had she been on finding Grace Harrington that she couldn't remember the last time she'd thought about Milly. She guessed some would say it was healthy, but for Laurie it brought a fresh surge of guilt.

As she approached the house, she was taken by the absurd impulse to break into a run. She wanted away from the place, from the thoughts troubling her head. Running was something she could rely on, and she sensed the restlessness deep within her muscles. She wondered if Grace had felt that way when she'd taken the run the other night; if she'd been pushing herself to the limits, so that simple fatigue would help her forget herself.

And as Tilly opened the front door for her, Laurie's thoughts returned to Annie Randall, the twisted figure of her corpse playing in her mind as if she'd seen it for real that morning, and not on a computer screen. What strength of bitterness and rage had caused Frank Randall to take her life, and disfigure her in such an inhumane way?

◆ ◆ ◆

The same questions were still bothering Laurie later that evening as she sat behind her desk, double-checking the interviews and notes from that day. Filmore had told her to go home an hour ago, but with David being away for the next three weeks, the thought of a second night alone in the apartment, with no real insight into the missing girl, was not much of a motivation to get her moving.

The team had ordered takeout a couple of hours ago—her share of it a burrito, smothered in congealed cheese—and she regretted joining in. She was bloated and lethargic, and that, coupled with the frustration of the Grace Harrington case, made her restless, her calf and thigh muscles tight and in need of a stretch.

She checked in with Remi before leaving. He was staying the night in Houston, keen to chat with Glen Harrington's work colleagues in the morning, when Filmore and Laurie were due to hold a press conference. With every hour passing, the chances of finding Grace dwindled. If twenty-four hours missing was crucial, forty-eight hours was a milestone no one wanted to reach.

Deciding to run home, she changed in the lockers and ran a couple of miles to warm her muscles before stretching. As the ground disappeared beneath her feet, Laurie struggled to rid herself of the bloated feeling in her stomach. She felt full of air, despite the tightness of her stomach muscles, Milly's absence more pronounced than ever. She hadn't spoken to David since his departure to the refinery, and that added to her despondency. She had the absurd notion of running toward Rebecca Whitehead's house, but had the sense to resist it and headed for home instead.

She was still breathless as she opened the front door, but this time her exhaustion was doing little to dispel her thoughts. Changing into her nightwear, she poured some water from the fridge, and found herself staring at the wedding photos on the mantelpiece in the living room. Every time she saw an image of David recently, it was like seeing a different person. In this instance, he was nothing like either the boy she'd seen in the photographs at Frank Randall's place or the man she'd first met during the Annie Randall investigation. Here he was smiling and carefree, as if getting married was easing all the concerns of his past.

How she longed for that man to return. When she pictured David now, it was yet another different version she saw: the grief-stricken man she'd lived with these last fourteen months.

Laurie thought again about the parallels between the two of them and Glen and Sandra Harrington. She tried to tell herself that her relationship with David would never end up that way, but as she struggled to find some sleep, it dawned on her that maybe it already had.

Chapter Eleven

The morning light, breaking through the cracks in the blinds, tore Randall from a fitful sleep. The air inside the house was cloying, reminding Randall of the hours of lockdown he'd endured in prison. He hadn't been outside since returning from Maurice's house and was going a little stir-crazy. He'd seen it in prison, convicts losing their sanity—sometimes temporary, sometimes not—during periods of forced isolation. Randall had only endured the indignity of solitary confinement once, after becoming indirectly involved in a prison yard fight. The three days he'd spent alone in the windowless cell had been an experience he never wished to repeat. It had left him with too much time to think, to dwell on how things in his life had so easily unraveled. That isolation had been forced on him, and this was self-inflicted, but still it took all his will to push himself out of the armchair by the fire and move toward the front door.

Changing, he was surprised to find his walking boots were damp, and the smell of saltwater fresh on his rain jacket. He couldn't for the life of him remember what he'd worn or packed for Maurice's place, but it appeared to have included his raingear. No one had warned him how forgetful he'd become in old age. Or if they had, he hadn't appreciated it at the time. Growing old was likely impossible for the young to appreciate, he figured. Now, it was as if there was a piece of him that often went missing. An absence in his thought process, as if little gaps were being hacked into his memory. It seemed to have worsened since his return to Galveston, and staying inside wasn't helping any.

A gust of wind caught him off guard as he opened the door, forcing him to step back. That was another thing they didn't warn you about. When he'd married Annie, he'd felt like the strongest man on Earth, and nothing would or could take that away. Now it was as if that strength was draining from him on a daily basis, and it made him want to turn back inside.

Pull yourself together, you old geezer.

His younger self would be dismayed to see what was happening to him, and he owed it to him to at least try. He would walk to the shore and back, taking the easy route, and would ignore the pain in his knee that was already causing him to stumble every few steps.

He half expected to see Maurice waiting for him as he followed the well-worn track. Seeing him the other day had been like seeing a ghost, and when he thought about Maurice's house, and its adjacent church, a tight knot formed in his stomach, forcing him to stop and catch his breath. Annie had told him that she didn't like Maurice, and that had been enough for him. He'd never been that fond of his brother himself. But what if there had been more to it than that? Maurice had always been a little strange around women, even in high school. Randall hadn't quite understood it then, but Maurice had an uneasy way about him in their company. He'd never had a girlfriend that Randall knew of, and the thought made him feel a little uneasy. Annie had been unequivocal about her distaste for Maurice, but had refused to talk about it beyond that statement. What if Maurice had done something unspeakable to her when they'd stayed at his house? Randall hated thinking that way, but seeing his brother again had stirred these feelings of unease and it scared him to think that Annie had lived with something like that all her life in silence.

And if Maurice had done something to Annie, what else was he capable of?

The thought faded. The wind had picked up and he was carried along by it, the occasional grit of sand brushing his face, scratching his skin like sandpaper. *At least it'll make for an easy walk home*, he thought, as he listened to the distant drone of the sea, and the gulls with their never-ending operetta of squawking.

Time didn't behave in the way it used to, and he was on the shoreline without remembering anything else in between. A few people were on the beach, but it was easy enough for him to feel he was alone as he gazed out to the sight of an oil rig poking up from beneath the water, like a mirage. The decommissioned steel monstrosity was as much a part of the Galveston coastline as the rolling waves, but today it looked particularly alien and threatening in the gloom. Being back on the island was like being trapped in a memory. Every sight and smell was reminiscent of another time, and Randall's past here was full of memories of Annie and David. He guessed they called it déjà vu, but the arrangement of clouds, the rig, and the heady smell of the seaweed—all of it made him think he was back at the day Annie had been found. A devastating storm had been brewing then, and he wondered if another was on its way.

He half wished for a hurricane to appear out of nowhere now and carry him away. He wanted to be swept along on the twisting air currents, and forget who he was and what his life had become. After Annie's dad and his goons had attacked him that first day back, he'd been left alone, but no one wanted him back on the island. His only visitor was his delightful daughter-in-law, Laurie. Why she bothered, he didn't know, but her appearances were a wonderful highlight. She'd come by late the other evening and Randall had told her all about Maurice. She'd listened with a saintly patience and Randall had sensed she wanted to tell him something. He'd asked after David, as he always did, and had noted a moment of hesitation before he'd told her how Annie would have been proud of them both. She'd left not long after, and he'd felt her absence long into the night.

Randall shuddered as the sense of déjà vu returned. On that day, he'd reluctantly agreed to allow Warren to take him to the crime scene, and had looked on in horror at the sight of his wife's remains. It had all ended for him then. He'd become another person, in so many ways; the person he'd once been erased by what had happened to Annie.

He needed to get back, to escape the taunting weather. He half expected to stumble across Annie's remains as he staggered along the powdery sand back to the relative safety of higher ground. There were other people in the area, and he sensed them watching him. He was convinced they were judging him on every step he took, his bad leg catching behind him as he stumbled along the path, and he had to fight the sense that they were about to give chase.

And then all of a sudden he was back home, breathless and scared. Had he imagined it all? For now, he didn't care. Discarding his damp clothes, he lit the fire and wrapped himself in the blanket, hoping his memory would continue to fail until he reached the point where he remembered nothing.

Chapter Twelve

Laurie called David the moment she woke. Her fitful sleep had been disrupted by thoughts of him with Rebecca Whitehead, and she'd called without thought, determined to get some answers, only to regret the decision as she heard the phone ringing.

"Hey," said David, answering after four rings. "Everything OK?"

They tended not to speak during David's time away unless it was longer than a couple of weeks. David would always only be either working or asleep, but still, it felt like an unhealthy habit they'd slipped into. Laurie caught the familiar sound of static she always heard on these calls, and could at least rest knowing he was away at the refinery and not cozied up with the head of HR in her fancy old house. Though the possibility of that, however far-fetched it might be, angered her and she pulled the phone away from her ear for a second, noting how stubby her forearm looked. She jammed the phone back against her head. "Just checking in with my husband, if that's OK?" she said, squirming at the sound of her neediness.

"Of course it is," said David. "You sure you're OK, Laurie?"

Why couldn't she just come out with it? As a cop, she was used to interrogating in the worst of situations, so why was she unable to find the words *Are you having an affair?* Was it because she thought it was a ludicrous notion, or was she worried what he might say? "I didn't know that Frank had a brother," she said, the words falling from her mouth before she knew it. "Your uncle, Maurice?"

"What's this about?"

"Just something I'm looking into."

"You're looking into my dad's brother?"

"He was in town the other day."

David went silent, the sound of machinery humming in the background. "Was he? Why?"

"I went to see your dad. Frank told me Maurice paid him a visit, and that they went on a trip to Maurice's church."

Another pause. She pictured him on the other end of the line, taking deep breaths, disappointed in her once again. "Why did you go to see my dad?"

It dawned on her that David wasn't the only one who'd been deceiving. She hadn't wanted him to find out she'd been seeing Frank this way and regretted ever making the call. "He's a released convict. Police business."

"Jesus, Laurie," he said. "Why can't you ever let the past go?"

It was Laurie's turn to go silent. She thought he was referencing Milly, and the question felt like a gut punch. "What can you tell me about Maurice?" she asked, not willing to argue with him.

"He took him to his church?" said David, his voice deeper than before, a sign he was pissed with her.

"That's right."

"Why?"

"I don't know, maybe because they're brothers."

"I've never even met him. Mom always clammed up if he was ever mentioned. I always suspected something was up, but whenever I asked either of them about it, they refused to say anything beyond he was a preacher somewhere between here and Houston. What's all this about?"

"Just curious."

David's breathing was heavy down the line and Laurie wondered what thoughts were going through his head. "I better get going," he said, after an overlong silence.

"OK," she said, waiting for the line to go dead before placing the phone on the side counter. She was shaking, her left bicep pulsating as if electricity had been shot through her veins. Talking to David had accomplished little beyond putting them both in fouler moods. It had been the wrong time to call, and the wrong way for her to tell him she'd met with his father. Not only would David be furious with her, he would feel helpless and alone at the refinery, which may as well have been on the other side of the world.

As for his revelation that he'd never met Maurice Randall, that didn't come as much of a surprise. Frank had said as much when he'd explained that Annie had never wanted to see the man. The real question was, why was this bothering her so much?

The fallout from their call, and her lack of sleep over the last few days, had sapped her energy and she decided against a run. She'd work from home instead, having arranged to meet at the Harringtons' at 8 a.m. He was staying the night in Houston, keen to chat with Glen Harrington's work colleagues in the morning ahead of the press conference scheduled for later in the day.

When she did arrive at the house, it was Tilly who answered once again. One of Laurie's colleagues had interviewed Tilly's father, but seeing the girl had spent the night at the Harrington house again, it made Laurie want to speak to the man herself. Tilly was seventeen, and again it struck Laurie as odd that she wouldn't spend the night with her own family during such a turbulent period.

It didn't take long for Laurie to realize that things had taken a turn for the worse between Sandra and Glen. Glen was his usual sullen self as Laurie walked into the kitchen, but Sandra's eyes were red from crying. Not that this was such a surprise. The ordeal parents in situations like this went through was unimaginable to most people. It would either destroy or strengthen the Harringtons' relationship, and with what Laurie had so far witnessed of the pair, her money was firmly on the former.

"You OK?" she mouthed to Sandra, as she took the offered cup of coffee from her.

Sandra nodded but Laurie could see she was on the verge of breaking down in tears again. Now wasn't the time to prep the couple for the press conference. It was enough to be there for now, and Laurie quietly sipped her coffee and waited to be asked any questions.

"You not going into school today?" Sandra asked Tilly, as Grace's girlfriend joined them in the kitchen.

"I thought I'd be of more use here," said Tilly, glancing at Laurie for support.

Laurie shrugged, not willing to get involved.

"You'd be more useful going in and quizzing your friends," said Glen, speaking for the first time since Laurie had arrived.

"You leave her alone," said Sandra, her hand shaking as she filled a plate with freshly made pancakes from the pan.

It was another thirty minutes before Laurie began prepping the parents for the upcoming ordeal of speaking in front of the press. Grace's disappearance was already big news locally, and a number of state, and possibly national, outlets would be present at the news conference. "The more we get Grace's picture out there, the more chance we have of finding her," she told them, Sandra nodding noncommittally. What Laurie refrained from telling them was how much bullshit they would have to trawl through to find anything of use. Public appeals like this always brought out the crazies, and by that night they would have unreliable sightings of Grace nation-wide, but Laurie was convinced it was the right way forward. All it would take would be the slightest lead, a sighting that rang true, and they could be in business.

When she'd finished with them, Sandra walked her to the door and stood outside with her as she lit a cigarette.

"We'll see you both at the station shortly?" Laurie asked.

The breeze was up once more and Sandra's long hair fluttered behind her as she sucked on her cigarette, the lines on her face momentarily aging her. Laurie felt small and inconsequential next to the woman. Sandra was much taller, and up close to her, Laurie felt more like Tilly than the lead detective on the case.

"Of course we will," said Sandra, taking another drag, squirming as if she was inhaling poison.

Sandra remained outside the house as Laurie walked away, Laurie catching a final glance of her imposing figure as she rounded the corner: her long legs and flowing hair, the serene way she gazed out into the distance. Laurie imagined it was the way Rebecca Whitehead would look visiting the viewing platform at the refinery, as all the male workers vied for her attention. She wondered if she was onsite now, if she'd seen David at breakfast that morning, if they'd purposely ignored each other so as not to attract attention.

Arriving back at her car, she tried to shake the feelings of jealousy. She was sure she was projecting something that wasn't there, and had to admit part of her was succumbing to fantasy. How much easier it would be if David was having an affair. It would give them both a way out, a chance to start again. She wasn't sure if that was what she really wanted, but it was proving to be too much of a distraction. What she really needed to do was go for a run, and she regretted not having done so that morning. Restlessness crept over her body, and she couldn't clear her mind. The interconnectedness of the troubled relationships—the Harringtons; Grace, Tilly, and Mia; Frank, Annie, and David; and her own struggles with David—played through her head, as if they could possibly have any relevance to one another. It was ludicrous, of course. Relationships broke down all the time and nothing about her or the people she knew made them any different. But she couldn't shake it.

She thought about Frank and Annie arguing that awful day sixteen years ago—maybe it had been over Maurice?—and what could possibly have triggered a rage blinding enough for seemingly gentle Frank to take his wife's life in such a savage way. That led to thoughts of her and David, the more passive uneasiness they'd endured since Milly's death. She even briefly wondered if David had the same latent temper as his father, before shutting her eyes and hating herself for ever thinking such a thing.

That didn't stop her from heading out toward Frank Randall's place. David had accused her of being fixated on the past, and if he knew she was headed back to his father's house, it would only cement that opinion of her, but still she kept driving.

Galveston was at its windswept best as she drove past the seawall, the waves up, the dark clouds hovering close to the gulf. The sensible thing would be to turn back toward the station, but she couldn't fight the desire she had to see Frank Randall again, as if some sort of answer lay in his presence.

As she headed inland, it dawned on her that Frank didn't know about Milly; about how close he'd come to being a grandfather. She wondered how he would take the news. If she hadn't known about his past, she would have accepted Frank as the kind and thoughtful person she'd come to know these last few weeks. As it was, her cop instincts stopped her from fully accepting this side to him, knowing that it could all be an act. But even if it was, she was sure there was some compassion left in the man. David rarely talked about the past, but when he did he never had a bad word to say about his father—at least until that day that changed everything. People made mistakes, even terrible, violent ones, and she hoped it wasn't all a performance for her sake; David would never be able to forgive his father, she understood that, but maybe Frank had learned from the terrible thing he did, and was the kind and generous father-in-law she'd thought he might be.

Laurie didn't stop as she reached the turnoff to Frank's house, continuing along the road toward Camino Real. Whatever she made of her father-in-law, seeking him out now made no sense, not with everything that needed to be done that day. Pulling to a stop, she realized she was less than half a mile away from where Annie Randall's body had been discovered all those years ago.

Laurie didn't believe in serendipity, but she was here now and had forgone her usual morning exercise. It would do her good to at least take a quick hike, would help prepare her mentally for the rest of the day.

She was deceiving herself, but she didn't care. Pulling her raincoat from the back seat, dark clouds blacking out the midday sun, she locked up and began walking the narrow dirt path toward the grasslands. When she'd last been here, sixteen years ago, the place had been swarming with police officers and emergency vehicles. She'd walked this very same path with David, who'd been a stranger at the time. He'd insisted on accompanying her, Warren having already taken Frank earlier to identify what remained of Annie Randall's body.

It was a different walk now. Laurie was aware of how isolated she was as she crossed over the damp land, despite her proximity to her car. Feeling for her firearm, she was relieved to find it in place, even as she wondered what was making her so nervous. She was used to assessing threat levels, and could detect none now beyond the rough terrain and short sightlines, but still her pulse quickened as she reached the opening to the beach.

Some distant part of her understood she was denying her true thoughts. This had always been her destination, from the moment she'd set off from the Harringtons'. She would never call it a hunch, as she didn't believe in such nonsense. Hunches came from good detection, and her detection skills had subconsciously told her to make her way here. It was probably nothing, but then, most of what she did was fruitless. Detection was a numbers game, and she was here simply to eliminate a natural suspicion.

Still, she didn't call it in. She didn't want Filmore or the others to use it as ammunition against her. She was operating on little beyond her imagination linking Annie Randall's death and Grace's disappearance. Each had been out for a run after a quarrel with a partner. She knew her colleagues would tell her she was reaching, so would keep it to herself for now.

It was impossible to find the exact spot. Nature and time had changed the area beyond recognition. The tall grass seemed more abundant than before, and the water level was lower. Annie Randall's body had been found a good fifty yards above the maximum tide line. Most had seen this as an admission of guilt, that Frank Randall had wanted to get caught, otherwise he would have let her be carried out to the gulf. Laurie tried not to dwell on all that would have meant, beyond the fact it would have made it extremely unlikely that she would have ever met David. This thought sent a shudder of pain through her, as she guiltily thought that she would never have had to carry Milly for nine months; would never have had to experience the awful reality at the end of that period.

Her black thoughts were interrupted by a splash of color catching her eye in the reeds by the water. She darted across an inlet and, as she pulled aside the long grass, a vine whipping back and stinging the skin on her forearm, she discovered she'd made the right decision in coming here.

Chapter Thirteen

Randall felt more and more like a helpless child, as if his world was regressing. No sooner had he managed to get to sleep than he'd been woken by banging on the door. Such had been the intensity of the knocking, he'd expected the door to be taken off the hinges, and when he'd finally managed to struggle from his bed he'd been more than surprised to see his brother waiting for him.

"You left on bad terms," Maurice had said. "Let me make that up to you."

That had been hours ago. Now he was back at the rectory of Maurice's church, dipping a heavy spoon into the chicken broth Maurice had prepared for him.

He'd argued but Maurice had a way about him that Randall struggled to resist. Maybe it was the older brother thing, or the hound-dog look in Maurice's ancient eyes, but he'd eventually agreed to accompany him. It was only when they'd arrived back at the church, and Maurice had shown him to the bedroom once more, that he recalled the reservations he'd had last time he was here.

"What happened between you and Annie?" he said, before he lost his train of thought.

Maurice eased the spoon away from his mouth and placed it next to his bowl. "We've already discussed this, Frank," he said, as if talking to a child.

Randall couldn't recall any such conversation, though that in itself didn't mean it hadn't happened. "Well, we're discussing it again."

Maurice ran his hand over his mouth. "What exactly is it you want to know, Frank?"

"We came here once. When we were newly married. You remember that?"

"I remember."

The thought of Annie as a bride sent a flutter through Randall's chest. He'd never understood the meaning of having your breath taken away until he'd met Annie, but her beauty had done that to him over and over again. "Close your mouth, honey," she'd have to say to him when he gawped at her. He pictured her now in a long, flowing summer dress, her red hair billowing behind her, and the memory was almost too much to bear.

He needed to focus. "Something happened between you two," he said.

"Nothing happened, Frank, beyond a friendly disagreement over religion."

Randall shook his head, the smell of chicken broth souring in his bowl. "She never wanted to see you again after that. She insisted on it."

"Don't I know it. I lost my only brother."

"Come off it, Maurice. You never cared for me."

"That's not true," said Maurice, raising his voice. Man, he looked so old when he lost his temper. His face wizened as the wrinkles spread from his face to his mottled neck.

"You used to beat me. I remember that."

"For that, I'm sorry. Neither of us had a good role model when it came to acts of physical violence."

"I never beat anyone in my life," said Frank.

Maurice raised his eyebrows, and pushed his spoon into the thick liquid in his bowl. This time, a different image of Annie appeared in Randall's mind and he came close to letting out a scream.

Maurice wiped his mouth with his napkin and stood, his chair scraping on the wooden floor as he placed it under the table. "We had an argument over religion, nothing more, nothing less."

"What, specifically?" said Randall, remaining seated.

"I don't know, Frank, it was so long ago. I loved Annie like a sister, but she sure could be stubborn."

Heat rose in Randall, and he got to his feet. "You take that back, Maurice," he said, dismayed to see his hands shaking in front of him.

Maurice's expression had gone perfectly blank, as if he'd retreated into himself. It was the same blank canvas presented there whenever he'd been dishing out his beatings. "Very well," he said, after a long pause. "I'm sorry. Please, let's start again. Go and change. I have a quick meeting here, and then we can go for a walk."

By the time Randall had changed into his warm weather gear, he could hear voices in the kitchen. He didn't want to interrupt but curiosity got the better of him.

"Ah, Frank, come on over. I'd like you to meet Gerald Spencer and Neil Mosley. Gerald is the church's accountant, Neil the church's lawyer. Gentlemen, my brother."

Both men stood and Randall shook hands with them, the accountant surprising him with a vice-like grip that almost brought tears to his eyes. The lawyer's grip was easy, as was his manner.

"Sounds like a very corporate meeting for a church," said Randall.

The lawyer smiled, his deep-blue eyes looking intently at Frank. "So much red tape, you wouldn't believe," he said. "But we're all finished here now, I think? Gerald, shall we leave these two to it?"

The accountant nodded, and Randall was pleased that he didn't offer to shake hands again.

Maurice saw the pair to the door before pulling on his coat. "Shall we?" he said.

The weather was a little less blustery than in Galveston, but still had a kick to it that sent shivers through Randall's body. He disliked the little town as much as he disliked Maurice's church. Although Randall lived in all but perfect isolation in his house, this was a different type of remoteness. If felt like the town had been lifted from somewhere else and planted down in the middle of nowhere. The houses, each with its Stars and Stripes proudly on display, had their blinds shut tight as if hiding secrets from the world. When they did come across people, they all stopped to say hello to Maurice. It became apparent that his brother commanded respect in the area, and everyone was keen to meet Randall and to find out more about him.

"We have a very forgiving community here," said Maurice, as they continued walking to a wooded area on the outskirts of the town.

Randall tripped over a loose stone just then, the thigh muscle of his bad leg pulling as he struggled to regain his balance. "Forgiving? What does that mean? You've told them . . . about me?"

"Careful, now. They know what happened, Frank. It's not like it's recent news. You were in all the papers, on the television. It didn't take much to put two and two together, to match the Randall brothers. I answered their questions and took comfort from their kindness and support. We prayed for you, Frank. We prayed for you and Annie."

I know what you can do with your prayers, thought Randall, though he opted to keep his opinion to himself for the time being.

Maurice continued along the muddy path to a small ravine. "Remember when we played Pooh sticks as children?" he said.

Randall remembered the game they'd learned from *Winnie-the-Pooh*, one of the few books in the house; remembered, too, that Maurice had always seen to it that he won. He would claim that whatever twig emerged from the other side of the bridge was his, and if Randall didn't like it, he would take a beating.

Maurice bent down with a grunt and picked a loose stick from the ground. Snapping it in two, he offered Randall a choice. Randall held his brother's gaze, wondering what in hell he truly wanted, and took the larger of the two sticks. Leaning over the edge of the bridge, they counted to three and dropped the sticks into the stream.

"Quick," said Maurice, moving with some speed to the other side of the bridge.

Randall grimaced, the cold reaching his knee, as he swiveled around and made it in time to see his twig arrive first in the stream below. "Who won this time?" he said.

"I think you did, brother," said Maurice, with a smile.

"First time in sixty years, huh?"

Maurice placed his hand on Randall's back, the touch so light it was as if there was no contact at all. "Things change, brother. We only have each other now."

Randall eased away from his touch and began walking back to the church. Once, he'd made the mistake of telling his father how Maurice had cheated at the game. He didn't think he was any older than six or seven, but his father hadn't been the type of man to listen to such grievances. Randall twitched at the memory of his father's belt snapping against his flesh. Three times, always three times. When Maurice had returned, he'd received the same treatment. They never played the game again.

"So what do you think?" said Maurice, as they retreated into the warmth of the house.

"What do I think about what?"

"My proposition?"

"Stop talking in riddles, Maurice."

Maurice shivered as he took off his coat. "A storm is brewing. About staying here, with me. Neither of us is getting any younger."

"I don't think that would work," said Randall, helping his brother load the fireplace with wood.

Maurice smiled. Randall imagined his brother thought it was enigmatic, but it wasn't. It was creepy and reminded him again of Annie's aversion to his brother.

"You won at Pooh sticks," said Maurice.

"I won lots of times in the past, only you refused to acknowledge it." How ludicrous it was to dwell on childhood games.

"My point exactly. We've both made mistakes, brother. You're not the only one who seeks forgiveness. I seek it on a daily basis. Stay awhile and we can seek it together."

Randall poked at the fire until the flames engulfed the chopped wood. He didn't believe in the type of forgiveness Maurice was talking about.

The only thing making him hesitate was Maurice's assertion that he, too, sought forgiveness. Maybe he was talking about the way he had treated Randall as a child, but Randall wondered if it went deeper than that. "OK," he said. "I'll stay for now."

"Splendid," said Maurice. His smile came and went, and they both stood back from the rising heat of the fire.

Randall briefly matched his smile, all the while wondering what it was Maurice truly needed forgiveness for.

Chapter Fourteen

Laurie knew immediately what she was looking at and as she edged nearer she drew out her firearm in case the perpetrator was watching her.

Wary of disturbing the crime scene, she took pictures before treading carefully toward it. Removing a plastic bag from her coat pocket, she picked it up: a size 8 Asics running shoe, purple and pink, the same make and size Grace had been wearing the night she went missing.

Any lingering optimism evaporated. Laurie's mind began spinning in a number of directions: the body must be nearby, why had the sneaker been left in plain sight, this was the same location where Annie Randall was found, Frank Randall would become an obvious suspect, she would need to cancel the press conference. And, worse than all of it, she would soon have to tell Sandra and Glen Harrington that their daughter was dead.

The noise in her mind was distracting, and she shook her head to dislodge the thoughts before calling it in. She had to focus. It was hard not to think the worst, but it wasn't over yet. She battled through the vines and moved further into drier land, her gun held out in front of her. She didn't get the sense that she was being watched, but wasn't about to take the risk.

In the distance, the surf roared. It felt as if the waves were nearby, ready to crash down on her, but the tide rarely reached this point. She stopped, frozen, as something brushed past her ankle, glancing down to see a grass snake disappear into the undergrowth. A vision of Annie Randall popped into her mind, the side of her face eaten away by wildlife, and Laurie shuddered before moving further inland.

Laurie was torn between two conflicting thoughts: she wanted to find Grace, but finding her would almost definitely mean the girl was dead and the thought of all that hope draining through her fingers was difficult to bear.

Fifty yards further in, the decision was made for her. Grace's second sneaker was standing unattended in a patch of open scrubland, the toe of the shoe pointing to a veil of branches and vines, as if playing a part on some lurid treasure trail.

She didn't bag the shoe this time but followed the line of the pointing toe to the tangled foliage, circling around it with her gun to make sure she wasn't being lured into it by someone on the perimeter, before pulling back the vines to reveal a second open space, where Grace Harrington's corpse lay.

At first glance, she appeared to be at rest, lying on her side, but as Laurie approached, she could see the violent dislocation of the ankles, the ghastly way her lower right leg dangled from the broken patella, and the zigzag mark around her neck where she had been cut. Laurie took an involuntary step back and fought to calm her breathing. The scene before her precisely mirrored the images of Annie Randall that had taken up permanent residence in her mind. Like David's mother, Grace Harrington had been brutally manipulated into this unnatural position, her arms and legs fashioned to give the impression that she was running. It reminded Laurie of the type of figure you would see on top of a sports trophy or on the hood of a luxury car, a stylized pose that bore little resemblance to real life. As she called it in, she wondered if Grace had still been alive when she'd been placed into the pose.

Laurie set about securing the scene as she waited for backup to arrive. She kept her distance from Grace. It was clearly the girl, and getting close to confirm her identity would only risk destroying potentially crucial evidence.

It was a surreal few minutes. It felt like time had slowed within the bubble of her vision as she heard the emergency vehicles arrive, and the teams followed the path she'd taken. She had seen dead bodies countless times before but had never come across one in such an odd way.

It was Lieutenant Filmore who emerged first from the barnyard grass, bulldozing his way through it. "What the hell?" he said by way of greeting, sweat pouring from his shiny scalp.

Laurie pointed behind her. "Grace Harrington."

Filmore stepped over and took little more than a cursory glance before returning to Laurie's side. "You OK? How did you know?"

Only the words *hunch* and *gut feeling* came to mind, so Laurie nearly chose to say nothing. But she trusted Filmore and could see no reason not to come clean. As the CSIs began working on the scene, she told him about the similarities between the Annie Randall investigation and Grace's disappearance.

"That is a hell of a leap," said Filmore.

Laurie couldn't tell if he was suspicious or impressed. "I got lucky. Shame it was too late."

Filmore sucked in a deep breath, as if he was savoring the sea air, his jacket tight against his stocky frame. "Murder weapon?" he asked, glancing at the red line along Grace's neck.

Laurie shook her head. "No sign of it, but I can't claim to have combed the area."

"We need to keep everyone away from her until CSI gets here." Then, without segue: "I understand you've been to see Frank Randall since his return from prison." He was staring with an intensity that dared her to ask him how he knew.

Not that she needed to ask. "Warren," she said, her grandfather-in-law being the only person other than David who knew she'd been to see him.

Filmore continued staring at her, his bushy eyebrows inching up his forehead again.

"Yes, I went to see him. He's an ex-con returning to the area."

"And he's your father-in-law."

"He didn't do this, if that's what you're thinking," she heard herself say.

"Is that right? Sure looks like he did."

"You haven't seen him. He doesn't have the strength to carry off something like that. He's a tired, scared old man now."

Filmore squinted. "He may be tired and old, but we can't ignore the connections. The bodies have been staged identically."

"Just telling you how I see it, Lieutenant."

"I appreciate your opinion, but we'll need to take him in for questioning. As soon as the press gets word of this, it won't take them long to piece things together."

"Yes, Lieutenant."

"This changes everything, of course. We'll need to cancel the press conference and . . ." Filmore was clearly alluding to the fact that Sandra and Glen Harrington would need to be informed of their daughter's murder. His unsubtle pause suggesting Laurie be the one to break it to them.

"I'll go there now," she said.

Filmore nodded, wiping beads of moisture that had reached his nose.

"And I would appreciate it if I can be the one to bring Frank Randall in for questioning."

Filmore pursed his lips, indicating he was thinking. "He's a family member."

"Hardly, Lieutenant."

"You're married to his son, Laurie. We can't risk being accused of bias, one way or another. I'm happy for you to remain in charge, but Remi should bring him in."

"He's in Houston."

Filmore scratched his neck. "Well, we can't delay. We'll have to send Rodriquez and Abbey."

Laurie lowered her eyes. She trusted both detectives, but worried about how Frank would respond, which only served to support Filmore's theory that she was too close. "Yes, Lieutenant," she said.

As first on scene, Laurie would usually be required to remain, but Filmore's presence eased her departure. She took one last, involuntary glance at Grace before leaving, again noting the "running" positioning of the body, as the CSIs carefully photographed and videoed the scene, taking samples from the surrounding areas before they would even start to examine the body. At some point, Sandra and Glen would be asked to identify their daughter, and though it was of the smallest mercies, Laurie was glad that scavengers hadn't had time to destroy Grace's features.

She called Rodriquez as she pulled away from the scene and instructed him to go easy on Frank. "Wait for me before you conduct the interview," she told him.

As she drove back to the Harringtons', she called Remi and told him everything that had happened. She was grateful when he didn't question her motives for going to the scene in the first place.

"You want me to come back?" he said.

"Have you finished what needs to be done there?"

"I have a few more people to speak to."

"Do we have a sighting for Glen Harrington on the night of Grace's disappearance?"

"He left work on the Tuesday at 3 p.m. Not that unusual, apparently. He often worked from his apartment."

"Do we have a sighting of him at the apartment building?"

"He was keyed in at 3.30 p.m. Left at 6 p.m., and back again at 10 p.m."

"Just long enough to get to Galveston and back."

"It would be a push, unless he gave someone else the key code. You really think he might have something to do with it?"

Laurie hadn't made her mind up about Glen Harrington just yet. His sullenness could be put down to stress over his daughter's disappearance, but Remi knew very well that parents and close family had to be considered as suspects in such cases as this. Glen wouldn't be the first father to kill his daughter, and there was still much for her to learn about the Harringtons. "Search for a sighting of him on the night of Grace's disappearance," she told him. "I'll question him again about his movements."

"He won't take kindly to that."

"I'm sure he won't," said Laurie, pulling up outside the house. There was nothing much she was going to say that either parent was going to like to hear, she thought as she made her way up the stairs and knocked on the front door.

Chapter Fifteen

This time, Sandra Harrington answered the door. Laurie had given many death notifications over the years. They never became any easier, and they often went this way. Laurie paused before speaking and Sandra saw it in her eyes.

"No," said Grace's mother, shaking her head, staring blankly at her as if she could see straight through her. "No," she continued, as Glen joined her side.

"What is it?" he said, glancing at Sandra, who was now in tears, and then back at Laurie.

"Please, can I come in?" said Laurie.

"What is it, what's happened?" said Glen, his voice rising in tone and urgency.

Laurie did her best to stay detached but it was impossible not to be empathetic to the situation. "I'm afraid Grace's body has been found," she said softly, not wishing to prolong the parents' misery any further.

Glen Harrington turned away, took a couple of steps and fell to his knees as Sandra continued staring at Laurie, dumbstruck.

"Let's go inside," said Laurie. Placing her arm around Sandra, she drew her inside and shut the door, silencing the menacing whistle of the wind.

It took a few seconds for Sandra to go to her husband. Glen was by now prostrate on the wooden floor as if he'd been knocked out, and Sandra fell into hysterics as she bent down to him. Laurie wanted to look away, but needed to see the interaction. As heartless as it felt, the pair couldn't be ruled out as suspects and she had to gauge the genuineness of their grief, and if it was tinged with guilt.

As she watched Sandra console her husband, easing him up onto his knees so she could embrace him, Laurie was reminded of one of her first cases as a detective working alongside Jim Burnell. That had been a missing person case too, a ten-year-old boy whose body was eventually found near Jamaica Beach. Laurie had been present with Burnell for the death notification. He'd told her to study the parents' reactions—this time a mother and a stepfather. Both had broken down in grief, in an almost identical way to the Harringtons, but Burnell had seen something in the reaction of the mother when being comforted by the stepfather—a simple shrug as he'd tried to embrace her—that had led him to suspect foul play. The stepfather was eventually successfully prosecuted for homicide, the mother for aiding and abetting.

That incident had taught Laurie many lessons, the most important being that nothing could be trusted at face value. That was a tough and sad lesson to learn, but one that had been necessary for her to succeed on the force.

As Laurie looked away from the grieving couple, she noticed Tilly for the first time, her short figure resting against the door frame of the kitchen area. As Laurie moved toward her, arms outstretched, the girl began repeating Sandra's gesture of shaking her head in denial.

"It's my fault," said Tilly, tears streaming down her face.

Tilly may have become part of the family recently, but the last thing Sandra and Glen needed at the moment was the girl breaking down in front of them. Laurie led her into the kitchen. Putting her arm around her, noticing how broad the girl's shoulders were, she asked why she thought she was to blame.

"You don't understand," said Tilly, through increasing hysteria.

Like the parents, Tilly had to be considered a suspect, and Laurie waited for her explanation, though she wasn't expecting an admission of guilt. She poured her some water as she waited for her to calm down.

"If I hadn't gone crazy about Mia, then she would never have gone out for a run in that direction," said Tilly through rushed gulps of water. "This would never have happened."

Mia will have to be brought in for questioning too, thought Laurie as she took the glass from Tilly's shaking hands. Despite the girl's protestations, Laurie didn't think their argument had any bearing on the killing. The similarities to the Annie Randall death suggested to her that Grace had been targeted and that the abduction had been planned, and she didn't want Tilly blaming herself.

She sat with the makeshift family until one of the junior detectives, Gemma Clayton, arrived. Gemma would spend the next few days with the family, and would report back directly to Laurie. Her role would be to offer support, at the same time studying the Harringtons for any clues, a similar role to the one Laurie had taken during the Annie Randall investigation.

Once Laurie had settled Gemma in with the family, she made her goodbyes. So many formalities still had to be concluded, but for now she didn't want to burden the three of them with anything more.

Rodriquez called as she headed back to the crime scene, informing her that Frank Randall was not at home. "Shall we put out an APB for him?" he asked.

"I don't think that's necessary just yet. Post someone there. Let's give him a few hours."

Was she being naive? After everything Filmore had said to her about being too close to Frank, Jim Burnell's instruction never to take anything at face value, and her own semi-dispassionate view of the grieving parents, could it be that she had somehow allowed her father-in-law to hoodwink her? She'd told Filmore that Frank was too frail to have carried out the attack on Grace Harrington, but what if that had just been what he'd wanted her to believe?

Panicking, she feared she'd been using her time with the man as a kind of therapy session. With her relationship with David breaking down, hadn't she been using Frank as a sounding board? And what if that was what he'd wanted all along? Laurie usually trusted her instincts, but what if she'd been so distracted with the problems she'd been having with David that she'd let Randall get to her? At the very least, the positioning of the body was undeniably linked to Annie Randall; of course he had to be considered a possible suspect.

He didn't do this, if that's what you're thinking. Would those words come back to haunt her? Where that certainty had come from, she didn't know, but one thing she was sure of: she needed to find Frank Randall, and fast.

Chapter Sixteen

It was late afternoon by the time Laurie returned to the murder scene, the dark clouds looming over the gulf still yet to burst. The first thing she saw was Warren's imposing figure. It was hard to see anything else. Wherever he went, Warren took center stage, and next to him Lieutenant Filmore appeared smaller, his authority diminished by the appearance of the ex-chief.

Laurie had expected the confrontation at some point, but wasn't ready for it now. She dragged her sluggish body over to the two men, ignoring the awkward glances from colleagues.

On seeing her, Warren's face changed. The last time she'd seen that blank visage had been outside the house on the day Frank returned. All humanity vanished from Warren for a split second, and in that time Laurie thought him capable of anything.

"Now, Warren," said Filmore, as her grandfather-in-law stepped toward her.

"What did I tell you?" said Warren, the veins in his neck swelled to bursting. "What did I tell you?" he repeated, raising his voice.

Laurie didn't engage. Warren wasn't thinking straight and it would be impossible to reason with him when he was this angry. "Let's go somewhere private and talk, Warren."

"We can talk right here, thank you very much. You should never have let him come back here."

"That's enough," said Filmore, placing his hand on Warren's shoulder.

"I wouldn't be putting your hands on me, Filmore, if I was you."

Laurie held her ground. "I've just been to see Glen and Sandra Harrington. Now isn't the time for this."

"I told you he was bad news, Laurie, and you did nothing to stop him. This . . . this girl's death is on you."

Laurie took a step closer to him. She loved the man, and could forgive him for what he'd said, but she was angry. "If you had your way, Warren, Frank Randall would be in the hospital now, or in the ground. You may remember that I could have arrested you then. If you continue like this, I will."

"Arrest me? Where the hell is Randall?"

Filmore glanced at her, as if she should answer the question.

"I realize you're concerned, Warren," she said, "but I can't divulge any details of the investigation. You, better than anyone, should know that."

Warren spoke through gritted teeth. "I'm the ex-chief of police, for Christ's sake. My daughter was the first victim of this psychopath. You tell me you've arrested Randall, or I'm going to go to his place now and do the job for you."

"Everything is in hand. Now, I need you to leave the crime scene," said Laurie, slightly aggrieved to be doing something Filmore should already have done.

Warren held his ground for a few seconds, as if daring anyone to approach him. He was hurting and Laurie hated seeing him this way. "You tell me when he's in custody," he said at last, the demand aimed at Filmore rather than her.

"Before you go, Warren," Laurie said. "What do you know of Frank Randall's brother, Maurice?"

It was slight but it was there, a flicker of doubt in Warren's eyes. "The preacher. What of him?"

"What did you think of him? Frank Randall told me he was visited by him the other day."

"So, you're on speaking terms with Randall now?"

"I keep an eye on him. He told me Annie never took to Maurice."

At the mention of his daughter's name, Warren's face crumpled, all the anger and hatred deflating from his body. Laurie understood his pain all too well, and it was harrowing to see the effect his daughter's death still had on him all these years later. "Annie never mentioned anything like that to me. Why do you ask?"

"Annie never told Frank why she disliked his brother so."

"Bad blood runs in that family. The father was a nasty piece of work."

"He still around?"

"No, long gone."

"If you don't mind me asking, Warren, did you get an alibi for Maurice?" It was a loaded question, and Laurie was reluctant to ask it, but with the similarities in the two homicides it had to be asked.

"He wasn't a suspect," said Warren, puzzled.

"OK, good to know. Thanks, Warren. And please, don't go paying Frank Randall any visits."

Warren sucked in his cheeks, offering her a brief shrug before moving off.

"What's this about Maurice Randall?" asked Filmore, as they watched Warren shuffle back toward his car.

"I'm going to need to look at the Annie Randall investigation. The whole thing."

"I thought you were certain that Frank Randall wasn't responsible?" said Filmore, not trying to hide his sarcasm.

"I may have been a bit hasty there."

"Annie Randall would have been your mother-in-law," said Filmore.

"I'm aware of that. But she wasn't at the time, and I didn't start seeing David until much later." Laurie had gone through so much over the last forty-eight hours, she had no intention of letting the investigation be taken away from her now.

"I may need to speak to the chief."

"You're kidding me," said Laurie, heat rising to her face. "Lieutenant," she added, as an afterthought.

"This is going to be news, Laurie. The lead detective happens to be the daughter-in-law of the original victim." He shook his head. "We can't risk anything undermining the investigation."

Laurie inched closer. "Annie Randall died sixteen years ago. I have nothing to gain from this investigation other than finding out who did this," she said, pointing toward the crime scene where Grace's broken body was still being examined.

Filmore nodded. "I appreciate that, and I'm on your side. Hell, maybe they won't even pick up on it. You carry on as normal for now." He nodded down toward the crime scene. "Crosby wants to speak to you."

Terrence Crosby was the lead CSI. Laurie had known him for ten years and they'd always got on well, rising through their respective ranks together. He nodded to her as she approached the knot of white-overalled figures still gathering evidence, the search for the murder weapon extending out into the grasslands.

"You remember the Annie Randall murder?" said Laurie, as they watched the paramedics preparing Grace Harrington for her transfer to the mortuary.

"Bit before my time," Terrence deadpanned.

"You suggesting you're younger than me, Crosby? I know for a fact that isn't true."

He made a little doubting sound. "If you say so, Laurie."

"Well, *I'm* old enough to remember, and from what I can see of this poor girl, there are a number of similarities."

"Of course I remember Annie Randall," said Crosby. "I'll have to look at the old pictures, but I agree the positioning of the bodies is similar, if not identical. It will be interesting to see if the cut to the carotid artery was by the same blade."

The murder weapon that had killed Annie Randall had never been found, but the laceration had been caused by a blade 4.44 mm thick. "And the fractures to the legs?"

He nodded. "It appears both patellae have been fractured as well as the ankles, as I believe was the case with Annie Randall. Again, I'll have to check, and obviously the autopsy will tell us more."

"What else can you tell me?"

Terrence grimaced. "We're going to have to wait for the ME's report, but I would estimate the time of death to be within the last ten to twelve hours."

If that was true, it suggested the killer had kept Grace in captivity prior to killing her. Laurie took in a deep breath. Her chest felt heavy, as if she was recovering at the end of a long run. They both knew there was a question being left unasked. Laurie wasn't sure she wanted to hear the answer, but Terrence wasn't going to volunteer the information. "The injuries," she said, her voice wavering. "Post or pre-death?"

"Again, we'll have to wait."

"Come on, Terrence."

He shook his head again, his eyes downcast. "From what I can remember, Annie Randall's injuries were sustained when her husband attacked her and he fractured her legs before killing her. I would say something similar happened in this instance. If I had to guess, I would say this poor young lady was still alive when her legs were fractured."

Chapter Seventeen

Laurie waited until Grace's body was in the back of the ambulance before leaving the scene. Terrence and the CSIs would remain for the time being, working with her team in a final sweep of the surrounding area before darkness fell. She left Rodriquez in charge and returned to her car, calling Remi as she made the short journey to Frank Randall's house.

"I've found Glen Harrington's ex-lover," said Remi, on answering. "A young intern by the name of Bonnie Webb."

"You've spoken to her?"

"On the way to her office as we speak. And when I say young, I mean young."

Laurie shivered. "Age?"

"Nineteen, eighteen when they were seeing each other."

"His daughter's age."

"I'm afraid so," said Remi. "And I don't think she was the first. Bit of a Romeo, our Mr. Harrington. A string of broken hearts."

"Any complaints? Reports of indecent behavior?"

"HR have given him the all clear, but there is a sense of unease about him, you know what I mean? As if people are holding something back?"

"Through fear?"

"Quite possibly. He's a senior figure in the corporation. Not someone you want to get the wrong side of."

"Okay, let's see what this Bonnie Webb has to say," said Laurie, ending the call as she arrived at Frank Randall's place.

Leaving the car, she half expected to see Warren Campbell and his cronies making their way along the dirt track toward Frank's place, ready to serve another helping of the ready-made justice they'd introduced him to earlier in the year. Although she sympathized with Warren, she now realized it had been a mistake not to report the incident. And by the way he was acting at present, it could become a decision she would live to regret.

Birdsong accompanied her as she walked up the dirt road. When the house came into view, she noted that Frank had transformed the surrounding area since his return, making it a much more hospitable place to live. Two uniformed officers were stationed outside the house, and Laurie was relieved when they told her they hadn't seen Warren or anyone else. "Only Detectives Rodriquez and Abbey," said one of the pair.

It was nearly 5 p.m., seven hours having passed since Laurie had discovered Grace's body. From what she knew of Frank Randall, it wasn't like him to spend so much time away from the security of his home. He'd told her that he liked to take an occasional walk to the water, but that his injured leg meant it was impossible for him to stay out too long.

She peered through the frosted panes of glass at the front of the house, unable to see more than the blurred outlines of Frank's furniture. "You've checked all the doors?" she asked, knowing before she'd finished asking that it was a pointless question.

Both officers nodded, then one asked her if she thought Frank Randall was inside. "I think we have to check," she said, radioing headquarters for permission to enter without a warrant.

"Do you think Mr. Randall is in danger?" asked the dispatcher.

"He's elderly and in ill health. It's unlike him to be away from his home for this long," said Laurie, giving the necessary answers to provide her with reasonable grounds to enter the building.

Once confirmation had been given, she withdrew her firearm and knocked on the door once more. When there was no answer, she nodded to one of the uniformed officers, who aimed a strong kick at the ancient lock. The wooden door frame splintered with barely any sound, and the door opened easily.

"Frank, are you in here?" said Laurie, easing the door open. Fearing the worst, she switched on the light, revealing an empty living room. It didn't take long to secure the rest of the house, and Laurie called in her findings, understanding only too well what would be made of it.

"Where the hell are you?" she said, lifting the framed photograph of the teenage David with his smiling parents. Could the handsome man with his arm wrapped around his son really be responsible for the gruesome killing of Grace Harrington? The certainty about Frank's innocence she'd felt earlier had all but evaporated. Frank's absence heightened her doubts, and would provide Warren, and anyone else who thought Frank Randall had struck again, with all the evidence they would need to make their minds up.

"You're not making this easy for me, Frank," she mumbled to herself, as she left the house and told the uniformed officers to remain in position until instructed otherwise.

A cold wind rustled the bushes next to the house, the breeze containing flecks of sand. So many thoughts rushed through Laurie's mind that she struggled to compartmentalize them all. Her main focus was naturally on finding Grace's killer, but she couldn't shut out her worry about David and Rebecca Whitehead, and the more immediate problem of finding Frank. Remi's revelation about Glen Harrington's teenage lover was an interesting development, but nothing beyond finding Frank today would be considered a success. She needed to reexamine Annie Randall's murder, but without Frank in custody it was going to be too easy for everyone to jump to conclusions.

Sheltering from the blustering storm in her car, she found the number for Maurice Randall's church. She hesitated when the call rang through to voicemail, before hanging up and calling the state police. She spoke to a detective there who agreed to assess the situation at Maurice Randall's house and to hold Frank, if he was there, at the premises until she arrived.

Chapter Eighteen

Laurie called in her destination before leaving for the church on the outskirts of Dickinson. Sandra, Glen, and Tilly would all have to be brought in for official questioning at some point soon, and leaving the island town at that moment felt like a dereliction of duty. But bringing in Frank Randall had to be the priority, whether she was sure of his guilt or not. State police had arrived at Maurice Randall's church and were waiting for her to arrive.

Images of Grace and Annie played through her mind as she drove over the causeway, the refineries burning in the evening gloom like some dystopian nightmare. Despite the decades separating them, the visions of the two victims merged into one. Both bodies with their long, willowy limbs broken and arranged into the strange running pose. Annie's injuries had been attributed to the wild, so-called *sudden passion* attack by her husband. When Frank had finally pleaded guilty, he'd been questioned about the positioning of the legs, but part of his *sudden passion* mitigation was denying he remembered attacking Annie. No doubt due to the plea bargain, which had meant an easy prosecution for the DA, no significance had been given to the multiple fractures to Annie's legs, beyond the uncontrollable rage attributed to Frank during the attack. "Not everything has to mean something complex," Jim

Burnell had told her at the time. "He went crazy and started hacking at his wife's limbs."

Things were different now. If Frank Randall had killed Grace, it all but proved that both killings were premeditated, and that was something Laurie struggled to understand. She found it difficult to believe that Frank Randall would have not only planned to kill Annie, but purposely mutilated her body with foresight. The *sudden passion* angle she could just about buy, but not *that*. If nothing else, Frank would have known how killing Annie would impact David, and she didn't believe he was capable of such horrendous forethought.

The words of Jim Burnell came back to her once more. *Don't trust anyone.* It was a lesson that had taken her a long time to accept, and again she worried she'd let her guard down with Frank. So eager had she been to hear stories of David's youth, it was feasible she'd given too much credence to the role Frank Randall had been playing for her.

Her stomach lurched as she left the causeway. It was a feeling she'd endured every time she had to leave the island, ever since Milly's death. It was as if the cord connecting them both was being stretched to breaking point, and she had to fight the urge to turn back round every time she made the crossing. The trauma of the separation was manifested in her body, her limbs going stiff and uncomfortable in the cramped confines of the car. It felt like ages since she'd exercised, and she rested a hand on her bloated stomach, sensing the fat congealing in her flesh.

A message appeared on her dashboard twenty minutes later as she approached the town limits of Dickinson. It was David, telling her he was coming back early from work and would be home tomorrow. Laurie tried to fight the image of him already back in town, nestling into the tall and slender body of Rebecca Whitehead. She wondered why she continued to punish herself with these perverse fantasies as she drove through the quaint village on the outskirts of Dickinson toward St. Saviour's church, where the blinking lights of a Texas state police vehicle were waiting for her.

◆ ◆ ◆

The smell of woodsmoke and the sight of floating tendrils of ash in the fireplace failed to distract Randall from the commotion by the front door. Since the police had arrived thirty minutes ago, Maurice had marched ceaselessly through the house, seething about how their rights were being violated by the authorities' presence on his property, or as his brother had so vehemently put it, "my place of worship."

So far, the two uniformed officers had been content to wait outside. This had struck Randall as odd, and he'd looked away as one of them peered through the dusty windows and caught sight of him by the fireplace.

This house of Maurice's played tricks on Randall. Time was a tricky customer nowadays, but in this place—in this town as a whole—it had utterly stopped making sense. It sped up and slowed down, distorting Randall's memories of the last few days. Maybe that was what had so freaked out Annie during their visit here, though every time he asked Maurice about the source of the friction between them, he sensed that wasn't the case. There was a look in his brother's eyes Randall didn't much care for every time Annie's name was mentioned, and Randall was determined to get to the reason why.

"How dare they come here, to this holy place," said Maurice, passing by once more on his agitated circuit of the house. His pale skin was close to translucent as he moved toward the fire, his insubstantial body shivering as he rubbed his eyes.

"What do they want?" asked Randall, moving to the window and sneaking a look outside where the police car was still waiting, the blue lights flashing silently like a lighthouse warning others not to approach.

"They want to know if you're here, dear brother," said Maurice. "I told them you were, but they were not allowed to enter. I should call my lawyer."

That much Randall had heard. He recalled the lawyer he'd seen in the kitchen earlier and wondered what use a lawyer working for the church would be in a situation like this.

Why they should be so interested in his whereabouts was a mystery to him. He looked back toward the fire. Maurice had his back to him, phone in his hand, and Randall noticed the curve in the older man's spine and briefly wondered what sort of pressure would force those bones to crack. Somewhere within him, he sensed a different type of breaking. His stomach was tight, his bad knee flaring in pain as if there was a change in the weather. He tried to hold on to the memory of the last few days, but every time an image or memory came to mind, it faded like dust in his hands. He pictured himself in various incarnations—on the beach, alone in the house, lying on the sand when Maurice had first found him, back at the house with Laurie for company—but nothing remained solid. Instead, his mind turned to firmer, more distant memories. Getting married to Annie, holding David for the first time, being led to the Camino Real area where Annie's corrupted body was waiting. He coughed, the woodsmoke invading his lungs, making him breathless. *What have I done?* he thought for the millionth time, as a second car appeared in Maurice's driveway.

When Randall moved away from the window, he grimaced in pain as his knee gave way, the crippling agony in his leg reminiscent of the day it had happened. He could picture those two convicts with much more clarity than anything he could recall over the last few months back in Galveston. Their shaved heads, slick with sweat, as they took turns kicking him before the smallest of the two brought the metal bar down onto his knee and whispered the words, "This is from Warren Campbell."

"What is it?" said Maurice, reaching him in time to stop him falling to the ground.

"Let them take me," said Randall, as his daughter-in-law left her car and walked toward the house. He didn't know how he knew, or what it meant, but he was sure his greatest fear had come true and that someone else had died.

Chapter Nineteen

After checking with the officers waiting outside, Laurie rang the doorbell. It was almost a surprise when Maurice Randall answered the door. The officers had told her about their run-in with the pastor, but it was still surreal to see the man—technically a relative—for the first time in the flesh. He looked older than in the file photos she had of him. Loose skin dangled from the angular frame of his face, his eyes sunken, his back arched as if he were crumbling under the force of gravity.

Laurie displayed her badge. "Detective Laurie Campbell," she said, noting the hint of recognition in Maurice's narrow eyes.

"You're Frank's daughter-in-law?"

Maurice was sharper than his withered body would have suggested, and Laurie chided herself for once more reaching conclusions based solely on outward appearances. "Is Frank inside?"

"He is safe."

"Can I come inside and speak to you both?"

Maurice straightened up. "Frank is very tired at the moment."

"As am I, Mr. Randall. I've come a long way, and I've had a very hard day. I would appreciate your cooperation."

"What is this about?" he said, his thin arm stretching across the door as a barrier.

"Laurie?" came a voice from behind the man. "Is that you?" said Frank, coming into view.

"Hello, Frank. I was hoping to speak to you."

"Well, what are you waiting for, Maurice? Let her through."

Maurice held Laurie's gaze, his distaste evident by the way he tightened his thin lips together. "Very well," he said, moving his arm.

Laurie followed Frank into the sitting room, where a fierce fire billowed in the hearth. Sweat prickled her skin as she unbuttoned her coat. "Everything OK, Frank?" she murmured.

Frank nodded, but couldn't hide the confusion in his eyes. He had the look to Laurie of someone in shock.

"So what is this about?" Maurice demanded again.

"Please, sit," said Laurie, before telling the brothers about Grace Harrington's death.

Maurice appeared unperturbed by the news, but Frank was visibly shaking. "Would you like some water, Frank?" said Laurie, glancing at Maurice, who reluctantly left the room to fetch it for him. Laurie waited until he'd gone before asking, "You know what this means, don't you, Frank?"

"It's exactly the same?" said Frank, trembling.

"The body was left in a very similar position to Annie, yes."

For an old man, Maurice was sprightly, returning with some water before Laurie had a chance to question Frank further. "And what has this to do with us?" he said, placing the glass in the shaking hands of his brother.

"I need you to come in for questioning."

"Don't be ludicrous," said Maurice. "Frank has been with me for the last few days. When did this girl go missing?"

"You collected Frank from his house?" asked Laurie.

"That is correct."

"When?"

"Last Saturday."

"And returned him?"

"Wednesday morning."

"Can anyone corroborate that?"

Maurice snapped his head back as if he'd been slapped. "My word not good enough for you?"

Laurie stifled a laugh. "I'm investigating a homicide, Mr. Randall. I'm afraid I need more to go on than your word, however honorable that may be."

"Ridiculous."

The dynamic in the house troubled Laurie. Maurice was doing all the talking.

"Frank, I need you to come with me," she said, ignoring the preacher's protestations.

"That's fine," said Frank.

"No, it is not," said Maurice. "I have called my lawyer. We will wait for him."

"Listen, Mr. Randall. I understand your concerns, but I'm afraid you're not in a position to argue. Your brother is an active suspect, and due to your proximity to him, I have to insist that you accompany me back to Galveston as well. Your lawyer can meet us there."

"And if I don't? I know my rights, you know."

Laurie took a deep breath in through her nose. The heat inside the room was stifling. She longed to be on a run with the biting fall air in her face. "If you don't come in voluntarily, I'll have no option but to arrest you. Now what will it be?"

◆ ◆ ◆

Twenty minutes later, Laurie was heading back to the island with Maurice and Frank in the patrol car behind her, the state cops happy to assist. She was glad to be free of the rectory, with its oppressive heat and uneasy atmosphere. Maurice Randall had complained so much as he and his brother had been led to the car that they'd been forced to cuff the pair. Even that hadn't stopped the pastor, the sound of his threats to sue the whole police department continuing until the patrol car door was mercifully shut on him. It was hard to imagine Maurice as a man of God, let alone to picture him in front of a congregation. Harder still to imagine him being related to Frank and David.

Laurie glanced in the rearview mirror, searching for sight of Frank in the back of the patrol car. The news of Grace's death had clearly rattled him, and she was trying to determine if that was because of a guilty conscience. The brothers' alibi needed to be verified, but Frank had allegedly been away from Galveston when Grace had gone missing. She thought again about the possibility that Grace had suffered the injuries to her legs when she'd been alive, shuddering as she imagined the pain and helplessness Grace would have endured.

But that was all conjecture. There was a danger in trying to arrange the details so they conformed to her preconceptions. It was something she was going to come across when she returned, as most people had already reached their conclusions. Laurie understood that—Frank had only been out of prison a few months, and Grace's death was identical in so many ways to Annie's—but she wouldn't be forced into thinking along those lines unless there was proof. She still found it hard to believe that Frank had anything to do with Grace's death, and not just because she'd found him good company these last few weeks. He was frail, and his bad leg would have greatly hampered any attack. That didn't mean he didn't do it, and with Maurice as an accomplice, it was definitely something they could have achieved together. But there were still so many unanswered questions, none more important than why target Grace Harrington?

News had spread of Frank's arrest, and the station was full by the time she returned. The state cops accompanied her to the charging desk with Maurice and Frank still in their cuffs. No official charges were made, but the pair were led to separate holding cells to await questioning.

Laurie noticed the looks her colleagues trained on Frank's hunched figure being led away, and marveled at her own sense of defensiveness on behalf of the man. She'd behaved the same way herself in the past, assigning a guilty verdict to a suspect before they'd even reached trial. It was wrong to presume anyone's guilt, but sometimes you just knew. Cops didn't always need a court of law to tell them when someone was guilty and, in Laurie's experience, once her colleagues made an absolute decision on a suspect, they were rarely wrong.

Remi had returned from Houston and walked over to her. "I'm glad you've found our man," said Remi. "Can I buy you a coffee?"

By "buy," Remi meant pouring her some of the lukewarm liquid from the breakroom, but she readily agreed. As she took the coffee into the bullpen, which was full of colleagues despite the late hour, she was dismayed to catch sight of Warren in Filmore's office. "What the hell is he doing here?" she said, taking a seat.

"You can't really blame him, can you? It would appear that the person who killed his daughter has returned, one way or another."

She supposed Remi was right, and she did sympathize with Warren. He would be reliving the agony of losing Annie all over again and she couldn't blame him for playing the ex-cop card. "As long as he doesn't interfere with the investigation. So you're on the Frank Randall bandwagon for this?" she asked, grimacing as she sipped her coffee.

Remi's youth and inexperience meant he wasn't as jaded as the majority of her colleagues, and he never reached any conclusions without a train of logical thought. "That's why I wanted to speak to you. Actually, I'm growing concerned about Glen Harrington."

"Concerned?"

"It seems Bonnie Webb wasn't the only young woman he'd been seeing. I managed to speak to another former intern, Natalie Morton, nineteen years old. She interned for Harrington last summer." He showed Laurie a picture of a young woman with flowing auburn hair. "She had an affair with him pretty much the whole time she worked there."

Laurie rubbed her face as she looked at the image of the smiling girl. "When did it end?"

"That's the thing that makes this all the more unpleasant, if that's possible. She was eighteen when they were seeing each other. Ended not long after her nineteenth birthday."

Laurie sipped her coffee again, fighting the wave of nausea from both the taste and from what Remi was telling her. "The same age as Grace," she said, shaking her head.

"It gets worse. They split up when she found out Mr. Harrington was fucking one of her college pals, Regan Yates. She's in Europe at the moment. One-night thing, by all accounts, but still."

"Have you spoken to her?"

"Not yet."

"Let's make sure we do. Christ, this is one headache I can do without. What the hell is he thinking?" She sighed. "Rhetorical question, I know." Glen Harrington clearly had a serious thing for very young women. That his obvious age preference coincided with the age of his daughter could be just queasily coincidental, but it might not be. Harrington wouldn't be the first sick bastard to have a fixation with his child, and it was easy to see how that obsession could have caused him to attack his daughter. If Grace had denied him what he wanted, or threatened to reveal him, then it was feasible to imagine him taking her life. And, with Frank Randall back in town, what better way to disguise his actions?

Laurie realized she was making some great leaps, but at the very least it was apparent that Glen Harrington needed to be questioned in depth, along with Sandra and Tilly. "How far did you question Natalie Morton?"

"Just the basics. She's happy to speak to me again. She's not Mr. Harrington's number one fan."

"OK, go see her again. Find out what they used to get up to. See if there were any role-playing fantasies. You know the sort of thing."

Remi looked momentarily confused before the horror of what Laurie was suggesting dawned on him. "No," he said, swallowing. "You don't think . . ."

"I hope not, but it's an angle we have to look at."

Laurie remained at her desk as Remi arranged another meeting with Natalie. She wondered if Sandra knew the age of her husband's ex-mistresses, and what her reaction would be to the news. It wasn't the sort of question she wanted to be asking her on any day, let alone on the very day she'd discovered her daughter had been brutally murdered.

She called Gemma Clayton, the junior detective who had been placed with the Harringtons. After checking on the parents' wellbeing, Laurie suggested she prep them both for the possibility of questioning the next day.

When she closed the call, she became aware of the tension in the bullpen, her colleagues all on edge, as if desperate for her to begin interrogating Frank Randall. She checked in with the front desk, but Maurice's legal representation had yet to arrive, so for now her hands were tied.

She took the time to revisit Annie Randall's homicide investigation. Like Grace, Annie had died in October, the dates only eleven days apart. With the images of Grace's stricken body still fresh in her mind, she studied the photographs of Annie Randall in detail. It soon became apparent that if Grace's killer was a copy-cat, then they would have to have had intimate knowledge of the original crime scene. The bodies were laid out in nearly identical fashion, the snapped and twisted bones giving an unreal quality to the victims, who in their stillness and deformity looked like mannequins washed up on shore.

Next, Laurie looked at the postmortem report. Grace's autopsy had been fast-tracked for tomorrow but the CSI had raised the possibility that Grace had been alive when her bones had been fractured; although Annie's body hadn't been found for three days, the autopsy had revealed that her bones were likely to have been broken prior, or very close, to her death.

Much more was still to be read. Witness reports and testimonies, including those from Warren Campbell and David, as well as the tapes and notes from the various interrogations of Frank Randall during the period between his arrest and eventual conviction. Like it or not, Frank Randall was the prime suspect in this new case and every detail about the old case potentially had some bearing on the current investigation.

"Laurie," said Filmore, sticking his head out of his office door. "A word."

Everyone's eyes were on her as she made the short journey across the bullpen. The tension was palpable. Many of Laurie's colleagues had children the same age or younger than Grace, and she knew they couldn't help but put themselves in the Harringtons' shoes. Just like the community at large, they were looking to Laurie to resolve the investigation as soon as possible, so they could return to some sort of equilibrium. Laurie sensed that pressure, and couldn't deny that a part of her thrived on it. Even so, she resented the sight of Warren Campbell talking to Rodriquez and Abbey as if he was still the chief of police.

"Shut the door," said Filmore.

Laurie did as instructed, sitting down without invitation. There was no point bitching about Warren being in the bullpen. The man commanded more respect than anyone in the station, the current chief included, and his legacy had been cemented by the terrible ordeal he'd endured with his daughter. Lieutenant Filmore was a good man, and a good leader. She tried to see it from his position, and decided Warren being around was a burden she could carry for now.

"The lawyer has arrived," Filmore said. "Out-of-towner by the name of Neil Mosley. He's been hired by the brothers Grimm and representing them both. Even tried to argue for a joint interview."

"OK. I'll start with Frank, then move on to Maurice. See if their stories match."

"I have heat coming on me from everywhere, you appreciate that, Laurie?"

Laurie sat up straight, fearing that Filmore was about to take her from the investigation. "I've got it covered, Lieutenant."

"A quick result would be great for everyone, get the vultures off us."

Laurie sucked in a breath as a cramp attacked the calf muscle on her right leg. She didn't immediately respond, waiting for Filmore to fill the gap.

Filmore appeared to study her for a time before continuing. "Of course, the most important thing is we find the right person," he said, as if he thought she'd been testing him.

Laurie could feel her calf muscle vibrating, as if something foreign were wriggling within her veins. She waited for the pain to ease before speaking. "On that front, you should be aware that we have some information about Glen Harrington."

"Do I want to hear this?"

"Probably not," said Laurie, proceeding to tell the lieutenant about Harrington's extra-marital affairs.

Filmore rubbed the stubble on his face, grimacing as if he wished he'd never let her speak. "You had any inkling of this before?"

"We knew he'd had an affair. Sandra Harrington had made that clear. No idea of the ages of his conquests."

"This gets out, the man is going to be ruined."

It was Laurie's turn to pull a face. "That's your concern?" she said, incredulous.

"Don't get me wrong, I think it's disgusting as well. But Frank Randall is a fit for this case. Imagine losing your daughter, then having your reputation ruined."

Laurie couldn't quite believe what she was hearing. "Sorry, but you are kidding me, Lieutenant. If Harrington didn't want his reputation ruined, then maybe he shouldn't have coerced young women into his bed."

"He coerced them?"

"He's forty-nine. He was their boss. They were eighteen and nineteen. That sound right to you?"

"You misunderstand me."

"No, I don't think I do, Lieutenant. You must see this makes him a potential suspect?"

"They were of legal age."

Realizing her mouth was hanging open, Laurie closed it. "He is over twice their age. I know some older guys are prone to this sort of behavior, but a man having an affair with young women close to the age of his daughter—you know what that could mean."

As Filmore rubbed his hands down his face, Laurie tried to control her breathing and the rapid thud of her heartbeat. She'd entered Filmore's office giving him the benefit of the doubt, telling herself he was a good man, and now this?

"Just because he sleeps with young women, doesn't mean he has an unhealthy fixation on his daughter."

"It might."

"Yes, all right, it might, but the point is we have a very strong suspect in Frank Randall."

"I am going to question Glen Harrington over this, Lieutenant," said Laurie, daring him to object.

"Let's just see how the interview with Frank Randall goes. Who knows, we might get a confession from him."

Wouldn't that be convenient for the boys' club, thought Laurie, leaving the office before she said something she would forever regret.

Chapter Twenty

Randall tried to fight the perverse sense of comfort he felt from being in the holding cell. This wasn't a reward, it was a punishment, but he'd spent nearly all of the last sixteen years in confinement and, aside from the last few months, it was all he knew. Rules and order were something you became used to, and though he couldn't say he loved being back inside, at least he knew where he was, and what was expected of him.

Two cells down, the bickering tones of his brother reached his ears. The man could sure raise hell when he wanted and had barely shut up since the cops had arrived at the church.

What really troubled Frank was Laurie's involvement. That disappointed look of hers wasn't something he would be able to shake any time soon. She'd looked at him as if he'd been conning her these last few months, and he could imagine her going back to David to tell him he'd been right all along. His father was the good-for-nothing so-and-so he'd always thought he was.

Any minute now, he would have to face her again and would displease her even more. Maurice's lawyer, Neil Mosley, whom he'd met at the rectory, had instructed him not to say anything. According to Mr. Mosley, he was only being questioned on the basis of historic events, and they had nothing beyond the similarities in the killings to link him at the moment. The lawyer didn't even ask him if he'd done it. "Keep quiet, let me do the talking, and we'll be out of here in the next couple of hours," he said, giving Randall the same unnervingly intent look he'd given him back at the church.

It didn't seem right, but what option did he have? During the humiliating journey from Maurice's house, Randall had tried to piece together the last few days. Laurie had told them a young woman had been found by the shore, but nothing else beyond that. Randall understood the gaps in his memory would be viewed as a guilty conscience, but for the life of him he could only hang on to snippets from the last few weeks. How could he remember the past with such pinpoint clarity, yet fail to recall what he'd been doing these last few days? Nowadays, it was as if each day bled into the next. What he could say for certain was that he had visited the beach, and had sensed a storm forming, and that Maurice had visited him once more and persuaded him to return to his house. Other images flashed through his mind—the loneliness he'd felt down by the water, playing Pooh sticks on the bridge near the church, meeting his brother's parishioners on the walk, and the accountant and lawyer at the rectory—but if Laurie was to ask him where he'd been on a specific day or time, he wouldn't be able to answer with any clarity, even if he wanted to.

Mr. Mosley returned with one of the guards. "They'd like to talk to you first, Mr. Randall," said the lawyer, his compassionate smile the kind you give a helpless child. "Remember what we discussed. Let me do the talking."

Randall didn't like the way the police officer looked at him as he opened the cell door. The man went to cuff him, but Mr. Mosley cut that short. "My client hasn't been charged with anything and is here voluntarily," he said, his brow furrowed in disdain.

The officer hesitated, seemingly weighing whether it was worth the argument, before putting the cuffs away. "Right. This way," he said, guiding them to an interview room.

"You OK?" said Mr. Mosley, as the officer shut the door.

What Randall wanted to do was to tell the lawyer, and anyone else who wanted to listen, that he was innocent. He glanced at the two-way mirror and pictured Laurie staring at him dispassionately. He didn't know for sure, but this appeared to be the room he'd been taken to on the day he was arrested for Annie's death. He recalled the lawyer from that time telling him a similar thing about remaining silent. He couldn't recall if he'd done so that first time, but once the evidence began piling up he'd continued pleading his innocence until he'd been instructed that the plea bargain was the best way forward. But as the interview room opened, and Laurie and a second detective entered the room, Randall decided that this time he would take his lawyer's advice and not talk.

It only took Laurie a few seconds to realize the interview was a waste of time. The way the lawyer, Neil Mosley, sat bolt upright, his arms crossed, with Frank Randall shrinking away to his side, made his opening words inevitable.

"My client would like to assert his right to remain silent," said the lawyer, as Laurie took a seat opposite with Remi.

"We're not charging Mr. Randall with anything. We would just like to ask him some questions," said Laurie, looking past Mosley to Frank, who shifted in his seat.

Had she really got it so wrong about him? He'd done a terrible thing in his past and that had to be taken into account, but Laurie hadn't thought him capable of killing Grace. If he had, then she feared what it said about her. She'd thought Frank was someone who had killed his wife, for reasons even he wasn't sure about, but had never considered him a potential habitual murderer. If Filmore and the others knew about the time she'd spent with the man over these last months, she would be ridiculed; and if he was guilty, rightly so.

"That's fantastic," said Mosley. "Then Mr. Randall can be on his way."

"Answer a few questions and we'll see what we can do."

Mosley chuckled and Laurie didn't much care for the sound. "That's a good one."

"Frank, just tell us where you were on Tuesday night." Maurice had claimed to have dropped Randall off on Wednesday morning, but they hadn't been able to verify that yet.

"Don't answer that," said Mosley. "Please, Detective Campbell. I know you're doing your job, but Mr. Randall has asserted his rights. He won't be talking tonight, and I don't believe you have any reason to be holding him here."

Remi leaned toward the man and his client. "A young woman has just been killed in the same manner as Mr. Randall's former wife, Annie Randall," he said as Laurie placed pictures of Grace Harrington's corpse on the table. "The wife Mr. Randall murdered."

Frank squirmed and looked away from the photos; Mosley seemed unaffected by them.

Laurie wanted to pull Frank aside and demand he tell her what had happened. It still just did not compute that Frank had attacked and killed Grace Harrington. He wasn't that old, but his mobility was severely limited due to his leg injury. And even if he had the strength, that type of brutality seemed beyond him.

But maybe that was what Annie Randall had thought, too.

She'd make one more attempt at questioning him.

"All we need is a reason not to keep you here overnight, Frank. Just tell us your movements on Tuesday evening and I'll see about letting you get home."

"I believe you'll be allowing my client home the second this interview is over," said Mosley. "Unless you want to charge him, which I would strongly advise you against."

"Thank you for the advice," said Remi.

"Let me remind you that you have nothing beyond a dubious link to a very old homicide investigation."

"At present," said Remi.

"Exactly, Detective Armstrong. If you should ever be in a position to offer us more, then we'll be happy to discuss. Until then, my client will not be speaking."

"Frank," said Laurie, "this will only make things worse for you."

"I am presuming that is not a threat, Detective?"

"If he leaves here without so much as an explanation for where he was that night, everyone will presume his guilt. I'm trying to protect him."

"Very commendable, I'm sure. Now, if we could wrap this up."

The song was the same during Maurice's interview. Like Frank, he'd been advised to assert the right to remain silent, though he had to be reminded of this on a couple of occasions by Mosley. Laurie understood why the lawyer had instructed the brothers to take this course of action, but that didn't make it any less frustrating. What she needed was for forensics to be pushed through, but those results could be days away.

"I don't think we have any option but to let them go," she said to Filmore, back in the lieutenant's office.

"Who is this Mosley guy?" said Filmore. "Never come across him before."

"He's employed by Maurice Randall's church group. A coalition of some thirty churches nationwide."

"That's all we need. Some high-octane attorney throwing wrenches into the works." Filmore shook his head. "You've been looking through the Annie Randall case. Anything there that can help us?"

"The injuries seem identical, but we need to wait for the autopsy report. Annie Randall's body wasn't discovered for three days after she was killed, whereas we think Grace Harrington died in the last eighteen hours. I think it's too circumstantial to charge him now."

Filmore sighed. "We won't even have enough to get a warrant to search his house for the murder weapon. Fine, do your best to keep this quiet, and send a patrol car to watch Randall. He's not to leave Galveston, though. Tell that lawyer that, will you?"

Laurie left the office and told Remi of the decision not to charge Frank. "That will not go down well," said Remi, glancing over at Warren, who was busy diverting the attention of some of the civilian staff from their work. She made the agreement with Mosley that Frank would be released on the condition that he stayed in Galveston. The agreement wasn't legally enforceable, but Mosley agreed to it readily enough.

As Laurie watched the lawyer drive Frank and Maurice away, it dawned on her that she would no longer be able to visit Frank in his house. He was an active suspect now, and she would only be able to see him on police business. She hadn't appreciated how much she'd enjoyed those visits, and she was surprised by the intensity of her sadness now that they were denied to her. She understood that talking to Frank had been a way of keeping close to David during a period where they were anything but. She'd learned some things about David's childhood, and his relationship with his mother, both things David had always been reluctant to talk about. Ridiculous as it felt, without Frank in her life she wondered if she and David had any future together.

◆　◆　◆

The thought occupied her during her run later that evening. Filmore had left for the night, and insisted her team go home and get some rest in preparation for the days ahead, but Laurie had been too hyped to sleep. She'd left her apartment building with no destination in mind but soon found herself following the same route Grace had taken on her final run. She'd stopped outside the Harrington house, and had considered checking in on the family, but it had been late and they would be in mourning. She tried to put herself in Grace's position as she started her run again, imagining what it was like once more to be a pissed-off teenager and what would have motivated her to take a different route. The obvious answer to that was the lure of her ex-girlfriend, Mia Washington, who she'd spoken to on the day she'd gone missing. Mia had been informed of Grace's death and would be at the station tomorrow for further questioning. Laurie ran by the girl's apartment building and wondered what she was thinking. If she was anything like Laurie had been as a teenager, she would be shouldering all the blame for Grace's death. It highlighted the unknown impact that unexpected death, especially violent unexpected death, had on the wider world. Grace's death would be felt way beyond her immediate family and friendship circle. It would touch on everyone at her school and in the community. If Annie Randall's death was anything to go by, it would rock the island city and the state for years to come. Even if it wasn't needed, that was motivation enough for Laurie to make sure the person responsible was brought to justice.

Returning to the seawall, Laurie ran through a stiff crosswind that ruffled her clothing and stung her skin. It was painful to run in, but she refused to turn back. It was a challenge she welcomed, her lungs bursting, her muscles screaming in pain as she pushed through the invisible barrier.

She kidded herself she didn't know where she was heading and let the lie play out even as she reached the turn onto Rebecca Whitehead's street. It was beyond foolish, but she ran down the road and stopped two houses away. She didn't know what she hoped to achieve. Any sign of David being here would devastate her, but the masochistic side of her hoped to see him. She wanted the pain of not knowing to subside, and if that meant catching him in the act, then so be it.

For one ludicrous moment, she even considered climbing the stairs to the porch and ringing the bell. She wondered if Rebecca would know who she was, and if her eyes would betray her. Laughing to herself, she turned and retraced her route back to the seawall and charged again into the wind.

Returning inland, Laurie passed the spot on Sealy Avenue where the GPS signal on Grace's Fitbit had cut out. She imagined a passing truck stopping and bundling Grace inside. For those practiced enough, it was a simple enough maneuver, and in the darkness, with little traffic, it was possible that it could have gone unnoticed.

By the time she returned to the Harrington house, she was forced to stop. Her running had been erratic tonight, her speed dictated by the power of the wind and the urgency of her thoughts, rather than her reliable steady pace. The lights inside the house were off and she hoped Glen and Sandra were able to have some sort of rest. Tomorrow was going to be difficult for all of them, their grief tempered by the ongoing murder investigation, which Glen was about to become directly involved in.

Laurie walked away from the house, waiting for her breath to return. She'd put to the back of her mind Filmore's concern over Glen Harrington's future, but now it returned and left a bitter taste in her mouth. Glen hadn't technically done anything illegal, and Laurie's years in law enforcement had taught her not to take a moralistic high ground, but the fact that he was having relations with young women the same age as his daughter was definitely a red flag she had to investigate. It might not be a motive for him to kill his daughter, but what if his attraction to the young women was related to an unnatural obsession with his daughter? Laurie had seen it before, and she needed to find out more about Glen Harrington. As far as she was concerned, his reputation could be damned. It would be easy to focus all their attention on Frank Randall, but at that moment she thought Glen Harrington was a worthy secondary suspect.

That notwithstanding, she had sympathy for the family as a whole. At the very least, Glen's dalliances would inadvertently reflect on Sandra, and would cheapen Grace's death. Laurie wished there was something she could do to stop that happening, but press management wasn't her job.

She returned toward the gulf, upping her pace until she was running again, thoughts of Grace's death bringing back memories of Milly. As her legs found a steady rhythm, she wondered for the millionth time what Milly would be like now. She'd probably be taking her first steps, and uttering her first words. It would never get any easier to accept that she'd never even taken a breath, that her little body had ceased to live in her womb. With all the monstrosities in the world, it still seemed brutally unfair that her little girl could be taken away without even enjoying the simple act of filling her lungs.

By the time Laurie reached her apartment, she didn't know if the salt on her face was from sweat or tears. Try as she might, she'd been unable to fight the urge of her mind to take her back to that time. She recalled the varying advice she'd been given after the stillbirth, the hardest of all being that she could try again, as if Milly had been some kind of failed experiment. It was hard enough that she had been stillborn, but for her girl to be treated as if she hadn't really existed was the cruelest thing of all. She and David had named their little girl and buried her, and now they both grieved for her like all parents grieved for their children. That she had died before her birth didn't mean a thing, and Laurie would honor her for the rest of her life.

"Right," she said to herself, as her pulse rate plummeted. She tried to refocus as she climbed the stairs, and only heard the sound from within her apartment once she'd opened the door.

Chapter Twenty-One

Laurie would have reached for her gun had she been carrying, and it took her a few seconds to realize that would have been a mistake. David had returned early and was in the living room with his earphones on. He jumped up on seeing her, his hand to his chest as he said, "God! You scared the crap out of me."

All the tension of the last few days hit Laurie at once, heightened by her recent thoughts of Milly. Seeing David sent a wave of conflicting emotions through her. She wanted to embrace him, to seek comfort in his arms, at the same time wanting to hurt him for the way he'd been making her feel. "I thought you weren't back until tomorrow," she said, hearing the coldness in her words, wanting to take them back but not knowing how.

"Last-minute change of mind. Bad weather brewing. You haven't seen it on the news?"

The weather forecast had been background news for the last few days, but she hadn't paid it much attention. Already this hurricane season, islanders had twice received warnings about storms hitting the island, only for both storms to veer away to sea. Storm and hurricane notices were a way of life in Galveston. The Great Storm of 1900 was the deadliest natural disaster in US history, and Hurricane Rita and Hurricane Ike were still recent memories, the latter in particular causing incredible damage to Galveston and the

Bolivar Peninsula. Laurie had stayed put during Ike, and could still recall the dread of being on the island during the storm, and the harrowing days that followed without power or facilities.

"I didn't realize it was that serious," she said.

"Who knows? They say it might be changing course. They ain't going to be taking any chances, so you're stuck with me earlier than you thought."

He was trying to be cute, but a few minutes ago Laurie had run past Rebecca Whitehead's house and was in no mood to play happy couples with him, even if the lure of his arms felt momentarily welcome. "I need to shower," she said, leaving him looking confused as she went to the bathroom.

Running the shower, she sat on the toilet and allowed herself to cry again. Instead of easing her tension, the run had somehow compounded everything. The release of her tears gave her some perspective, though, and she realized that in all the commotion of finding Grace's body and interviewing Frank, she hadn't really given any thought to how today's events would affect David. His estranged father was now a suspect in another murder, and images of Grace Harrington would naturally bring with it devastating memories of his mother. It didn't matter how angry she was with him, he needed to know and she needed to be the one to tell him.

She showered first, feeling sluggish as she noted signs of weight gain around her middle and on her arms. Her training was haphazard at the moment, and with the current investigation she wasn't eating the right things. She ran her hand over the slight curve of her belly and found it difficult to believe it had once protruded so hugely from her body, full of life.

"David," she said, as she left the bathroom, a large towel draped around her. The living-room lights were switched off, so she went to the bedroom, ready to face the difficult task of telling him about today, only to find him lying on the bed. She spread the wet towel over the back of a chair and climbed into bed next to him, the sound of his gentle breathing lulling her into sleep.

◆ ◆ ◆

Laurie was up first. She brewed some coffee and sat in the living room waiting for David to wake, the sound of wind rattling against the windowpanes keeping her company. On the television, the only news was of the potential hurricane making its way to Texas. Galveston's mayor was on, talking about a possible evacuation of the island. That had happened both for Rita and Ike, and both times it had been a catastrophe, people getting trapped for hours as they fled the coast; during Rita, more people had died on the road than during the storm itself.

Laurie muted the television, unable to deal with the idea that a hurricane could be making their lives even worse in the next few days, when she had more pressing concerns. The most pressing of which was telling David about Grace Harrington.

She had played out what she was going to say to him over and over in her head, trying to predict his responses, but gave it up. It was impossible to guess how he would react. He could go withdrawn and sullen, or he could turn angry and blame her for going to see his father and helping him to adjust back to life in Galveston so easily.

In the end, she was forced to wake him. Bringing him a coffee, she nudged him awake. "We need to talk," she said, as he stirred from his sleep.

David nodded as he sat up and accepted the coffee, as if he knew this moment was coming. It struck Laurie that maybe he thought she was going to question him about Rebecca Whitehead, and she almost asked the question, before deciding it would only confuse matters at the moment.

She sat next to him on the bed and told him what had happened. He barely reacted as she told him the news about Grace. Staring straight ahead, now and then sipping at his coffee, he failed to meet her eyes as she mentioned that Frank had been questioned.

"Be one hell of a coincidence if it ain't him," he said, after a prolonged period of silence.

"Not necessarily. It could quite easily be a copycat killing."

David gripped the coffee cup, still staring ahead as if he could see something invisible to her on the far wall. "Why, Laurie?"

"Why what?" she said, her hand hovering near his.

"Why do you insist on trying to see the good in him? You stop Warren giving him the justice he deserved, then you go see him, and now you think he might not be responsible?"

"You knew about that, with Warren?" said Laurie, troubled that David thought she'd somehow prevented justice being served.

"He killed my mom, Laurie. Warren's daughter. And now he has killed this poor girl."

"We don't know that, David." Even as she said it, she doubted her words. Was David right? Not for the first time in the last twenty-four hours, she wondered if she'd been deceived by Frank Randall.

"He killed my mom," repeated David, placing his cup on the bedside table before turning away from her and putting an end to the conversation.

Laurie did a hundred crunches before showering, her body stiff as she changed for work. She left the apartment without checking on David, her mood oscillating between sadness and anger. Somehow, he had made the whole situation about him. Even as she approached the station, she had to resist the urge to return to the apartment and confront him over whatever he had going on with Rebecca Whitehead. Maybe then he wouldn't be so sure of himself, and could check his righteous indignation about her methods of investigation.

Such was the overheated whirl of her thoughts that she shouted "What?" at the figure who'd dared stop her at the door to the station.

The young man, his jeans a size too small on his skinny frame, was momentarily taken aback, but recovered himself sufficiently to repeat the question: "Any comment on the similarities between Grace Harrington's homicide and that of Annie Randall?"

"No comment," Laurie muttered, only now taking in the numerous television trucks that had invaded the parking lot. How had she not seen them when she pulled in? Stepping into the station, she cursed herself for staggering around blind and losing her temper so easily.

Within a minute of reaching her desk and opening a browser, she understood how much media attention Grace's death was attracting. It was national news. But of course it would be, her cynical side told her. It involved a rich white family. Only last month, two African American boys had gone missing in Louisiana, their bodies discovered a week later, abused and abandoned by Cross Lake in Shreveport. Laurie had only found out about the incident after speaking to a local cop from the area during a joint investigation. As far as she was aware, it had never made much dent in local news, let alone national. But Grace had been white, young, and beautiful, and that made certain people take notice.

"For you."

Laurie looked up from her screen at the sound of Remi's voice as he dumped a file box on her desk. "What's this?"

"And good morning to you. The rest of the case notes on the Annie Randall investigation. Everything yet to be digitized, brought to you by order of our illustrious lieutenant."

At least he's forgotten about taking me off the case, she thought, as she opened the top file.

As she flicked through the case notes, alighting on the day Annie Randall's body was found, she could almost smell the nicotine and bourbon on the paper, the vices of choice of her old mentor, Jim Burnell. She would need more time than she had now to go through it all. She'd worked on cold cases before, had crawled through her old case notes, and it never ceased to amaze her how written memories could differ so much from what was stored in the mind. She hadn't had much of a part to play in the Annie Randall homicide investigation itself, but she could picture the murder scene as if it were a photograph. Only, if these reports were to be believed, Burnell's recollection of it differed from hers. His report was matter-of-fact, detailing the time the body was discovered, its positioning, and the initial findings of the CSI, who believed Annie had died from a laceration to the neck. But there was no mention of the weather—a storm brewing, just like now—and he omitted all the drama of that time: the chaos of the emergency services, Frank Randall's traumatic response as he was led to the sight of his crime, and the number of men it had taken to hold Chief Warren Campbell back from killing his son-in-law.

"Gemma is bringing Mr. and Mrs. Harrington in shortly for questioning," said Remi, dragging Laurie back into the present.

"We'll need to question them separately. They probably won't like it, but it has to be done," she said, scratching the back of her head and returning to the old investigation notes as she waited for the Harringtons to arrive.

◆ ◆ ◆

Twenty minutes later, the Harringtons were led into the office by Detective Clayton. Laurie did a double take as she saw that Tilly was with them, following behind Glen and Sandra like a dutiful daughter. Laurie's colleagues couldn't help themselves, the office falling silent as they walked through to the interview room.

"Back to work," said Laurie, as she signaled for Remi to join her in the interview room.

Words were all but useless in these situations. Laurie bowed her head slightly as she greeted the grieving family. Sandra and Glen sat at the table, hands interlocked. Laurie understood that whatever their differences at that moment, the grief at the death of their daughter would bond them for the time being. Laurie shot a look at the young detective, Gemma Clayton, communicating her displeasure at Tilly being present. Gemma shrugged, as if it was beyond her control.

Laurie and Remi sat across from the temporary family, as if they were about to begin an interrogation. "I am so sorry for your loss," Laurie began, a vision of Milly's lifeless body flashing before her eyes and disappearing in an instant. "And I know this is the last place you want to be, and talking to us is the last thing you want to be doing. We'll try to make this as quick as possible. Our role now is to find whoever is responsible, and I promise you my team and I will do everything in our power to do that for you."

Sandra Harrington made eye contact with her for the first time since arriving, and offered her the briefest of smiles. Laurie knew very well that the emotional and physical impact of grief couldn't be underestimated. She had to tread carefully, as the next few moments could easily turn either or both of the parents against her.

"To make things easier for you," she said, "we're going to interview each of you individually." Noting the confused looks on all three of their faces, she added, "It's just procedure."

"Is that necessary?" said Glen.

"It will be much quicker this way," said Laurie. "Sandra, if you stay here with Remi. Glen, if you're OK with coming with me. And Tilly, I'll find someone to speak to you. None of this should take very long, and we can get you all on your way. Whenever you finish, just wait for the others in the reception area."

Laurie couldn't be sure, but it looked to her as if Sandra was relieved to see her husband and Tilly escorted out of the room. "We'll be back soon," said Laurie, nodding to Remi then closing the door after them.

Laurie placed Glen in a separate interview room before quizzing Gemma. "How has the mood been at home?"

"All but silent. They put down a lot of alcohol last night, and I had to help Sandra up to bed."

"And Tilly?"

"She's been a great help, actually. Really supportive of them both," said Gemma, before hesitating. "Any new developments I should know about?"

Laurie updated the officer on Glen's extramarital activity. "You hear any discussion about that?"

"No, but I have to say I was a bit surprised to see them holding hands just now. If anything, they've been avoiding one another at home."

"OK, keep your ears open for any mention. Awful question, but is there anything to suggest something going on between Glen and Tilly?"

Gemma winced. "I haven't noticed anything, but I didn't know about what he's been getting up to. I'll look out for any signs."

"Don't you find it a bit strange, Tilly spending all her time there?"

"From what she's told me, she doesn't have much of a home life. Single dad who sounds like he's alcohol dependent."

"That makes sense," said Laurie, heading over to the interview room where Glen was waiting, deep into a call on his cell phone.

Laurie shut the door and signaled for Glen to end his call. He sighed, as if talking to her was an inconvenience he was being forced to endure.

"Thanks, Glen. Probably a stupid question, but how are you holding up?"

"As well as I can." Everything about him, from his folded arms to his furrowed forehead, screamed defensive to Laurie.

"And Sandra?"

"Not that well. It would be helpful if we could get her out of here."

"Of course, this shouldn't take long," said Laurie. "Again, this is just procedure, but I will be asking questions and need to inform you that you have the right to legal representation."

That got his attention. He unfolded his arms and sat up straight. "What the hell is this?"

"As I said, it's just standard procedure. Sandra and Tilly will be told the same. Would you like legal representation, Glen?"

The question had thrown him. As he slowly shook his head, his mouth open, Laurie didn't waste any time. She started recording, confirming for the record that Glen had waived his right for a lawyer to be present. She began gently, asking him where he was on the night Grace had gone missing and the night before her body had been found, before changing her tone. "I understand you and Sandra having been going through some relationship troubles?"

A smirk twisted his lips. "Someone been talking?"

"Quite a few people, actually. Including Bonnie Webb and Natalie Morton."

His face went ashen at the names of his former lovers. "What the hell?" he said, now much more alert to the situation.

"I believe Natalie was the last person you had an affair with. According to her, you put a stop to it early this year."

Glen heaved a deep sigh, as if the line of questioning was pointless. "What can I say? I'm away from home most of the time. I get lonely. I won't be the first married man to look elsewhere, and certainly won't be the last."

"How old was Natalie when you broke it off with her?"

"I don't see the relevance—"

"How old?"

"Eighteen, nineteen," said Glen, color returning to his cheeks.

"Eighteen years old, Glen. A few weeks before her nineteenth birthday."

Glen raised his voice as he leaned in toward Laurie. "And your point is?"

"You like them young, Glen?"

Glen recoiled in disgust. "Nothing illegal. She was very mature for her age."

"And Bonnie? Sandra knows about Bonnie, doesn't she?"

Glen shook his head, his clenched teeth making it clear he wasn't used to being spoken to this way. "This is none of your business."

"Would your company see it that way? Both women—I say women, but they were little more than girls—were the same age as Grace." Laurie wasn't there to moralize. Glen was right in the fact he'd done nothing legally wrong, but he was nearly three times the age of the women in question and had been in a position of power over them. "Something you're not telling us, Glen?"

Glen's thought process was evident on his twitching face. "What are you saying? You think because I slept with some slutty college girls that I killed my daughter?"

At last, the man appeared to be revealing his true self. Laurie wondered what Grace would have thought of him, talking about

151

the college girls that way. "No one mentioned you killing Grace. Is there something you want to tell us?"

"You should have told me you were going to ask these questions," he said, getting to his feet.

"You're free to leave, Glen, but we will need to continue this interview. Maybe you should appoint a lawyer."

"Don't you worry," he said. "I'll be retaining a full team of lawyers, and when they're done with you, you'll no longer have a job."

Chapter Twenty-Two

Every time Randall closed his eyes, all he could see was Annie's mutilated body. It was like those first months after her death, when his memories of her felt forever tarnished by all he'd seen that day. Over the years, he'd been able to compartmentalize those images so they only appeared in his nightmares, or at moments of stress. Now, like then, every time he tried to think of their life together, the memory of her gentle beauty morphed in the space of a strangled breath into that lifeless figure in the sand.

It was so cruel that death had ravaged her in such a way. They'd occasionally talked about what would happen when they died, Randall readily accepting Annie's pact that they both be buried. "I want to be worm food," she'd told him. "I want to be part of the earth."

She'd become food for more than worms in those three days she'd been left alone in the weeds by the dunes. Animals of all sorts had had their fill of her, until only the left side of her face had been recognizable, her red hair, still ablaze in the autumn sunshine, covering the savage wound that had bled her dry. Randall tried to shake that vision, clinging on to happier times. Forcing himself to recall their wedding day—the short ceremony in the Strand followed by a party on the beach, Annie impossibly beautiful as they ran hand in hand toward the gulf.

From the other room, a fresh salvo of Maurice's snoring shook him from his reverie. Mr. Mosley had suggested they remain on the island, not wanting to give the authorities any grounds to incarcerate them. Already it was claustrophobic having his brother pressed into these rooms with him. In prison, he'd grown to accept tight quarters, but having Maurice in the house felt like a disservice to Annie. He still couldn't pinpoint the source of her hatred for him, but she'd never allowed Maurice to stay here when they'd been together. Despite the circumstances, it felt like a betrayal to have him sleeping in David's old room.

He left his bedroom and set water to boil on the stove. Funny how having someone stay over could make him feel so lonely. The only person he would have liked to see now was Laurie—or David, if he would ever consent to such a thing—but that was something unlikely to ever happen again. He'd seen the disappointment on her face as she'd shown him the photographs of that poor young girl. He'd tried not to look, but his eyes had sought out the images as if they wanted to punish him. The similarities were unmistakable and he'd struggled to keep the scream lodged within him from escaping. The girl had been a runner. She shared Annie's long legs, her hair a darker shade of Annie's fiery color. Like Annie, she'd been placed in that strange position, as if she'd been running on the sand; like Annie, her legs had been cruelly broken, and her neck severed.

It was as if time had come full circle, and as he sat in his armchair, the sound of Maurice's snoring competing with the shrills and hoots from the wildlife outside, a never-ending kaleidoscope of images played through Randall's mind of Annie and Grace, and the other girl who had started this all off.

Chapter Twenty-Three

Glen Harrington's threats were nothing new to Laurie. She'd heard similar hundreds of times before, usually from those in privileged positions who didn't think the law fully applied to them. She didn't care how uncomfortable the questioning made him, or anyone else for that matter. All she cared about was finding Grace's killer and if that meant upsetting some people on the way—and in particular those conducting sordid affairs with young women the same age as their daughters—then so be it.

Sandra, Glen, and Tilly had left the building thirty minutes after Laurie's interview with Glen. As Laurie watched them file out, the distance between Glen and Sandra had been noticeable. All three had been questioned along the same lines at Laurie's request, and she wondered what Sandra and Tilly were thinking about Glen as they left the building.

Shortly after, Laurie had attended Grace's autopsy. It was never an easy experience, and Grace's was no exception. The pathologist confirmed the worst fears of the CSI team. The injuries to Grace's legs had been inflicted when she'd still been alive.

The fact haunted Laurie now as she worked through Annie Randall's case file. Due to the delay in finding Annie's body, it had never been determined for sure if Annie had endured the horrific fractures to her legs when she'd been alive. When Frank had finally admitted guilt, he'd claimed not to have remembered the attack. From the records, it appeared the DA had been torn between staging a big court case and pushing for a tougher sentence or—the decision that had finally been made—accepting the plea and with it the guaranteed prosecution. They had chosen the latter, and because of that no details were ever offered from Frank about the attack. He wouldn't have been the first innocent person to accept a plea when facing overwhelming evidence. What if he had only accepted guilt to prevent a court case and the threat of a longer sentence, and possibly execution?

Either way, the rest of her colleagues still considered Frank Randall to be the only possible culprit in Grace's death. A car was positioned close to his house, where he was currently staying with his brother. Lieutenant Filmore was one of many convinced that forensic reports would definitively link Frank to Grace, and that it was only a matter of time before they could arrest him and put him back behind bars.

Laurie couldn't afford to think that way. She'd assigned Rodriquez and Abbey to work on the Frank Randall side of the investigation. The pair were currently in Dickinson, speaking to members of Maurice Randall's congregation, trying to pinpoint the Randall brothers' movements over the last few days. Laurie still felt it odd that David had never once mentioned his estranged uncle. As her tour of the Annie Randall case file reached the notes on Jim Burnell's interview with Maurice Randall all those years ago, she again wondered what else her husband had been hiding from her.

Closing her eyes, she pinched her nose and set about the by now grimly familiar business of trying to dismiss the images of Rebecca Whitehead from her head. Grace was the only person who deserved her attention at that moment and she needed to stay focused.

Jim Burnell's interview notes with Maurice Randall were succinct. He had only spoken to the pastor by phone, when Maurice had told him that he hadn't seen Frank in over three years. Jim hadn't seen any need to call Maurice in for further detail—despite him being the only surviving member of Frank's extended family—and had closed the report.

It was no wonder Laurie couldn't recall Maurice. Maurice's involvement didn't sit well with her and she wanted to know more about his relationship with Frank, especially considering the fact the two brothers were currently each other's alibi.

The more she read through the Annie Randall notes, the more apparent it became that Burnell's investigation had been single-minded from the beginning. It was clear there had only ever been one credible suspect and that Jim had gone after Frank Randall from the start, to the exclusion of all others.

Not that she could blame him. The evidence was substantial. There were witness reports of Annie and Frank arguing on the day she died, a fresh wound on Frank's eye he admitted had come from Annie, and Frank's DNA was found all over her body. Most telling of all were the abrasions found on Frank's body, and his skin found under Annie's nails, suggesting a struggle between the pair.

Perhaps a better lawyer than the court-appointed one Frank received would have fought harder on those two facts. As a married couple, it was natural that Frank's DNA would have been found on Annie's body, and the skin under her nails could have occurred during sex.

Why are you trying to defend him?

Laurie closed the file. Her job right now wasn't to reinvestigate Annie's death. She was reading the case to uncover direct links between the two murders, and so far the only link was Frank Randall. She understood that some distant part of her wanted Frank to be innocent. The thought that Milly's grandfather was a murderer was hard for her to accept. It was futile thinking along those lines, but she'd long ago acknowledged that it was impossible to think rationally about her daughter's death.

"Boss, call just came out I thought you'd want to know about."

Laurie looked up to see one of the uniformed officers standing by her desk. "Tell me."

"It's nothing really, some sort of domestic dispute. A fight between two teenagers that got out of hand. Only, when I read the names, I thought you'd want to know."

"Get to the point."

"It was Grace Harrington's . . . girlfriend?"

Laurie gave the officer a hard stare, wondering why it was so hard for the man to speak the words. "Tilly Moorfield?"

"Yes."

"And who was she fighting?"

"I believe it was Grace's ex, Mia Washington."

Laurie took a deep breath and released it. "Right. I'll get right on it."

Outside, Laurie felt like she was walking in molasses as she made her way to the car. She'd all but ignored the weather report this morning. Among the problems presenting themselves, it had been easy to shove aside. But as she hauled the car door shut after her, she began to realize how important it could become. No one wanted to take chances in the city, and there had been more noise about a possible evacuation. The fact that David had been sent home early was a worrying sign, and as she drove along the seawall, her mind started overthinking the situation. It felt as if the gulf was lying in wait for the town. The waves were up, the tide creeping toward the shore. The sight of the seawalls being breached, cars having to crawl through seawater, was too recent a memory for her, and the threat of another tragedy all too vivid.

Driving the route she'd run yesterday evening, Laurie parked next to the two patrol cars already stationed outside Mia Washington's apartment building. She instructed the officers to switch the flashing lights off as she glanced into the back of one of the cars, where a disgruntled-looking Tilly was sitting.

Ignoring her, Laurie walked over to the front of the building, where Mia Washington's mother pulled out of a full-blown argument with two of the uniformed team to glare at her. "About time you got here," she said, the calming personality Laurie had encountered the other day nowhere to be seen. Now, the woman's face was contorted into uncontrollable anger.

"Shall we go inside and you can tell me what happened?" said Laurie.

"What happened is that little . . . *lady* over there"—she jabbed a finger toward Tilly—"assaulted my daughter, and I want her prosecuted."

"Where is Mia? Can I see her?"

Mrs. Washington fell still in the doorway for a long, furious moment, clearly internally debating the situation, before turning and calling over her shoulder for her daughter. Mia appeared moments later, an ice pack held to her forehead.

"How are you doing, Mia?" said Laurie.

"Look at her," said Mrs. Washington.

Laurie couldn't see anything with the ice pack to the girl's face. "Could you take Mrs. Washington inside so I can talk to Mia?" she said to her colleague.

"No way," said Mrs. Washington.

"Mom, *please*," said Mia, raising her voice.

"I want that girl arrested," said Mrs. Washington, as she was reluctantly led inside.

"Well," said Laurie, "let's see it."

Mia pulled the ice pack away to reveal a small lump on the side of her forehead. "Sucker punch," she said, replacing the ice pack.

Laurie couldn't quite imagine diminutive Tilly striking out at someone, though grief could change a person as quick as liquor or drugs. "What exactly happened?"

"That was it. She rang the doorbell, I opened the door and she just punched me."

"Did she say anything?"

"No."

"And did you hit her back?"

"No. I wish I had. Mom was standing behind me and she grabbed Tilly before she could get away. Then she told me to go and put some ice on it before calling you guys." She turned and glared Tilly's way through reddened eyes. "She thinks she's the only one grieving."

The wind thrashed their hair as Laurie gave Mia a few seconds to compose herself. It whistled down the street, seeking out pockets to rush through. "Why would she do this?" Laurie asked at last, brushing her hair from her forehead.

Mia shrugged. "I guess she's still jealous of the other day. What can I say?"

"You know I'm conducting a homicide investigation, Mia?"

"Of course I do."

"Then I need you to tell me the truth. Is there anything else I should know? About you and Grace? Or you and Tilly?"

Mia's shoulders rose up to her head, as if she was trying to hide herself. "What else can I tell you?"

"It will all come out, Mia. Tell me now and it will make it so much easier for you."

"Honestly, I've told you everything."

Honestly. Laurie had heard that so many times before that to her it was almost a liar's creed. She told Mia to go back inside, and went over to the patrol car, where she climbed in next to Tilly.

It was a relief to be out of the wind. Laurie hadn't realized how intrusive the sound outside had been. "Tough day?" she said.

Tilly stared ahead, not meeting her gaze. "You could say that."

"Mia's got quite a knot on the side of her head."

Tilly bit her lower lip. "I shouldn't have taken it out on her."

"No, you shouldn't have. But you're still in shock."

Tilly turned toward her. "You don't understand," she said, eyes downcast.

"Don't understand what, Tilly?"

"I've really messed up."

Laurie could tell she meant something beyond hitting Grace's ex-girlfriend. "You can tell me. You're not going to get into trouble, at least not much more than a slap on the wrist for your little punching fit. I want to find Grace's killer. That's all."

"I should have told you, but I hid it," said Tilly, all the pent-up frustration of the last couple of days coming out in a wave of emotion as she started to cry.

Laurie wanted the girl to tell her what she meant, but there was no point in rushing her. When she appeared to have cried herself out, Laurie asked, "Hid what, Tilly?"

"Grace's diary. I should have told you about it, but I wanted to keep it safe. I read it when I got back today. It was for the first time, I swear. I confronted him about it and he told me to leave the house."

"Glen? Mr. Harrington?"

Tilly nodded.

"Was Sandra there?"

"No, she'd gone for a walk."

"What was in it that made you confront Mr. Harrington?"

"Don't you get it? That was the reason Grace and Mia split up. She never really cared about me. She was just using me because she was still in love with Mia."

"Slow down, Tilly. Start again."

"I never read the diary until today, I promise," said Tilly, repeating herself. "I took it when Grace went missing. She always left it in sight. She liked to test me, to see if I could be trusted."

"And what did it say when you read it today, Tilly?"

"It was Glen all along. That was why they split up."

"Mr. Harrington told Grace to split up with Mia?"

Tilly shook her head and Laurie had a sickening feeling about what she was going to say next. "No—well, probably, but that wasn't the reason. Grace saw them, you know?"

"No," said Laurie, but there was an inevitability as to what was to come. "Tell me."

"Glen and Mia. Together. You know, making out. She wrote about it in her diary. That was why I hit Mia. I couldn't believe she would do that to Grace."

Laurie ran her hand through her hair. "You told Mr. Harrington you read this?" she said, already making her way out of the car.

Tilly nodded.

"Stay here," said Laurie, calling in backup as she returned to her own car.

Chapter Twenty-Four

If Tilly was telling the truth, this potentially changed everything; making out with your daughter's girlfriend wasn't the behavior of a man in control of himself. She made a number of quick calls on the short journey to the Harringtons' house in Offatts Bayou before calling Gemma Clayton to double-check that Glen Harrington was still at home.

"He went out an hour ago," said Gemma, a hint of nervousness in her voice.

"Out? Where exactly?" said Laurie, already fearing the worst as she watched a trash can lid caught in an updraft sail past her car roof.

"Said he needed to clear his head. I didn't know I was supposed to keep them inside," said Gemma defensively.

"Wait there." Laurie hung up, her impatience outweighing any compassion for her colleague's mistake.

Parking outside the Harringtons', she called Rodriquez and told him to concentrate his efforts on finding Glen. She decided not to tell him why for the time being but insisted that it be the team's number one priority.

Gemma answered the door. "Sorry, ma'am," she said. "I would never have let him leave if I had known."

Sandra Harrington was in the sitting room, curled up on a four-seater leather sofa, a cup in her hand, staring through the ceiling-high windows at the pattern the wind was making on the surface of the ornamental pool outside. She greeted Laurie with a vacant look before glancing over at the television, where a rerun of *Modern Family* was playing on mute.

Laurie sat down next to her. "Do you know where Glen is, Sandra?"

"Out. I hope he never comes back," she said, not looking away from the television.

Remi had questioned Sandra about Glen's extramarital affairs. He'd even gone so far as to ask her if she thought her husband capable of killing Grace. Remi had told Laurie that she'd been surprised by the question, but perhaps not as surprised as she could have been.

"We really do need to speak to him, Sandra. Is there anywhere you think he may have gone?"

"He took the car, so he's probably heading to Houston to fuck one of his college girls."

"You knew about that already though, Sandra, didn't you? About Glen and young women?"

Sandra placed her cup down. From the smell, it seemed it had been full of white wine. She was wearing jogging sweats and an oversized hoodie with Texas A&M emblazoned on it. "What can I say, he likes them young. I didn't mind so much in the beginning, but that was twenty years ago. It's sad and pathetic now."

"He's been doing this for twenty years?"

"That's not the worst of it. I'm one of his affairs. He was with someone when we hooked up. I didn't know about it at the time, but it explains a lot. I wouldn't have lasted if I hadn't got pregnant."

Laurie's stomach lurched at the word "pregnant." She wanted to ask Sandra why she'd stuck it out with the man for so long, but she wasn't there to judge anyone. "I understand Glen and Tilly had an argument?"

"Did they? I've been sleeping."

Laurie looked over to Gemma, who nodded. "I heard some shouting," said Gemma. "Tilly left, and Glen not long after."

"What's happening?" said Sandra, glancing from Laurie to Gemma and back again.

Ideally, Laurie would have liked to have seen the diary before proceeding, but she suspected Sandra knew much more than she'd been letting on. "Can you think of a reason Tilly and Glen would argue?"

Sandra shook her head, but Laurie could see the realization dawning on her. Her life had been a lie and it had now reached a terrible conclusion. "Tilly found out something about Mia," Laurie said. "About Mia and Glen."

She knew immediately that Sandra understood what she was saying. The woman shrank back into the sofa, but there was no denial. "Grace told me," she said, hugging herself. "But I just couldn't, you know . . ."

"Couldn't what?"

"I couldn't let it be true," said Sandra, shrugging her shoulders as if that explained everything.

After Sandra had composed herself, Laurie asked her to call Glen. "Tell him you need him back here as soon as possible."

The call went straight to voicemail. "He usually has it switched off," said Sandra, by way of explanation.

After trying Glen's work and apartment building with no luck, Laurie called Filmore and requested that an APB be put out on Glen Harrington. Filmore's tone of voice suggested he wasn't happy with the request, and Laurie had to spell out her concerns. "He'd made out with his daughter's girlfriend, and for all we know he may have gone much further."

"That's not a capital crime," said Filmore, his sights still solely on Frank Randall. "And it's not a natural progression that he would do something with his own daughter."

"I agree, but I don't like the fact that he went AWOL the second Tilly confronted him about this. With his kind of wealth and connections, he could become a difficult man to find. I'm trying to spare us some issues in the long term."

Filmore's sigh was audible down the phone line. "Fine, but let me know the second he returns to the house so we can take it off the system."

Laurie hung up. In the rush to reach the house, she hadn't asked Tilly where she'd found the diary and where it was now. As was procedure, a thorough search of the house had been undertaken when Grace's body was discovered, but no diary had been uncovered. Laurie called the station, where Tilly had been taken on possible assault charges, and arranged to speak to the girl on the phone.

"Are you alone?" asked Laurie, when Tilly answered.

"The officer from before is here but no one else. You said I wouldn't get anything more than a slap on the wrist."

"You probably won't, but Mia's mother has insisted you be processed, and to be honest at this moment, Tilly, I have more pressing concerns. Where did you find Grace's diary?"

"It was in her locker at school."

"What? When did you retrieve it?" Like the house, the school had been searched, including all the contents of Grace's locker.

"When she first went missing. No one noticed."

"And where is it now?"

"In the spare room where I've been staying, in the bedside table drawer."

"Stay on the line." Laurie took the phone upstairs to the spare room, where she retrieved the diary. Shutting the bedroom door,

166

she asked Tilly softly if Glen Harrington had ever tried anything on with her.

Tilly's laugh in reply was cold and mirthless. "I'm not his type," she said.

◆ ◆ ◆

Laurie didn't understand why, but she was fixated on what Tilly had said. She glanced at her short, stocky legs as she made her way downstairs. Like Tilly, her shape was a stark contrast to Mia's, and to the long-limbed Harrington women's. Glen clearly did have a type but Grace Harrington, like Annie Randall, hadn't been sexually assaulted. Maybe Glen hadn't been able to go through with it, or maybe he'd had nothing to do with his daughter's death. Either way, it was imperative that she speak to him.

As she reached the kitchen, Sandra Harrington was opening a bottle of wine. "Please, Sandra, you'll be much more use to us sober." Shooting Gemma a fierce look, she took the bottle away from the woman. "Come and sit down. Maybe Gemma could make us some coffee?" said Laurie, holding Sandra's arm as she guided her to the sofa.

Laurie wasn't shocked by the situation Sandra found herself in. Loveless marriages, particularly ones where the female spouse felt trapped, were all too common. Even Glen's predilection for teenagers didn't feel that uncommon and she'd met many women over the years who'd turned a blind eye to such behavior, and sometimes to things even worse. "Did you ever try to leave?" she asked Sandra, sitting next to her.

"I certainly made a lot of noise about it. That's why we ended up getting the place in Houston. His little fuck pad. Out of sight, out of mind, that's what they say, isn't it?"

"Did Grace know?"

Sandra shook her head. "Not until she saw him kissing Mia. Jesus Christ, what a night that was. All three of them crying. Glen begging Grace's forgiveness. She worshipped him, you see. Well, they worshipped each other. I could never have said a bad word about him. She would either not have believed me or taken his side anyway. You know how it is."

Laurie thought about Milly. Would she have turned out to be a Daddy's girl? David had so looked forward to being a father that it broke her heart even to think about it. "And after she found out about Glen and Mia?"

"She hasn't spoken to him since. Never will now, will she?"

"How did Glen take it?"

"What do you mean?"

"Was he sad? Angry?"

"Glen is not great at emotion. Truth is, we haven't seen that much of him these last few months. Very busy at work, you understand," she said, with cutting sarcasm.

"And Grace? Tilly thinks Grace only got together with her because she was on the rebound."

"Tilly's a sweet little thing. I don't know if that's true or not. Fact is, Grace and I weren't on great speaking terms, either, after Glen left. I think a part of her blamed me. And you know what, that part was right. I should have kicked that man out long ago. He is poison, and he destroyed my daughter's last few months on this Earth."

Laurie paused, preparing for the question she'd wanted to ask since arriving. "I'm sorry that I have to ask you this, but I'm afraid I have no option," she said.

Sandra frowned, smudges of mascara breaking out on the side of her eyes. "Ask me what?"

"Do you think Glen ever tried anything with Grace?"

This time, there was no pause for reaction. Sandra's face contorted into a mask of rage. "Of course not," she said, heaving herself to her feet. "What the hell is this? You think Glen and . . . and . . ."

Laurie slowly got to her feet. Even in her shoes, she was a few inches shorter than the barefooted Sandra and was forced to look up at the woman. "I know it's an awful thing to think about, but please, Sandra. For Grace's sake."

Just like that, the anger drained from Sandra, and she fell back into the sofa. Laurie remained standing, this time looking down on the woman, who looked beaten and worn out.

"You think Glen may have killed her?" Sandra's voice was ragged, empty, the true horror of that potential truth beginning to resonate.

"It's something we have to explore. It would help if we could speak to him."

"I can't believe he would sink this low, though I said the same thing when I found out about Mia. I don't know where he is, I truly don't. I didn't think Tilly knew about the situation between them. I've been sleeping and . . ."

Gemma walked over and handed Laurie her phone. "Station has been trying to reach you."

Laurie took the phone. "Detective Campbell."

"Laurie, it's Rodriquez. I thought you'd want to know first. Been a bit of trouble in a bar on 23rd Street. A couple of arrests. I'm afraid we have Warren in custody."

"Is he OK?"

"Yeah. Evidently someone said something about Annie and he took it the wrong way. Busted the guy up pretty good."

"OK. Let him sleep it off, and I'll come and get him soon."

Chapter Twenty-Five

Laurie tried Glen's phone again before leaving for the station. Leaving Gemma Clayton with Sandra, she told the officer to keep gently nudging the grieving mother. It seemed obvious to Laurie that Sandra was stuck in an abusive relationship. And even if the extent of the situation was beginning to dawn on Sandra, it didn't mean she wouldn't protect her husband, consciously or not. It was highly likely that Sandra knew where Glen was at that moment, and for everyone's sake they needed to find the man before he disappeared for good.

Laurie skimmed ahead through Grace's diary, alighting on the last entry, where she'd caught her dad and Mia together. That had been six months ago, and the diary hadn't been touched since. She tried to imagine what that would have done to Grace, but found it impossible to comprehend. Placing the diary in an evidence bag, she forced herself to listen to local radio as she made the short journey to the station, the wind rocking her car side to side as the waterline crept ominously toward the seawall. A category 4 hurricane, cutely named Heather by the National Hurricane Center, had briefly made landfall in Cuba and was now bearing down on the Gulf of Mexico. It appeared to be heading toward the coast of Texas, but no one could guess if it would make landfall or lose power over the gulf. Some islanders weren't taking any chances and had already begun leaving the island city, fearing the chaos of a last-minute evacuation, which in previous years had seen vehicles stuck in queues in excess of fifteen hours. The mayor had yet to announce any official evacuation plans, though a hurricane committee was closely monitoring the storm and all emergency departments were on standby.

The islanders were resilient, particularly the BOIs. Many had experienced Rita and Ike with stoicism, even during the dark days of no power or communication. Laurie had stayed herself during Ike, part of a small skeleton crew who'd manned the police station. David had been away at work and they'd gone six days without speaking to one another when the power cut. The relief of speaking to him again and, days later, seeing him, was a raw emotion she would never be able to forget. She'd been reminded during those times how fragile normality was, and how quickly it could be devastated by something as simple, yet powerful, as the weather.

News of an impending evacuation had obviously reached the station. Equipment was being packed for storage as Laurie made her way down to the holding cells to speak to Warren. Sergeant Nick Raynor was manning the holding cells and offered her a warm smile as she arrived. Nick was the longest-serving officer at the station and had worked under Warren's reign as chief, and no doubt would be doing everything to look after him. "Last time I looked in on him he was asleep, or pretending to be," he said.

"And the person he hit? Hear anything?"

"We managed to persuade him to drop charges," said Nick, grinning. "It was either that or face a charge himself. Thankfully he had two DUIs to his name, so he didn't want to risk anything stupid."

Laurie didn't want to know any more. "Can I take him home?"

"Sure, give me ten and I'll do all the necessaries."

Fifteen minutes later, Warren was led out by Nick, the pair sharing a joke as Warren collected his belongings. "You here to tell me off?" said Warren, eyes downcast as Laurie stood with her arms folded.

"If I didn't have so much going on, I would've pushed for you to stay the night like an idiot teenager. Come on, let's get you home."

◆ ◆ ◆

The drive to Warren's house—a small family home near Sea Isle Beach—had started with Warren apologizing, but quickly progressed to the man falling asleep. Laurie parked outside the house and let him sleep some more, content to sit in relative peace as the storm raged outside.

"Come on, let's get you in," she said, when Warren finally stirred twenty minutes later.

"You haven't told David, have you?" he asked as she walked him up the steep stairs to the front door of the stilted property and let herself in with her spare key.

"Not yet," she said, a shiver running through her as she shut the door, cutting all sound but the low, ominous white noise of the storm.

"I'd rather you didn't. He's going through a lot just now, what with his dad coming back, and now all this."

Laurie switched on the lights. The place looked tidy, the bookshelves well organized, but a closer look revealed a film of dust on everything. She and David had suggested Warren hire a cleaner, his wife having died some ten years ago, but the former chief was a stubborn soul.

"Have you spoken to him?" she asked him.

"Once or twice."

172

It was absurd to be feeling this way, but part of her was jealous that David had spoken to his grandfather when she couldn't get a word out of him. As she made Warren coffee, she wondered if he knew about Rebecca Whitehead. She watched him sip at the coffee in the same way David did, and decided she was being unfair.

"So you want to tell me what happened tonight, Warren?"

Warren's hound-dog eyes looked away from her. Laurie had always admired his strength and resilience as chief of police and hated seeing the change in him. He looked another notch older than he had when she'd stopped him from beating Frank. "What can I say? I had a few too many beers."

"Someone said something about Annie?"

Warren sighed, and Laurie heard so much emotion in the sound that she had to look away. Warren had been something of a surrogate father to David these last sixteen years, and had been a father figure to her, too, since she'd first started working for him. She'd enjoyed getting to know him better since she'd married David, and with her own parents having passed, she now considered Warren to be family. It pained her to see the weight he carried from Annie's murder. "It came at the wrong time," he said now, very quietly. "The guy was trying to bait me. I shouldn't have responded in the way I did, but damn, he deserved everything he got"—for a second sounding like his old, fearsome self.

But Warren wasn't the man she'd seen at Grace's murder site, and then at the station. Maybe it was the hangover kicking in, or the stress of the last few days, but she knew there wouldn't be a better opportunity to question him.

Pouring him a second coffee, she told him about Glen Harrington.

Warren accepted the cup with trembling hands. "Never met the man, but I've met his sort," he said, some of the authority returning to his voice. "You think he may have killed his daughter?" he asked, sounding doubtful.

"We should get forensics back in the next couple of days," she said.

"I'm sure he'll turn up. Probably ashamed of himself, as well he should be."

"I'm glad I got to see you, Warren, even under these circumstances, as I wanted to speak to you about the original investigation into Frank Randall."

Warren shuddered at Frank's name, sipping his coffee before replying. "And here I was thinking you were being the dutiful granddaughter-in-law," he said, with a weary smile.

"I'll always be there for you, Warren, you know that. I just need to get to the bottom of things."

"You know how I feel. You'll see when forensics get back to us. That poor girl will be swimming in that bastard's DNA. Why they ever let him out is beyond me. They should have tied the key to a rock and sunk it to the bottom of the gulf."

Laurie knew Warren would have done everything in his power to persuade the parole board that Frank was still a threat. "I'm sure you're right, Warren, but I have to be prepared for all eventualities, you know that."

He grunted, then sighed. "Then how can I help you, Detective?"

"I've been going through Jim's notes from that time and although everything is above board, it does seem to me that his investigation was narrow in its focus."

"How so?"

"Frank was the only real suspect."

"You know as well as I do that sometimes it works out that way. Everything pointed to Randall being responsible, and thankfully *we* didn't have to wait long for our forensics."

Laurie couldn't tell if that was a jab at her, but chose to ignore it. "Have you met Maurice Randall before?"

"The brother? No, not until yesterday."

"You don't find that odd? David aside, Maurice was Frank's closest living relative, and Jim did nothing more than phone him up."

"Laurie, I don't understand this. Everything pointed to Randall being guilty. I know it don't mean anything, but I could see it in him. The guilt. Made no difference to me, I'll tell you that, but he was a guilty man."

"If he felt guilty about Annie, then why has he done it again?"

"Who the hell knows? Just because they feel guilt, don't mean they won't repeat it. You know that."

"What did you think of Frank before it all happened?" asked Laurie, a question she'd wanted to ask him ever since the day Annie's body was found.

A flicker of indecision crossed Warren's eyes as he went to answer, as if he was debating how much he should tell her. "I was never for it, if that's what you mean."

"Frank and Annie getting married."

Warren recoiled. "Wasn't a secret. I know all daddies say it, but he wasn't good enough for her."

"Why was that?"

"Just a feeling?"

"A feeling? Come on, Warren . . . Don't you think now might be a good time to start sharing?"

Warren linked his hands together and placed his chin on a bridge of fingers. A steeliness had returned to his eyes, and as he stared back at Laurie he was no longer her grandfather-in-law, but the former chief of police. "He was a good-for-nothing ladies' man, that's what he was," he said, but there was little conviction in his voice.

"Did he ever cheat on Annie?" asked Laurie, unable not to think about Rebecca Whitehead.

"Probably."

"You can do better than that, Warren."

"Hell, I don't know, but that ain't the point," said Warren, getting to his feet. The sudden movement and anger left him breathless. "I'm sorry, I shouldn't have raised my voice. You're doing your job, and you're doing an amazing one at that. You know how proud I am of you."

"I need to be sure, you understand that. If there is anything I should know, you need to tell me."

Again, she saw the indecision in Warren's eyes before he answered. "There's nothing. Wait for forensics, and put him away where he belongs. Now, if you'll excuse me, I think I need to sleep off this hangover."

David was asleep by the time Laurie got home. She glanced in on him, wondering how they'd ever got to this point—then admitting that she knew very well, each and every sad step. She made some cocoa and watched the news channels, all of which were focused on Hurricane Heather. After leaving Warren's, she'd been notified of an emergency meeting at the station the following morning with the chief, mayor, and members of the armed forces who'd been called in to deal with the possibility of a full island evacuation.

Had David been awake, she would have suggested that he take Warren off the island for a few days, though she had no idea where they would go. The storm appeared to be losing some power over the gulf, but now clearly had them in its sights. Neither man had ventured much out of the state in the past, and all their immediate family were located close by. David would resist leaving, especially when she told him she would be staying, but she hoped Warren's safety would compel him to take things seriously.

Why don't you drive him directly to Rebecca Whitehead's house and be done with it?

Lord, she was sick of herself. Surely some things were more important at that moment than her quite possibly—maybe even probably?—unfounded jealousy. She thought about Warren's dust-covered apartment, and how his drinking appeared to be getting out of hand. Recalling what he'd said about Frank Randall, she began to worry about him as well. Frank was all but under house arrest with his brother, but it was important to her—and, admittedly, to the investigation—that he remain safe. Although when it came to Lieutenant Filmore, *safe* was interchangeable with *not absconding*.

On the television, a giant illustrated cloud loomed over the Gulf of Mexico. Laurie felt her eyelids getting heavy, the last few days' workload finally taking its toll. She wanted to get up and sleep in the same bed as David, despite their current difficulties. In her weary state, she tried and failed to generate the proper panic about the storm arriving and causing unimaginable havoc.

Falling into sleep at last, she pictured the gulf itself lifting up and tearing through the city, wiping everything in its path.

And in the remains, on every coastline, and in the wreckage of every building, she saw the ravaged corpses of Grace Harrington and Annie Randall.

Chapter Twenty-Six

Randall wasn't sure why he was here, battling the stiffening breeze that threatened to take one or both of them away in the next gust of wind. Like he seemed to be doing more and more of late, he was following Maurice's lead. His brother may have been weary and frail, but he carried an inner strength Randall begrudgingly admired.

"We can't let them think you're afraid," Maurice had told him as they'd dressed for their little expedition. By "them," he'd meant the officers who'd been stationed outside his house since the indignity of his police questioning. Heat rose in Randall's cheeks at the very thought of that time in the station. The interview itself had been bearable for Randall, were it not for the disappointment painted so firmly on Laurie's face. Randall had remained silent, as instructed by his lawyer, and had soon been free to leave. What had been unbearable was the way everyone had looked at him. It was more than disappointment he'd seen in the eyes of Laurie's colleagues. Their disgust and anger was palpable, and in one corner he'd caught the eye of Annie's dad, whose hostility threatened to boil over at any second. And through it all, all Randall could think was how much he deserved it. Not for the death of the young girl—his memory may no longer have been sharp, but he wasn't responsible for her death—but for everything that had happened to Annie, which he thought about every waking second, and most of the time when asleep. The argument they'd had had been avoidable. He'd been keeping secrets from her, and if he'd only been honest they would never have had that fight, and she wouldn't have stormed off, never to return. He may not have dealt the blows to her, but if not for him she would never have come within range of the madman who'd delivered them.

The police were with them now, two uniformed officers following them like shadows as they crossed over to the muddy brown sand of the beach. Maurice said something to him, but it was inaudible in the noise of the swirling wind. Randall didn't want to be here. The weather aside, his leg was causing him a great deal of pain and every step brought with it painful memories both of his time inside and of those days leading to Annie's death.

A storm had been brewing back then as well and had eventually hit after Randall was arrested. It was strange how so many of his past memories were picture-perfect clear, like being at the movies, while so much of his recent past was such a cloudy, indecipherable mess. He followed Maurice onto the sand, the boisterous water only yards away, and recalled how he'd walked this very spot with Annie two days before she'd gone missing.

She'd been angry then, after Randall had told her what he'd done; he'd been angry with himself for his deception. He'd come close to telling Laurie about it yesterday, though he couldn't see the possible relevance, and may well have done so had it not been for the insistence of the lawyer.

Betrayal came in many different forms.

When they'd first got together, they'd discussed their former lovers. Randall had been forced to fight his ego, and his pathetic male jealousy, as Annie had counted off her former partners as if reciting a rosary. When it had been his turn, Annie had smiled at his awkwardness and had tilted her head at every name he mentioned.

He'd come close to not mentioning Sadie, and that filled him with a double regret: that he'd come so close to lying to Annie, and that he'd wanted to betray Sadie's memory.

"Do they need to stay so close?" said Maurice, interrupting his reverie as he looked back at the two police officers following them across the sand.

"They're only doing their job, Maurice," said Randall, grimacing as his right foot caught in the sand, sending a jarring pain up the side of his body.

"It's humiliating," Maurice said, oblivious to Randall's pain.

Randall shuffled onward, the loose sand morphing into wet, dank mud, as he tried to recall what he'd been thinking about. Lately, holding on to recent memories was like recalling a dream a few minutes after waking. Snapshots lingered just out of reach, so Randall did what he always did on these occasions and thought of Annie.

So many memories came to him when he thought about her that it was often unbearable. He closed his eyes, and let the sounds and smells of the gulf dissipate until all he could see was Annie running along the beach, her red hair flowing behind her. The warmth from the vision was enough to give him strength. "I want to go back," he said to Maurice, "and I think maybe you should go home too."

Maurice was too involved in an embittered war with the weather to pay him much attention. The wind billowed against his rain jacket, a ruffling noise escaping as he ran his hands across his face. "What?" he shouted.

"Home," said Randall, turning back inland. He still couldn't understand why Maurice was there, why all of a sudden he was taking an interest in him after all these years.

The police officers didn't avert their gaze as he walked past them. Randall understood he was prejudged and couldn't blame them for their conclusions. All he cared about now was getting back to the house, sending Maurice away, and spending some time alone.

Chapter Twenty-Seven

David was still asleep as Laurie left for work. She suspected he was pretending and considered calling him out on it, before deciding she didn't have the energy to start the day with conflict.

Laurie's first duty of the day was to attend the emergency evacuation meeting with the mayor, the city manager, members of the armed forces, and the chief of police, where it was ultimately decided that an advised evacuation would begin immediately for the West End, where properties were not protected by the seawall. Hurricane Heather was still a category 4, and the Hurricane Center was concerned that it could make landfall in Texas within the next few days. The most pressing challenge was getting the news out without causing panic. Thankfully, many people had already begun preparations, so it was hoped there would be no repeat of the excess delays experienced during Rita and Ike.

The meeting had now thinned out and it was just her, Lieutenant Filmore, and the current chief of police, who was all of a sudden taking a strong interest in Grace Harrington's murder. "We now have a missing father to add to our woes?" he asked them.

"I'm afraid so."

Glen Harrington was indeed still missing. His phone was switched off and undetectable, and his work hadn't heard from him. Gemma had informed Laurie that Sandra and Tilly had spent the evening on the sofa watching black-and-white movies as Sandra had slowly drunk herself into oblivion. With their permission, Gemma had checked both Sandra and Tilly's phones and laptops, and no messages had come through from Glen.

"Doesn't look good, does it?" said the chief, glancing at Filmore, who shifted in his seat. "You think he's good for it?" he asked, changing his attention to Laurie.

"He certainly has a taste for young women. This all came about after Tilly Moorfield found out Mr. Harrington had been seen with his daughter's then girlfriend."

Both men squirmed a little in their seats. "Yes, I read about that in this morning's paper. Does it mean he killed his daughter?"

Someone had obviously been talking to the press. If she were to guess, Laurie thought the insight had probably come from Tilly. "I questioned him on his extramarital affairs. I didn't want to presume Frank Randall's guilt," said Laurie, giving Lieutenant Filmore a quick glance.

"Harrington didn't confess though, did he?"

Laurie managed to keep her composure. "Of course not. I questioned him over his ex-lovers, including a college intern who was practically the same age as his daughter. It definitely made him uncomfortable, as you would expect. We have no firm alibi for him during the estimated time of Grace's death. He was supposedly at his apartment in Houston, though we can't find anyone to corroborate that."

"I don't suppose he's there now, is he?"

"We'll be notified if he enters that building."

"And the murder weapon?"

The search of the local area was continuing now that it was light again, but, as during the Annie Randall investigation, it felt unlikely the weapon would be discovered. "The Harringtons consented to a search. We haven't applied for a warrant for Frank Randall's house yet."

"OK, Detective Campbell. That reminds me, how is Warren? I hear he got into a bit of mischief yesterday."

"He's fine."

The chief nodded absently, as if he wasn't really listening to her. "Good. What is your gut on this, Laurie?"

"Something is definitely off with Glen Harrington. We'll know more when Forensics get back to us."

"Which will be when?"

"I've been told tomorrow by the latest."

The chief clasped his hands together. "Maybe give them a nudge, Filmore? Would be prudent to search the Randall place for the murder weapon sooner rather than later," he said, glancing down at his paperwork to signal the end of the meeting.

"You going to give them a nudge, Lieutenant?" asked Laurie, once they were out in the bullpen.

Filmore smiled, the tension easing from him now they were away from the chief. "I'll give them a call and find out how long we'll have to wait. This hurricane warning isn't helping any. We still have eyes on Randall?"

Laurie nodded, even though Filmore already knew a team were stationed outside Frank's house. "He went to the beach yesterday evening with his brother."

"In *this* weather, as frail as he is?" Filmore cracked, walking off to his office before she had a chance to respond. Like seemingly everyone else, he clearly considered Frank Randall plenty spry enough to abduct a fit young woman, kill her, and take her to a remote beach area.

Returning to her own desk, she found a cup of hot coffee was waiting for her. "This your work, Remi?"

"Yes, ma'am. Thought you'd need it after meeting the board of governors in there."

"Anyone tell you you're an angel, Remi?" said Laurie, sipping the nectar.

"Only my mom."

"Well, you tell her I said she's a great judge of character."

◆ ◆ ◆

Every time Laurie looked up from her laptop screen, she caught a glimpse of the large television glued permanently to the Weather Channel, trailing Hurricane Heather, which still seemed to be on a direct course to Galveston.

When she could tear herself away from the image of the looming cloud system, Laurie caught up with some of her outstanding cases. Although investigations were active in Grace's case—the hunt for Glen Harrington the current number one consideration—it felt as if they were playing a waiting game on that front. Not for the first time, Laurie wished that the CSI worked like they did on TV and film, with an almost instantaneous response. As it was, they were using the Forensic Science Center in Houston to process the results from the Grace Harrington crime scene, and it could be some time before they received what they needed.

Laurie searched through an unrelated missing person case, a fifty-seven-year-old man who hadn't turned up to his work on board a local fishing boat three weeks ago. Everything that could be done had been done, and Laurie signed the investigation off. The missing man had no immediate family in the States; a brother in his native Puerto Rico had been notified but hadn't responded beyond an email of acknowledgment. The fisherman would become another name to add to the list of thousands of people who went missing nationwide each year, and Laurie sighed as she filed away the report.

"Laurie," mouthed Remi, nudging her as he took a call on his cell phone. "Hey, Alex, what's up?" he said into the phone, as Laurie looked on. "Hey, that's great. You saw him go into this apartment?"

"We've got him," he said to Laurie as he hung up the call a moment later. "My contact at the apartment building in Houston saw Glen Harrington enter the building five minutes ago."

"What are we doing sitting here, then?" said Laurie, shutting down her laptop.

It was a relief getting out of the building. Remi coordinated with local officers in Houston, who had been instructed to detain Glen Harrington if he left the apartment block.

As they drove along Seawall Boulevard to the causeway, it was apparent from the steady stream of traffic leaving the island that notice of the evacuation had already been announced. Many low-lying areas of Houston were also on standby, and there was concern that an evacuation order might be issued in the city as well. The last thing Laurie wanted was to get cut off in Houston. She needed to get in and out as quickly as humanly possible. As they approached South Houston, she switched on the inbuilt siren and lights, and they made the apartment building twenty minutes later.

One of the concierge team met them inside and showed them live video footage of the hallway outside Glen's Houston apartment, which was one of three on the penthouse level. "Fancy," said Laurie. "You've had eyes on that door since you called Detective Armstrong?" she asked the doorman.

"Ain't looked up once, ma'am."

"Keep up the good work. Call us if you see Mr. Harrington leave before you see us arrive on his floor." The doorman returned to the screen as if his life depended on it.

Although an APB was out on him, Glen Harrington wasn't an official suspect. They weren't there to arrest him, merely to check on his safety and to ask him a few more questions. Yet as she and Remi stepped into the elevator, cheesy Muzak accompanying them on their upward journey, Laurie felt as if she was in the eye of the storm. Glen hadn't absconded for no reason. At best, he'd kissed his daughter's eighteen-year-old girlfriend. What else he'd got up to with her was anyone's guess. Whatever the reason for his disappearance, Glen Harrington had shown himself to be unpredictable, and unpredictable people could be dangerous.

The elevator pinged to a stop, the strained cries of a lounge bar version of Lionel Richie's "Hello" still assaulting their ears as they made the short walk to Harrington's apartment.

Laurie unclipped her gun holster as she knocked on the door. She gave a count of ten before nodding to Remi, who produced the all-access card the doorman had given him. The light on the door flashed green and Laurie stepped into the apartment building, her hand ready by her holster. "Mr. Harrington?" she called, securing the hallway before seeing the shape of Glen Harrington on the floor of the living room.

Rushing to his side, she dropped beside his prone body and searched for a pulse. Even as she did so, she knew it was an empty gesture. Glen Harrington stared at the ceiling, wide-eyed, flanked by an all but empty bottle of Macallan Rare whisky. The syringe he'd used to inject the poison that had taken his life hung from his arm like a weird appendage.

Chapter Twenty-Eight

Laurie moved away from Glen Harrington's corpse and told Remi to secure the room. She scanned the area for a sign of a potential suicide note before retreating into the hall, where they called Houston Homicide and waited for the CSIs to arrive.

In a perfect world, Glen Harrington would have left a suicide note detailing the murder of Grace, which would tie in perfectly with the forensic report they would be receiving at some point soon. That would be determined later, but for now, as was seemingly always the case, all they could do was wait.

And plan what she would say to Sandra Harrington.

The Harringtons' relationship may have been all but nonexistent, but losing her husband so soon after her daughter would still pour on one more thick layer of trauma.

She hated to think how much worse it would be for her if Glen had killed their daughter.

Although everything pointed to death by suicide, homicide couldn't be ruled out. Laurie updated the lead detective from Houston PD's homicide squad, Kevin Estrada, as his team and the CSIs arrived ten minutes later. She knew Estrada from previous joint investigations. In his early fifties, his hairline seeming to have receded a couple of inches since the last time she'd seen him, Estrada had the look of someone under permanent pressure.

"I heard about that beach murder," he said. "Same MO as the Randall killing from sixteen years ago?"

"Something like that. This is the dad," said Laurie, who then updated the detective on Glen Harrington's recent indiscretions.

If Estrada was shocked, he didn't show it. "Looks like suicide to me," he said, "though it could be staged that way. Anyone want him dead?"

"A few young women I know. His daughter's girlfriend was arrested yesterday for assault on one of his conquests, but I've already checked on her whereabouts."

Estrada's eyebrows knitted. "His daughter's girlfriend assaulted his teenage lover?"

"You're getting it. The lover was also his daughter's ex-girlfriend."

Estrada winced as if the situation's soap opera calculus was giving him a headache, then gave his head a little shake as though putting that all aside for the moment. "Work troubles?"

"Probably. News was already out on his affairs with young work colleagues. It wouldn't be long before the press found out about his dalliances closer to home."

Estrada shook his head. It didn't pay to get too judgmental in this line of work, but his disgust was evident. "Happy to hold up things for you here. I'll let you know if we find a note. I imagine you want to get back before that hurricane hits?"

"Thanks, Kevin, appreciate it. We are still looking for the murder weapon that killed Grace Harrington," said Laurie, summoning Remi, who'd finished interviewing the last of Glen Harrington's neighbors in the apartment building.

◆ ◆ ◆

Laurie would usually have stayed until Glen's body had been recovered from the apartment building, but Estrada had been right about beating the storm. After a deviation in its course across the gulf, the latest update had it making landfall in Galveston at some point tomorrow evening, and by the time they reached the island, what had started as the suggested evacuation of the West End was now a mandatory evacuation of the whole island. The northbound side of the causeway was already close to standstill, weary travelers inching along every few minutes.

"This is going to be a logistical nightmare," Laurie muttered to herself as they pulled into the station parking lot. It applied more generally as well, but she was thinking of the broadening Harrington investigation. Until forensics reports came back, or definitive evidence from Glen Harrington's death scene, they were still unable to arrest anyone for Grace's death. The evacuation would mean that Sandra, Tilly, Mia, and more importantly, Frank and Maurice Randall would all leave the island. It was just possible a court injunction could be imposed to keep Frank under police custody, but with only a circumstantial link to a historic case and with Maurice's pit bull of a lawyer taken into consideration, that seemed unlikely, especially in such a short space of time.

"Do you have anywhere you can go?" Remi called to her as they battled the wind on their way across the lot.

Laurie looked at him blankly. "Oh, you mean for the evacuation?" she yelled back at him. "I'm not going anywhere. I'll stay in the shelters if it comes to it."

"You can count on me to stay too," said Remi, struggling to hold open the door.

Remi had two children under the age of three, and one on the way, and there was no way she was going to let him stay on the island.

"No, you need to get out of here. Get that family of yours safe. There'll be enough people staying," said Laurie, who knew this was a conversation going on throughout the island. Hopefully lessons had been learned since Rita and Ike, when too many people had refused to leave. It was impossible to enforce a full evacuation, even with the threat of immediate loss of life, but surely the destruction and aftermath, particularly Ike's, would still be fresh enough in people's minds that they wouldn't want to stay.

That said, she knew many people would be weighing up the inconvenience of evacuating against the probability of the storm hitting. Too many predicted hurricanes never made landfall. Add this to the stubborn streak of so many BOIs—*a stubbornness that occasionally reaches stupidity level*, Laurie thought, as she recalled a group of surfers recklessly attempting to catch some breakers hours before Ike had started to wreak havoc on the coast—and she knew many would stay, or at least wait until the last minute to leave.

"Someone in interview room one for you, Detective Campbell," said the desk sergeant.

"Who?"

"Says he's your boyfriend or something like that," said the sergeant with a mischievous grin.

"Good one. Go on up, Remi, I'll see you in a minute."

Remi smiled. "Say hi to David for me."

"Just get going," said Laurie, giving the desk sergeant her best frown as she walked over to the interview room.

David stood as she entered and for a split second there was an awkwardness between them that she'd never experienced, before he reached over and kissed her. Despite herself, she sniffed his neck, pleased to smell only his familiar aftershave on his skin. "You didn't say goodbye this morning," he said, sitting back down.

"Didn't want to interrupt the snoring," said Laurie, smiling. Wishing she didn't know about Rebecca Whitehead, she sat in the chair next to him. She wanted to be happy to see him, but all she could think about was that evening at the coffee shop, the smile on David's face the same now as it had been when he'd brought the coffees over to the woman.

Whether or not he was having an affair felt irrelevant at that moment. Even if that meeting had been innocent, which the rational part of her brain told her it was, the fact David hadn't mentioned it was systematic of something wrong in their marriage, as was her continued worrying about it.

"Sorry about that," he said. "Catching up on my sleep, I guess."

"Anything up?"

David frowned, hesitating before speaking. "I just wanted to see what you want to do about this hurricane. I believe we're supposed to leave?"

Part of her wanted to come out, here and now, and ask him about Rebecca, but another, more powerful part of her feared what he would have to say. Confirmation of his infidelity threatened to unravel her, and she wasn't ready for that quite yet. "I think you should go and get Warren. Find somewhere upstate for a few days until it's safe."

"I'm not going to leave you here," said David, placing his hand on hers.

Laurie pulled her hand away, a little more forcibly than she'd intended. "I have no option."

"Jesus, Laurie," he said, his hand falling onto the table. "What the hell is going on? What have I done?"

"I'm busy, that's all."

"It's more than that, Laurie, and you know it."

"Just get Warren safe."

He gave a hollow laugh. "Warren. You've met him, right? There could be a full tsunami yards from his house and he'd still try and stand it down."

"Sweet-talk him, David. You're good at that."

He stared at her for a long, dead moment, then said, very quietly, "What the hell does that mean?"

Laurie lowered her eyes and tried not to think about Milly. None of this would be happening if her body hadn't betrayed her, and betrayed their little baby. By now, David would have already left the island with his little girl and she wouldn't have been far behind.

"I need to go," she said. "Just get Warren off the island. I'll be fine here. I can stay in one of the shelters."

"And my dad?"

It was the first time Laurie had heard David refer to Frank as his dad. "I'll make sure he's safe," she said. "You could always check on him before you go."

"That's not what I meant," he said, turning away from her.

She wanted to embrace him and take away all his pain. So many times, she'd wanted him to open up about his mom, and what Frank had done. Death had permeated David's life, and it had always felt impossible to talk to him about it. Not that she was any different, she knew. She wasn't the only one to lose Milly, and she knew she sometimes forgot that. She was guilty of clamming up as much as David was, and now they were at this impasse.

This time, it was David's turn to shrug her off as she placed her hand on his shoulder. "Just go on, then," he said, refusing to meet her gaze.

Laurie didn't know if David wanted his father safe or not, but she told him she'd look in on him before she ducked down into a shelter, if it came to that, then opened the interview room door and left him behind her.

Chapter Twenty-Nine

Laurie was trembling by the time she reached the all but deserted bullpen; she wasn't sure if it was out of rage or sadness.

She had to remind herself constantly that she wasn't to blame for everything. The rational side of her knew it was illogical, and definitely counterproductive, to blame herself for Milly's death, but it was a constant struggle. Especially when her darker side kept reminding her that it was her body that had failed Milly. And it was that same side of her making her feel guilty for the possibly unfixable state of her marriage. Trying to drown it out was taking all her strength, and at that moment there was just too much going on to put up a credible fight.

As usual, Remi was her temporary savior, planting a profoundly welcome cup of coffee in her hand. "Everything OK, boss?" he asked, his demeanor suggesting he didn't want to step over any boundaries between them.

"Has Sandra Harrington evacuated yet? I need to see her," said Laurie. "It's not right for her to wait so long to find out about her husband."

"I just spoke to Gemma. They haven't left yet. You need me to come?"

Laurie shook her head. "You need to get going. Have Ava and the children set off yet?"

"Yes, they went this morning."

"Get going, Remi. I told you. There's enough of us here."

"If you're sure."

"I'll drive you off the island myself if you don't get going, now get," said Laurie, smiling as Remi gave her a hug for the first time since they'd worked together.

◆ ◆ ◆

Laurie shut down her laptop and packed it away. It wasn't the first time the station had prepared for an incoming storm since Ike had struck, and anything of value had already been securely stored. Even though the wind was raging, the threat of a full-scale hurricane still felt distant to her. But as she left the building and drove to the seawall, the reality of the situation began to hit harder.

The waves were lapping at the seawall, as if biding their time. Laurie had seen the very same road covered by water before, but it was an ominous sign seeing the water this far in already. She sent a message to Gemma, telling her she was on her way, as she moved back inland to avoid the queues of evacuating islanders.

Gemma replied instantly. *Sandra has been in bed for the last two hours. Everything is packed so she's ready to go.*

Laurie drew in a deep breath and slowly released it. There could be no good time to bring her news like this, she knew, but the idea of delivering it when she was already laid out by grief seemed incredibly cruel.

It took another thirty minutes to reach the house. Again, Laurie circled back to it: a second death notice in a matter of days. She hardly needed reminding how quickly someone's life could unravel, but it was hard to fathom that only days ago Sandra Harrington had a husband and daughter, and now would be facing up to a future utterly alone.

Gemma met her at the front door. "Sandra is still asleep. I've been packing for her," she whispered, as she let Laurie in.

"Tilly?"

"Back with her father. They're planning to leave as soon as they can."

"Has Sandra said where she's planning to go?"

"To her parents in Dallas."

"I might need you to go with her," said Laurie, before telling the officer about Glen Harrington.

Gemma was speechless for a few seconds before replying. "Of course I'll go with her," she said. "I don't think she'll be in any fit state to drive anyway."

"Could you see if you can wake her up?" said Laurie, before catching sight of Sandra Harrington walking down the staircase wearing a thick navy robe, her hair darting in numerous directions, her face a fright mask of smudged makeup.

"Hello, Sandra," said Laurie. "Come on, let's get you some coffee."

Sandra didn't answer. She walked past them both toward the kitchen, where she began filling the coffee machine with beans.

"I can do that," said Gemma.

"No," said Sandra quite forcefully, before regaining her composure. "Sorry, I need to be doing something. You found him yet?" she asked, glancing at Laurie.

"Please, come and sit down, Sandra."

Sandra shook her head, pouring water into the coffee machine before switching it on. While the roar of grinding beans broke the silence for a few seconds, Laurie indicated to Gemma that she should take over in the kitchen.

Laurie led Sandra to the dining table, the smell of stale wine strong on the woman's breath. As they both sat, Laurie thought how similar they were. Both had lost daughters. Sandra was going through the early stages of grief and had turned to alcohol for comfort, whereas she was in a different stage, albeit one she suspected felt exactly the same. What had she turned to for comfort, she wondered, before glancing down at her hyper-toned body, which felt as devoid of curves as a slab of useless meat.

"This isn't going to be easy to hear, Sandra," she said.

Sandra smiled at her as if she was simple, as if anything could possibly be worse than finding out your daughter was dead.

"I'm afraid we found Glen's body this morning at your apartment building in Houston. I can't confirm for sure, but it seems highly probable that he has taken his own life."

Sandra sat open-mouthed as the news filtered through to her. "Did he kill her?" she said, taking Laurie by surprise.

"You mean Grace?" said Laurie, glancing over at Gemma, who came and sat next to Sandra. "We just don't know at this stage. We've been unable to find a note from him as yet."

Sandra allowed Gemma to put her arm around her but remained tensed, her back iron-straight.

"Do you think he killed her, Sandra?" asked Laurie.

"It wouldn't surprise me. He was a monster. He had no morals, no compassion, and I'm glad he's dead. Now, let's get this coffee. I'd like to get out of this town before that hurricane hits, and I don't ever want to come back."

Chapter Thirty

Laurie checked through Glen Harrington's office in search of a suicide note before leaving the house empty-handed. Gemma remained with Sandra, helping her to pack and secure anything left behind. Laurie wondered if Sandra would be as good as her word and never return to Galveston. Grace's body had been transferred to the pathologists in Houston, and Glen's body would be there soon, too, so there may never be a need for her to return. And if Hurricane Heather proved to be as destructive as everyone now seemed to anticipate, Galveston's infrastructure would be seriously curtailed in the coming months.

As she drove from Offatts Bayou, Laurie wondered if her own time in Galveston might also be coming to an end. She'd made a life on the island after getting posted here, but what was left of it now? Milly was gone, and David was receding from her. Her only real connection to the city was her job, and that was something she could do elsewhere. The hard truth was that every second in Galveston felt like it would always be a reminder of Milly. How could she run along the beaches, or swim in the gulf, without thinking about what could have, should have been? The three of them would have been so happy, and now making any kind of happiness here seemed like a distant dream.

Along the coast, it appeared everyone was thinking along the same lines, if only temporarily. The traffic toward the causeway crept along like a funeral procession, the faces in the vehicles haunted. There had been fatalities in Galveston during Ike, and in some ways the city was still recovering from that time. People had lost their homes and businesses, and many hadn't returned. Those who prayed would no doubt be in contact with their maker right now, and from the look of it more people than last time were taking the warnings seriously. Another truth was that little had changed since Ike. Plans had been floated of ways to protect the area from further storms, but all such ideas cost vast amounts of money and what money there was had been spent on rebuilding. If Heather did make landfall tomorrow, power would almost certainly disappear in most areas. No matter what, the next few weeks, at the very least, were going to be extremely unpleasant for anyone left on the island.

By the time she reached their apartment, David was back and had already boarded the windows. He was packing and didn't raise his head as Laurie entered the bedroom, the fallout from their earlier meeting still fresh. "I've packed away as much as I can," he said, not looking up as he zipped shut a suitcase.

"Did you manage to speak to Warren?" she asked, collapsing on the bed. Despite everything that was happening between them, she was already beginning to miss him. It felt like forever since they'd spent any proper time together. She cursed herself for having followed him to the coffee shop that night. How much happier would she be now, she wondered, if she'd just stayed home. David stopped packing and lay down next to her. "We can still leave," he said, as if reading her mind.

"You *are* leaving," she said. "I have the Grace Harrington investigation."

"Come on, Laurie, that can wait. You don't need to put yourself in danger's way because of a homicide investigation. They don't pay you enough, for one."

Laurie smiled. "That's true enough. You haven't answered me about Warren."

"He's as stubborn as you. It looks like none of us are going to leave."

"What are you talking about?"

"I'm going to stay around at his place. See if I can keep one of us alive."

"No," said Laurie. "That's not happening."

"What, so it's OK for you to stay, and not us?"

"You do know how old he is, David? Not to mention where he lives?"

"He's just been in a bar brawl, which he won, I might add. I don't think you need to worry about Warren."

"I'm worried about both of you."

"Then let's all go together. If he sees you're going, I'm sure he'll come too."

They were lying next to each other like nervous teenagers, their bodies not quite touching. Laurie felt bloated and tired, the last time she'd done any exercise feeling like a distant memory. She wanted to reach out and touch him, at the same time wanting to punish him for breaking her heart.

"I can't," she said. "They need emergency personnel anyway." She got to her feet and walked into their living room, where she stopped dead in her tracks.

David followed her out. "There was no room in the locker," he said, looking, as she was, at Milly's unused bassinet.

Laurie tried to fight the emotions swirling in her but was unable to stop her knees from buckling. David caught her before she hit the floor. She turned and sobbed in his arms, her tears falling for both Milly and the disastrous state of her marriage. "I'm sorry," she said at last, pulling away from David, whose eyes had also misted up.

"Come here," said David, reaching for her.

"We need to pack," she said, ignoring him.

"Seriously. What's going on, Laurie? I don't understand. I know things haven't been going well for us recently, but it's like you've reached some sort of decision that I'm not part of."

"Now's not the time, David. I have too much going on."

"Oh come on, you always have too much going on. If you're not working, you're going on your stupid runs."

Laurie bent down and touched the bassinet. She'd pictured Milly in it so many times that the fantasy felt like a memory.

David knelt down beside her. "Sorry," he said, placing his hand on her shoulder.

Laurie felt herself tensing, and David withdrew his hand.

"Is there anything you want to tell me?" she said after a long moment, but David had already left the living room.

Ten minutes later, she watched from the window as he drove away, neither of them having said goodbye.

Laurie found some eggs in the fridge and overcooked an omelet, washing down the tasteless dish with a bottle of Lone Star beer that David had left behind. Finding a solitary bottle of red wine in the rack, she took it to the living room and sat down next to Milly's bassinet. She unscrewed the top, wincing at the acidic smell wafting up from the bottle. It would be easy to drink herself into a brief oblivion, but it wasn't going to happen. She was already enough of a mess. What she needed was a good sleep, but there was just too much to do. She inhaled the wine's scent, which seemed less foul to her this time, before resealing the bottle, and answered her cell phone, which had been ringing these last twenty seconds.

"Campbell," she said, grimacing as she pushed her weakened body off the floor.

"Sorry to bother you, ma'am. This is Officer Hall. I'm over at the Randall residence."

"Frank Randall?"

"Ma'am. We are trying to evacuate Mr. Randall, and his brother, Pastor Randall, but both men are refusing to leave."

"Can you exert a little authority, Officer Hall?"

"Believe me, I have tried, but they're—well, Pastor Randall is threatening to sue, and it's not as if I can tase them and drive them off the island myself."

"OK, hold tight. I'll be there shortly."

If it weren't for the line of vehicles, their lights illuminating the night sky, it would be easy to forget that the island was on the verge of a hurricane. The darkness hid the rampaging sea and the worst effects of the brutal wind that buffeted Laurie's car as she drove over to Frank's place.

It was hard to believe that only a few days ago, such a journey had been a kind of mini-salvation for her. Frank had become a confidant of sorts, a sounding board. Already she missed their chats, and as she parked and used her flashlight to navigate to his house, she wished she was visiting under different circumstances. Although they rarely talked about David, at least beyond his childhood years, she had a sudden urge to tell Frank everything. About Milly and the troubles in their marriage.

She greeted the two uniformed officers stationed outside the house, who informed her that the Randalls' lawyer had arrived.

"Detective Campbell, nice of you to join us," said Neil Mosley as she entered the house. Mosely exuded the same confidence—no, call it arrogance—she had encountered at the station, and held her gaze as if testing her resolve. Frank and Maurice were sitting in the armchairs by the fire, Frank glancing over at her before looking away.

Laurie shook hands with the lawyer. "Any particular reason for your visit?" she asked him, fearing she was already in a losing game.

"I could ask you the same question, but that would be churlish," said Mosley, with an enigmatic smile. "Pastor Randall asked me to pop over. It seems he and his brother are being forced off their property."

"No one is forcing anyone or anything," said the uniformed officer who'd accompanied Laurie inside, falling silent as she raised her hand.

"You know there is a hurricane on its way," said Laurie. "We only want everyone to be safe."

"Mr. Randall and the pastor have made it perfectly clear they do not wish to leave the sanctuary of their house. I am not really sure why we're all here, if I'm being totally honest with you."

"Can we talk outside?" said Laurie.

"Be my pleasure," said Mosley, following her outside, where they could barely hear themselves speak over the sound of the wind.

"Frank Randall is under suspicion of homicide, Mr. Mosley. You can't expect me to allow him to stay here."

"Are you going to arrest him?"

The forensic report had yet to come back and Mosley would know her hands were tied. With the hurricane, the report could be delayed for days if not weeks. "It's for his own safety. We can put him somewhere for the next few days until this has all cleared."

"You're clutching at straws, Detective. Now, I have been very patient with you and your colleagues, but enough is enough."

Laurie was powerless to act. Had Mosley not been there, she would have tried to convince Frank to accompany her, but there was no way the lawyer was going to let her speak to his client and any further interference at this stage could jeopardize a successful prosecution. "You're going to take responsibility for Mr. Randall?" asked Laurie.

"I don't have to. He's a free man. Either charge him or leave him alone. And by that, I mean depart his property completely. I understand from him that you've had officers stationed outside his house ever since he came in for questioning?"

"No need to worry, Mr. Mosley. Anyone with any sense is getting the hell out of here."

"Well, that's something we can agree on. I will of course suggest to my clients that they leave Galveston, but if they choose to stay, then I'm afraid I'll be leaving them to it."

"OK then," said Laurie, summoning the officers, and wondering if Frank's home would still be standing the next time she visited the place.

Chapter Thirty-One

Randall had wanted to call out to Laurie as she left. All he cared about was her and David's safety, and if that meant giving himself up, then he'd have been prepared to do it. Maybe now was the right time to talk about everything; if not for him, then for the family of that poor girl who'd been murdered in the same way as Annie. But, coward that he was, he'd stayed in his seat as Laurie and the other police officers had left.

"Well, gentlemen, one last plea from me," said Mr. Mosley. "I listened to the latest reports on the way over and Hurricane Heather is due to make landfall tomorrow at some point. Some folks who should know fear that it will be worse than Rita and Ike combined. The safest thing would be for you to leave. I believe that if you returned to Dickinson, you would miss the worst of it. I would be happy to assist you in any way I can."

The lawyer meant well, but even the devil himself wouldn't drag Randall away now. "Thank you for your concern," he said, turning his attention to the crackling fire, which was doing its best to warm his injured leg.

"He's right, you know," said Maurice, once the lawyer had left.

"I'm ready to die here," said Randall. "Are you?"

Maurice looked as if he'd slapped him in the face. "I don't wish for either of us to die, brother."

"Then maybe you should get going. I'm not going anywhere."

Maurice slowly shook his head, the loose skin on his neck wagging. "You were always a stubborn one."

"Is that right?"

"It sure is."

"Is that why you used to beat me? Is that why Daddy used to beat both of us? I don't know why you're here, Maurice. You were never here for me before, and to be honest, I don't need or want you to be here for me now."

Maurice turned away and they both sat facing the fire in silence.

Randall had been in prison when Hurricane Ike had run riot in Galveston, as he had been for Rita a few years back. He remembered both occasions clearly. He'd been desperate for news of David, but it had taken ages for confirmation of his son's safety to reach him. Prior to that, he'd never once left the island during a storm. The legend of the Great Storm of 1900 was passed down by his daddy, who had boasted how the Randalls had fought every storm from that time onward, and that only a coward would let the weather chase him off the island.

It wasn't why Randall was staying. He had no urge to try to best a hurricane and had brains enough to know it wasn't a battle he could choose to win. If the hurricane wanted him dead, dead he would be. He was staying in part because he didn't have the strength to leave, but mostly because he didn't want to leave the house behind. It was all he had left of Annie. They'd made a life here, and although they'd had their ups and downs, they had been happy together and created a loving boy who, despite everything, had grown up to be a fine young man.

And he was ready. Ready to see Annie again, ready to leave th[is] poisonous world behind. He only hoped that he wouldn't have [to] share his last moments on Earth with Maurice, who was staring [at] the fire with unnerving intent.

"Why are you here, Maurice? I don't mean to be unkind, but I don't understand it," said Randall, throwing a couple more logs onto the fire, the delicious aroma of woodsmoke filling the room.

"I'll go, first thing in the morning," said Maurice. "I'm a foolish old man, Frank. It's taken me a long time to realize I wasn't a very good brother to you. In truth, I haven't been a very good person. Strange thing happened to me a few years ago, which you'll find difficult to believe."

"What was that, Maurice?"

Maurice turned to him, his face illuminated by the glow of the fire. "I found God."

Randall shook his head. "Spare me the sermon."

"No, you don't understand. By a few years, I mean two or three years ago."

"But you've been in the church since you left Galveston."

"Exactly. That was all a lie. I've been hiding all this time. I guess you could call it irony, or a great mystery, but finally God spoke to me."

Randall nodded. "Well, that's great. I imagine there is a reason that most congregations are full of elderly people without long to live, isn't there?"

"I don't blame you for your cynicism, Frank. And what you say is true. Facing death often brings people closer to God. And maybe that is what happened with me. I don't have long left now. When I found out you were being released, I wanted to reconnect. I knew we could never be really close, but I hoped perhaps you could forgive me for the person I was."

"If you've changed, Maurice, that's great. We're both different people now. If you're seeking my forgiveness, then you can have it if you tell me what happened between you and Annie."

Maurice bit his lower lip, and Randall wondered if his little speech had all been for nothing. "And you'll tell me about that girl, Frank?"

"What?"

"Grace Harrington. I'll tell you what happened between me and Annie, and you'll confess to me that you killed her. I can absolve you, brother. It's not too late."

"For heaven's sake," said Randall, trying to summon the energy to stand up and slap his brother. "I did not kill Grace Harrington, and you're not a Catholic priest."

"You had the opportunity, Frank. Your memory isn't what it was. You were here the night she was taken. I dropped you home that morning, remember? I told the police a different story, but when they find out . . ."

Randall didn't know if Maurice was right about the timings, but he was as sure as hell that he hadn't killed that poor young woman. "What did you do to Annie?"

Maurice lifted his chin. Randall couldn't tell if he was being proud, or shamefaced. "I made a move on her," he said defiantly. "I'm ashamed of it now, as I was then."

Randall couldn't stifle a laugh. "You made a move on her?" he asked, his initial humor fading fast. "What exactly does that mean? Did you hurt her?" he said, standing up and grabbing his cane.

"No, no, no. I tried to . . . Listen, Frank, I've never been able to understand women, now or then. I'm more or less a virgin. I wanted to kiss her. I guess I was jealous. I may have grabbed her too hard, but nothing beyond that happened. I'm so sorry."

Randall's hand cramped on the cane. Maurice looked so pale and pitiful in the armchair, but Randall still had to fight the rage welling up in him. He lifted the cane behind him, feeling its weight. "Did you kill her?" he asked, the cane lifted high above his head, ready to strike.

"Kill who?"

"Annie, of course."

Maurice's head darted from side to side. "What? No, no, Frank. You killed her, remember?"

"I didn't kill her."

"Then why did you spend all that time in jail, brother?"

It would have been a mercy to bring the cane down on his brother's head, but Frank resisted the urge. "I'm going to bed. If you're still here by the time I get up, God or no God, I will strike you down. Do you understand me?"

Maurice nodded, sitting back in his chair as Randall went to the bedroom, closed the door, and bolted it shut.

Chapter Thirty-Two

Laurie had no option other than to send the officers watching Frank's house back to the station. She couldn't justify leaving them there when every available body was needed to help with the evacuation, and what could be an imminent disaster if Hurricane Heather made landfall. She'd come close to going back and arresting Frank, but at this stage, and with the lawyer Mosley breathing down her neck, it was too much of a risk.

She thought back to that first day here, when she'd stopped Warren and his friends from giving Frank a beating. Maybe things would have been different had Frank left the island, as Warren had wanted. She'd enjoyed getting to know Frank, but at what cost?

Driving off, she reminded herself that she couldn't keep second-guessing her actions. What she needed was some rest and fresh perspective. Sleep felt like a privilege at the moment but things would feel much worse if she didn't catch even a couple of hours. Despite which, she found herself making a round trip of three houses before returning home, stopping outside the Harringtons', Tilly's father's house, and finally Rebecca Whitehead's. The lights were off at each place and no sign that anyone had stayed behind. Still, she lingered outside Rebecca's house on the chance that David would turn up.

The quiet was eerie, the only sound the hum of the wind rattling through the streets. To Laurie, it felt as if the storm had abated, which from previous experience wasn't necessarily a good thing. *The calm before the storm* wasn't just a saying.

As she drove away ten minutes later, she couldn't deny the feeling of disappointment. The night she had seen David and Rebecca together at the coffee house felt like a distant memory, yet she was no closer to finding out what was actually going on between them. She understood now that it was the doubt that was doing the most damage. If only she'd confronted him about it, then she would at least have known where she stood. As it was, she was in limbo and now she and David would spend the next days apart . . . and it was difficult to see that ever being reversed.

Back at their apartment building, she was pleased to see that nearly everyone had left. Although they were inland, the impact of any potential storm surge was unpredictable. It seemed that people were taking the warnings seriously, and even if that meant some uncertain and uncomfortable times trying to evacuate, it was good to see.

Inside, Laurie switched on the news and began to understand why more people than expected were leaving the island. The National Hurricane Center had adjusted their predictions. Any hope that Galveston would be spared now seemed unlikely and landfall was expected as soon as lunchtime tomorrow.

She needed to pack her last few essentials and leave, but was unable to switch her mind from the investigation. Gathering printouts from the case, she spread sheets of paper across the living-room floor, photocopied images of Annie Randall, Grace Harrington, and Glen Harrington's corpses taking center stage. It was hard not to think she was wasting her time. Glen's suicide didn't necessarily imply any guilt over his daughter's death, and until forensics came back there was nothing concrete enough to link either Frank or Glen to Grace's murder.

That didn't stop her from reading through everything again until her eyes ached. She was convinced something was missing that would open the investigation up, but as she'd told herself on many occasions, a feeling wasn't enough.

It was early morning before she finally put the files away. She needed some exercise, and completed a twenty-minute HIT session from a video she'd saved on her laptop. Dragging herself to the shower to wash off the sweat, she caught a glimpse in the mirror and froze. She barely recognized the harrowed features on her face, or the angular contours of her body as she pivoted where she stood. She was tired, overworked, stressed, her PMS was kicking in. Now wasn't the time to think about the changes she'd put herself through, but she couldn't help it.

Even now, the thought of looking at herself as she'd once been repulsed her. Not long after the pregnancy test had proved positive, David had decided to make a video diary of Milly. This had mainly consisted of recording Laurie changing shape as he sang absurd made-up songs to her slowly swelling belly. She chuckled at the memory, though as she showered, the water flowing over her toned, muscled body, it was hard to believe she'd ever been that way; that a life had existed within her.

She was self-aware enough to understand that, consciously or not, she'd purposely transformed herself over these last months. Her manic exercise routine employed to rid herself of any visual memory of her pregnancy. She was also self-aware enough to understand what a complete waste of time it had been. Health benefits aside, the exercise did nothing to rid her of the memories of Milly's stillbirth. She'd been literally running from her problems this last year, and it had only made things worse.

After drying, she climbed into bed, the darkened landscape eerily silent outside her window. She glanced at her phone, checking for any last messages, then allowed her fingertip to hover over the photos app, but she couldn't bring herself to look at the woman she'd once been. That person was a relic, an overblown representation of the mother she hadn't become. She knew without looking how much she would hate the images of her extended stomach, her cherry-red face round and glowing, her little pudgy arms and legs.

Though as she fell asleep, she knew there was nothing she wouldn't give to be like that again.

Chapter Thirty-Three

It was too late for reconciliation. It was a shame Maurice had waited so long to tell him what he'd done. Randall could have forgiven him. Their upbringing was in part to blame, he knew. Neither of them had been given anything remotely approaching a normal model of how someone should act with a member of the opposite sex. He and Maurice hadn't been the only ones who had taken a beating from Randall senior. Their mother had fled her abusive relationship when Frank was four, and Maurice had been the one to endure witnessing the damage their father had inflicted on her. Clearly it had messed him up.

Randall only wished that Annie had told him about Maurice's clumsy advances. He was prepared to take his brother at his word that nothing more had happened. He would have been angry as hell if he'd known, and there would have been no guarantee that the years would have passed any differently, but at least he could have explained Maurice's behavior to Annie, if not pardoning it.

But that could never happen now. He expected Maurice to be gone by the time he woke, and God help him if he was still here. It wasn't only what had happened between him and Annie. Maurice thought him capable of killing that young woman, thought he had killed Annie, and there was no coming back from that.

Randall may have been overdrawn in the memory bank, but he knew for a fact he hadn't killed Grace Harrington, because he hadn't killed his beloved Annie.

He'd considered telling Laurie that on each of her frequent visits to his place. Sometimes he'd thought it had been what she'd wanted to hear. Something grave had happened between her and David, and Randall sensed she was keen for him and David to be reunited in some way. But that was never likely to happen, and her weekly visits had been one of the few things keeping him alive and he hadn't wanted to risk that by pleading innocence.

And anyway, in a certain way he was responsible for Annie's death.

The letters had started to arrive three months before Annie was killed. At first, he'd hidden them from her. The letters had been from his high school girlfriend, Sadie Cornish. The correspondence had started innocuously enough, but by the third letter Sadie had started asking Randall for money. Annie had known about Randall's high school sweetheart from the beginning of their relationship, and Randall's guilt at how things had ended between them. Annie had insisted on little during their marriage, complete honesty being the main exception. Sadie had been diagnosed with fibrous dysplasia in the final year of high school. The disorder had reached the bones of her legs, and by the time of graduation she had to use a wheelchair. She had intended to go to Texas State to study medicine, but her parents had decided to move to Corpus Christi and he'd never heard from her again.

At least, they'd never spoken to one another again. It had been difficult, but he'd explained to Annie how badly he felt he'd treated Sadie. He could easily have kept their correspondence going, could have continued to see her, but he'd taken her departure as an opportunity to fully end things between them. Her illness had been difficult to deal with and he'd only been eighteen at the time. He'd told Annie this, shamefaced, but she'd held him and told him to stop beating himself up.

Together, they'd decided to ignore the letters and wait for Sadie to grow tired of bothering him. Randall didn't owe her anything, and even if they had wanted to, they weren't in any position to be giving money away.

But guilt had started to eat away at him, and finally he'd succumbed to Sadie's requests. She'd told him she needed money for medical treatment and he'd begun sending her any spare cash he had and, like a fool, he hadn't told Annie. He still had the letter that had started everything in motion. It was the last thing Annie had given him, and he retrieved it now from a box under the bed. How stupid he'd been.

Annie had found the letter and that was why they'd argued that day. It hadn't even been about the money. It had been his betrayal of Annie's trust that had set her off. It had torn at something deep within her; she was a passionate person, but he'd never seen anything like that kind of rage from her. When he'd tried to restrain her—the last thing he should've attempted—she'd lashed out viciously at him, struck the only blow either had ever delivered to the other. It had shocked them both, sent them staggering back from one another. Panting, wide-eyed, Annie had cupped a hand to her own face, as though it were her own flesh she'd raked, and then bolted out into the storm with Herbie on her heels.

It was pointless, retreading the past, but he was helpless to resist it. And it always brought him to the same desolate position: if only he'd confided in her from the start, Annie would never have thrown herself in harm's way.

And to this, he now added a fresh torment: but for the part he'd played in feeding the monster that first time, would there ever have been this second sacrifice?

It was still dark outside when he heard Maurice leave, the front door rattling shut as Randall zoned in and out of sleep. Maybe he should have left his bed and said goodbye to his brother, for he doubted they would see each other again, but the effort was too great and he had been dreaming of Annie and wanted to return to that blissful state.

When he awoke the second time, light was creeping through the blinds of his bedroom. The details of his dreams lingered just out of memory and when he tried to recall them, they faded altogether. He closed his eyes, wondering if he could fall back to sleep. Something felt off and it took him a few minutes to realize it was the silence. Usually at this time of the morning the birds were at their most vocal, but however hard he strained his ears, Randall couldn't hear anything besides a low hum. He didn't understand the science of it, but he knew why the wildlife was silent; they knew better than any weather forecaster what was on the way.

It didn't make much difference to him. Like a captain on a sinking ship, he was prepared to stay at the house until the very end. He doubted anyone would come for him now. That chance had come and gone yesterday evening. Either he would have to sit this hurricane out or, more likely, he would have to endure the consequences. All of which made it harder to get out of bed.

But some preparations would have to be made. He and Maurice had made a stop at the local supermarket, so provision-wise he was OK. He would spend the morning boarding up the windows and doors, making sure anything that could cause external damage was tied up or stowed away, and then it would become a waiting game.

He pulled on his robe, feeling his age in his creaking bones, and made his way to the living room, where he was surprised to learn that Maurice was still here.

And still more surprised to see that his brother wasn't alive, and that he had company.

Chapter Thirty-Four

Laurie checked the latest information on the storm as she drank her morning coffee, though all she had to do was look outside. Hurricane Heather may not have fully arrived yet, but her tendrils were already inland, the wind wreaking havoc on the island city.

She tried to call David and Warren but phone coverage was down in vast areas of the island. Sending them both emails on the off chance that they would get through, she changed and made final checks before leaving with the two bags she would take to the shelter that had been arranged at the high school. A harried-looking Remi was waiting outside, fighting against the wind as he got out of his car.

"What are you doing here?" she asked, her voice all but lost in the noise of the brewing storm.

"I'm getting the hell out of Dodge. I've been trying to call you all morning but I couldn't get through."

Laurie sighed. "Why haven't you gone already?"

"Thought I'd double-check."

"You've checked, now go."

"But what about you?"

"I need to check on Warren," said Laurie, omitting the fact that she also wanted to see David.

Remi hesitated. "If it wasn't for my family . . ."

"You don't need to apologize to me, Remi. Your wife is pregnant, for goodness' sake. You're not going to do any good staying. Get yourself to safety, and hopefully I'll see you in a couple of days."

Still Remi didn't move. "You should come too. I can take you."

"Don't worry, I'll go and get Warren and I'll be right behind you. Why do you think I have this?" she said, pointing to the bags, even though she had no intention of leaving the island. "Go," she added, surprised when Remi gave her a quick hug goodbye for the second time in as many days.

"Stay safe," he said.

"You too, Remi," said Laurie, tensing her legs to remain balanced as she waited for Remi to leave.

The evacuation line out of the city had eased since yesterday. The numbers were still near a record high, but many had already escaped. Laurie knew from the string of emails she'd been receiving over the last twenty-four hours that at some point soon the drivers of those vehicles would need to make a choice. Either risk getting caught on the highway or return to the island to ride out the storm.

Laurie had driven for a few minutes more when suddenly her phone reception came back to life. She pulled over and called Lieutenant Filmore. As they discussed the most urgent of the open cases, Laurie thought how this would be the perfect time to be a criminal on the island. She told Filmore about last night's visit to Frank's. Thankfully he agreed that she had taken the only feasible course of action under the circumstances.

"I'll check in on him if I'm able," she said.

"He's made his bed, he can lie in it," said Filmore. "Your priority is to keep safe. Don't wait until the last minute to get to the shelter."

"About that, I was hoping to bring in Warren and David to the shelter at the high school. Is that OK?"

"I thought they'd be long gone."

"It's Warren we're talking about."

"Good point. Of course they can go, but ideally you all need to be there before midday."

"Lieutenant," said Laurie, hanging up before heading out to Warren's.

◆ ◆ ◆

Laurie was going against the traffic as she headed toward Warren's house. The water had breached the seawall, and she feared it wouldn't be long before parts of the road were unpassable. Driving inland off the Termini-San Luis Pass Road, it was like heading into a ghost town. All the windows on the stilted beach houses were boarded, the garage doors sealed shut. Only a few vehicles remained in the area, one of which was the truck parked outside Warren's house. Despite which, the house felt abandoned as she climbed the steps to the front door, and Laurie was half surprised when David opened it.

"I've got you two places at the high school shelter," she said, not waiting for a response before stepping through the doors.

Inside, it was as if Warren had been preparing for the end of the world. The sitting room was stacked high with provisions, and the gun cupboard was unlocked, Warren busy cleaning an AR-15.

"You going to war, Warren?"

"Can't be too careful," he said.

Laurie repeated what she'd told David, but Warren didn't budge. "Ike never got me," he said. "This one won't either."

"This could be twice as bad as Ike," she said, sitting down next to him, the springs of the sofa soft and yielding.

"We're in no danger here. Too far inland."

Laurie couldn't hide her incredulousness. "Your house isn't hurricane-proof, Warren. You're surrounded by water, for heaven's sake."

"Won't reach this high," said Warren, his focus on his gun.

"David, will you talk some sense into your grandad?"

David lifted his hands in mock surrender. "Can be no harm in going to the high school," he said, with little conviction.

"That place is little better than here. We'd be cramped up. Horrible conditions. No, I ain't going anywhere."

"Coffee?" said David, nodding toward the kitchen.

Laurie sighed and eased herself up. "This is not over, old man," she said, retreating to the kitchen and leaving Warren with his guns.

"I've been trying to talk him out of this all night," said David, handing her a coffee.

It felt reckless to be sitting around drinking coffee as if nothing momentous was going on outside. "Your whole family is stubborn as hell," said Laurie, regretting the words the second they left her mouth.

"And what does that mean? Frank staying put too?"

"Tried to talk him out of it. If this damn hurricane hits, I don't think he'll survive." Laurie studied her husband's reaction to this, searching, but not finding, a hint of concern for his father.

"You not going to arrest him?"

Maybe he was concerned and the question was his way of expressing it. Or maybe she was reaching again for something that wasn't there.

"I would if I could. We're waiting on forensics results, but they'll almost certainly be delayed."

"You think he killed that girl?"

"I don't honestly know. Do you?"

David drank his coffee as if she hadn't asked the question. Laurie knew it was the wrong time, but she couldn't hold back any

220

longer. Who knew what today would bring? It may well be nothing, but if she didn't ask him now, then maybe she would never find out. "I saw you with Rebecca Whitehead," she said, the relief from finally saying the words dizzying.

David froze, except for his eyes darting up to her. "What do you mean, you saw us?"

"What do you think I mean, David? What do you need to tell me?"

David's face was blank, his mouth wide open like he was trying to catch flies. He'd been hard to read those months after Milly died. He'd broken down now and then, but most of the time he'd remained composed, unflappable even. "I don't have anything to tell, Laurie. Is this why you've been off with me these last few months?"

"Months?" said Laurie. "I only saw you the other week. At the coffee house over in the Strand."

"Is that so? Well, either way, you've been off these last few months."

"So, you've been fucking her all that time?" Laurie felt her heart beating against her rib cage. She couldn't quite believe it had come to this, but there was no turning back.

She couldn't tell if David was angry or disappointed as he took another sip of coffee.

"I haven't been fucking anyone," he said.

"Well, we sure as hell haven't."

David moved toward her, his hand held out tentatively. Laurie shrugged it away as if it were posing her some threat. He frowned and took a step back. "I started going to that group," he said.

Laurie felt her patience fading. She hated not being in control, but couldn't bring herself back. "Group? What group?"

"The parents' group," said David softly. "The baby loss group. I told you about it, but you weren't interested."

Laurie's heart rate began to slow. She recalled David mentioning something about a support group some time last year, but hadn't been able to face the idea of attending. "What has that got to do with Rebecca?"

David pursed his lips, as if disappointed in her. "There's nothing between me and Rebecca. She's just part of the group. She's gone through what we went through, Laurie. I had no one else to talk to. I tried to talk to you, but you always changed the subject. I lost her too, you know."

Laurie lowered her eyes. It wasn't quite how she remembered things. She'd tried to talk to David on a number of occasions, but maybe she hadn't been as open as she'd imagined. One thing she couldn't deny was that David had suffered as much as she had, and maybe she'd lost sight of that at some point. "I know you did, David."

"I swear, nothing has happened. In fact, I'd like you to meet Rebecca. She's a lovely woman and she's really helped me. She could help you too."

This time, Laurie let David place his hand on her arm, before grabbing him close. "I've been stupid," she said, allowing him to embrace her, breathing in his familiar scent.

"We've both been stupid. I should have told you where I was going. We shouldn't have secrets."

"You're right," said Laurie, taking one more sniff of David's sweater before pulling free. "What say we get Warren, and get the hell out of here? Once this hurricane is over, we can maybe both be stupid together, for a change?"

David smiled, and hugged her once more. "Sounds like a plan," he said.

Chapter Thirty-Five

It was another hour before they finally convinced Warren he had to leave, the Weather Channel swinging his decision. Even the most optimistic forecaster couldn't deny that Hurricane Heather was going to make landfall, and the satellite images alone—the swirling mass of white and gray, hovering within touching distance of Galveston—were enough to make Warren grudgingly pack a bag.

That didn't stop the former police chief sulking like a petulant child as Laurie drove his pickup truck, filled to the brim with provisions, to the makeshift shelter at the high school. As Galveston was usually a mandatory evacuation area during hurricanes, no official shelters had even been designed for the island. Only essential staff were supposed to remain. Contracts had been struck with hotels to offer such essential staff accommodation, and a last-minute decision had been made to use the local high school to accommodate more staff and equipment.

Anyone left who was still considering fleeing the island had now given up. Water was spilling over Seawall Boulevard. Laurie eased the truck through the deluge, David following behind in their car. The world felt like it was on pause, the road all but empty, and although Laurie still held on to the faint hope that the storm would either weaken or change course at the last minute, as had happened many times in the past, part of her just wanted it to arrive so they could be done with it once and for all.

The high school was situated on Avenue O, and although it was inland it was, like most of the island, less than a mile from the water. The surrounding field with the athletics track was filled with emergency vehicles and equipment, and the school building swarming with emergency personnel.

Laurie nodded to acquaintances as she walked Warren and David to one of the school halls, where cots had been arranged for the essential workers. The three of them secured a bunk each, before David walked her to the door.

She was still coming to terms with what David had told her. She had no other option at present than to take what he had said at face value. If it was a lie, then it was one hell of a bit of theater. No. She knew in her heart that he was telling the truth. In her grief, and self-induced isolation, she'd sometimes forgotten what David had also been going through. He'd remained strong during those terrible months following Milly's stillbirth. Instead of trying to help him, and therefore herself, she'd buried her emotions away, had fed them to her obsessive exercise routine. She'd been selfish, and if David had fallen into Rebecca Whitehead's arms, then who could have blamed him? She recalled the times he'd asked her to go to the group and she'd refused. She'd thought the pain would be too hard to face, but it seemed she'd been wrong about that, as she'd been wrong about so many things of late.

"What can I do to help?" asked David, as they stood in the corridor, both still a little awkward with one another.

"The best thing you can do is keep Warren safe . . . and out of mischief," she said, pleased when he smiled. "I'll make this up to you," she added.

"Make what up to me? You haven't done anything. I should have been clearer about what was going on. I could have told you about Rebecca, but . . ."

"I wouldn't have listened."

David continued smiling.

"Listen, I'll be back soon. I need to catch up on some work."

David nodded, and it was harder than she expected to walk away from him. In truth, she didn't really need to be on the island. If there were any active criminals in town, then they would be risking their lives staying here. Sandra Harrington, Tilly Moorfield, and Mia Washington had all left Galveston, as had everyone else involved in the Grace Harrington investigation except Frank and his brother.

All she could really do now was tie up a few loose ends, then wait for Heather to make landfall and help deal with the consequences. If she'd wanted to bring Frank in, then she should have done so yesterday evening. Yet, unable to get the investigation off her mind, she made one last call to the forensic center in Houston.

"I thought you'd be long gone by now," said the operative who answered.

"Should be. Somehow, I've found myself volunteering to stay. Any news for me?"

"Hold tight, you're on my to-call list. This place is like a goddamn ghost town right now. Let me see, Grace Harrington . . . Yes, some news for you, just came in the last hour. I'll email the full details now, but looks positive. Some DNA profile was discovered on the body of Grace Harrington. Nothing from either parent, but some matching Mia Washington, and, more importantly, a strong match for Frank Randall."

Chapter Thirty-Six

Laurie couldn't wait for the email from the forensic center. Ideally, she would have liked to obtain an arrest warrant, but that wasn't likely to happen this side of the hurricane. Fortunately, the presence of Frank's DNA profile being found on the body of Grace Harrington was enough probable cause to justify his arrest without a warrant. She called Lieutenant Filmore to confirm, but his phone was either switched off or he had no signal.

It was risky going alone, but she had no option. Although Heather had yet to make landfall, the storm was already battering the west end of the island. All available personnel were tied up either preparing for the storm or helping those who hadn't evacuated. Even if she wanted to, she couldn't justify taking someone with her. Instead, she called in to dispatch, which was now working from a remote center in Austin, and headed to Frank Randall's place.

The dirty gray sky appeared lower than she'd ever seen it. The rough sea was spewing onto Seawall Boulevard, which would soon be unpassable, the water threatening to seep further inshore as the wind increased its ferocity. If this was pre-hurricane, what would happen when Heather finally hit? One thing was for sure, she needed to be back at the high school by the time it did.

As she made slow progress to Frank's, she acknowledged how disappointed she was with the forensic report. Hard as she tried, there was no explaining how Frank's DNA profile could've been found on Grace's body. They hadn't known one other and from what she'd been told, it seemed to be conclusive. If she was being brutally honest with herself, it shouldn't have come as a surprise. She had been wrong about so much recently, and in retrospect, she'd been hoping for the impossible. She'd wanted Frank to be innocent because of David and Milly, even for Frank himself, whom she'd grown to like over the last few months. Now, it seemed like that was a great mistake, and that Frank had manipulated her from the beginning. Jim Burnell had always told her that the most logical explanation was usually correct, something both Warren and Filmore had tried to tell her from the beginning. Grace dying in the same way as Annie Randall, weeks after Frank's release from prison, could have only meant one thing and she'd been wrong to focus so much energy elsewhere.

Searching for a patch of elevated dry land to park her car, she decided it was too late for recriminations. All that would be determined when, *if*, they got through this. For now, the important thing was to detain Frank Randall.

Changing into her waterproof boots, she radioed in her location and made her way to Frank's house, noting his truck was not parked in its usual spot. He was fortunate that his building was higher above sea level than most, though if there was a storm surge there was a risk he would soon be stranded.

Hindsight was useless, but she cursed herself for not arresting Frank yesterday. Neil Mosley had talked a good game, but she doubted arresting Frank would have had any bearing on a successful prosecution—especially not now they had the new forensic evidence. Not that it mattered. All she cared about now was arresting Frank and getting back to the shelter as soon as she could.

As she passed the tree where she'd watched Warren deliver a punch squarely to Frank's jaw, she noticed that the door to the house was wide open and swinging in the breeze, hitting the door frame with some force, over and over. It was enough for her to remove her firearm. Chances were high that Frank had already left—Laurie had issued an APB on him before leaving the shelter—but she wasn't about to take any chances, especially now that she knew what he was capable of.

In any other situation like this, she would have waited for a backup, but backup wasn't arriving anytime soon.

"Frank," she called, creeping nearer, not wanting to risk taking him by surprise. "Frank, are you here? It's Laurie. Everything OK?" she said, edging closer, checking her surroundings as she moved, the creaking and banging of the door carrying over the shrieking of the wind until, finally reaching it, she wedged it open with her foot.

"Frank, are you in here?" She waited for the count of ten before entering, the gun held out in front of her as she secured the area. The rooms were empty.

It appeared Frank had left without packing. The duffel bag he'd carried back from prison was still on top of the wardrobe, and a cursory glance through his stuff suggested all his clothes were still here. *Maybe he's gone to his brother's house*, thought Laurie, cursing as she first tried her radio, which only returned static, and then the phone, which had no signal.

Securing the front door, she made her way around the house to the rear of the property, the gun still held out in front of her. She didn't think Frank could successfully run from this, storm or no storm, but then again, she hadn't thought him capable of killing Grace.

As she reached the backyard, she stopped in her tracks, reaching for her useless radio at the sight of the man on the ground. At first, she thought it was Frank who was face down in the mud, but as she approached she noticed the gray hair of the victim, who, like Annie and Grace, had been placed on his side, his limbs manipulated into that strange, all too familiar running position.

Pulling on sterile gloves, Laurie did her duty and checked the pulse of Pastor Maurice Randall, not needing the feel of his cold skin, only the telltale sign of the zigzag laceration across his neck, to tell her that he'd been dead for some time.

Chapter Thirty-Seven

Randall hadn't had time to ask the man the question that had been on his lips before he was struck a crushing blow to the head. As the floor rushed up to meet him, he nonetheless had time for a final glimpse of his lifeless brother, his neck sliced open, and who, like Annie, had suffered the indignity of being mutilated in death, his legs snapped at the knee and placed in that weird, striding position. His last thoughts after having met the floorboards were to wonder how he had slept through such an attack, then to decide it didn't matter. Maurice was gone now and he wouldn't be long behind.

His presumption now he'd regained consciousness was that he was in the trunk of his abductor's car—a thought more palatable than the other possibility that presented itself to him: that he'd been placed prematurely into his coffin. It was difficult to be sure of anything at the moment, but he appeared to be moving—occasional rays of light were leaking into the musty interior. At some point the engine had stopped, and the rocking motion within the trunk had suggested they were crossing water, but he couldn't be sure that hadn't been a dream. All he could be certain of was that he was cramped into a fetal position, the ache in his knee in a steady competition with his bruised temple, and that the pain that had been sending him in and out of consciousness for an indeterminable time period was now so intense he tried to will himself back into oblivion.

The vehicle moved over rough terrain, and Randall groaned as he was jolted from side to side, his knee crashing into something hard and metallic. His cheeks were wet with tears. He'd endured so much over the last sixteen years that it surprised him his current situation would be capable of bringing him to tears. He'd cried for Annie and David, of course, but when he'd entered Texas State Penitentiary, he'd learned quickly that he had to turn that part of himself off. Prison was no place for tears. He'd trained himself out of it, and until now he'd maintained that discipline. He tried to fight the memories but they came rushing at him. Somehow, they always started with Annie leaving that day. What he wouldn't give to reach out and touch her, to tell her not to go. But go she had, and she'd never returned. Randall had made so many mistakes over the years but that was the worst. It was why he was cramped up in this makeshift coffin, why he'd spent a good part of his life in prison, and why his son didn't talk to him.

Be true to yourself, goddamn it.

The car stopped. As the engine stuttered to rest, Randall prepared for the worst. He didn't fear death anymore. He'd contemplated taking his own life on more than one occasion, so that he could be with Annie again. But he did fear pain, and the killer had demonstrated an aptitude for that. He was old—far older than his years—and frail, his body as weak as his mind. Inside, he'd been able to deal with the physical and mental demands placed on him, but he was so tired now. His resolve had all but disappeared, and as the trunk opened and the killer looked down on him, he prayed that the man would be quick and merciful in his actions.

"I need you to meet someone," said the killer, seizing two fistfuls of his jacket and yanking him from the truck like a bale of straw.

Randall had been correct about them crossing water. He'd been here many times before when he'd been courting Sadie. They were on the Bolivar Peninsula to the east of Galveston, a narrow strip of land surrounded by the gulf on one side and Galveston Bay on the other. It had suffered catastrophic damage during Hurricane Ike; most of its homes had been wiped out. It seemed crazy that the ferry had been running in this weather, but maybe they'd caught the last one; the one that had, by the look of the desolate landscape, taken the remaining inhabitants of the peninsula to Galveston for evacuation.

"Why have you brought me here?" he asked.

"I think you know why," said the killer, grabbing Randall's arms behind his back and securing his wrists together with a zip tie.

Anyone with any sense had left a couple of days before, and the killer didn't need to worry about anyone seeing them as he ushered Randall up a dirt road to a decrepit beach house on stilts. "You remember this place?" said the killer.

The howling wind kicked up sand as Randall was forced onward. It blurred in front of him, stinging his eyes and filling his mouth. If the hurricane hadn't arrived, it was only a matter of time. Of course he recognized the place. He'd been here most days during high school, catching the ferry and walking inland just to spend a few minutes with his then girlfriend, Sadie. "I was told she'd moved," said Randall.

"She did, but she came back here one final time to rest."

Randall didn't like the way the killer said that. He'd always been racked with guilt for leaving Sadie when she'd fallen ill. The condition that had claimed her when she was eighteen would have eventually meant a life of care. Randall had told her he would stay with her whatever the circumstances, and a small part of him had probably even meant it. But when the opportunity had come to leave her, he'd taken it. It had been at her insistence, but he hadn't needed to be asked twice. They'd made love one last time, in the house he was now being forced toward, and he'd never seen her again.

The guilt had stayed with him long after he'd started seeing Annie. She'd understood his guilt and had helped him own it. He'd never forgotten, but had managed to more or less put it behind him before that first letter arrived.

Every step was torturous. The wind seemed to be blowing in all directions at once, and it took the killer's strength to guide them both up the wooden steps to the screen door. An unholy smell greeted them as Randall was pushed through the opening. He fell to the floor and kept his face down, not wanting to look up and see what was waiting for him. He screamed with pain as the killer grabbed hold of his hair and yanked his head back.

"You need to look. To see what you've done."

Randall looked up at the source of the stench. A couple of yards away, still in her wheelchair, sat what he somehow knew to be Sadie's corpse, which, by the state of its pallid skin and yellowed eyes, had been in this condition for a few days.

The killer yanked him up off the floor, a manic smile on his lips. "What do you think, Dad?" he said. "Isn't it nice for us all to be together for once? One, big, happy family."

Chapter Thirty-Eight

Laurie did another sweep of the property, the wind now so powerful that she struggled to keep her balance. She'd sensed the tension between the two Randall brothers, but couldn't understand why Frank would have done this to Maurice—or how he could possibly have carried it out, as fragile as he'd seemed to her. But then, it seemed she'd horribly misjudged him all along.

Returning inside, she was astonished to find bars on her phone. She called Filmore before they disappeared.

Filmore's phone crackled with static. "Laurie?" he shouted down the line. "Hang on, let me try and get some shelter," he added. "That's better. Where are you?"

Laurie explained the situation. "No sign of Frank Randall," she said.

"Listen, Laurie, I don't know if it's hit you, but there has been a storm surge, I've never seen anything like it. I'm on the corner of 46th and Avenue S and it must be two feet here already. If there was ever a time to make a run for it, now would be it. You need to get the hell out of there or you risk getting stranded or worse."

Laurie took a look at her watch, wondering how long she'd been away. "I'm at a murder scene. I can't just leave it."

"Well, CSI isn't going to be with you anytime soon. Everyone's been called in, did you not hear? Maurice Randall will still be there afterward."

"Unless the water gets to the house. I could bring him in?"

"God, no," said Filmore. "You wouldn't be able to reach anywhere to safely keep the body. Take photos and video, and anything else you see that might be relevant, but you need to get the hell out of there as quick as you can. That's an order, Laurie. You understand me?"

"Lieutenant."

Laurie closed the call and looked outside. The thick gray clouds were so low it was as if she could reach out and touch them. She feared what would happen when the storm surge reached Frank's house, but there was no time to dwell on the possibility. Pulling on another pair of sterile gloves, she returned to the crime scene. She'd worked with CSI before, so knew the basics of what they did. She wouldn't be able to take any samples, but knew enough to take the correct photographs of the corpse, which was all but floating on a river of blood. She zoomed in on the deep, ragged mark on Maurice's neck, which appeared to have severed the carotid artery. Videoing the mark, she made a comment suggesting this was the cause of death, before moving downward to capture Maurice's disfigured legs.

She cleaned herself up in the bathroom before taking a final sweep of the house, stopping in Frank's bedroom. Had the man killed his brother and then just upped and left? If he was out there in the wild, chances were high that the hurricane would take him one way or another. But no, his truck was missing. It was feasible that he'd joined the thousands evacuated and had already escaped the island, and possibly the state. This was frustrating for so many reasons, and Laurie wondered if they would ever find out why he'd done what he'd done.

She was about to leave when she caught sight of something beneath one of the pillows on Frank's bed. It was an envelope addressed to Frank. The paper was dry, the ink faded. Putting on another pair of gloves, she took out the letter and began to read.

It was a note to Frank from someone named Sadie, thanking him for some money he'd given her. "I know it must have been hard for you, hearing from me all these years later," she wrote. "I have wanted to write you for so long now. There are so many things I wish I had told you. It's so good to see you're doing well, that you are married and have your son, David. I wish I'd had the chance to meet him."

Who *was* this Sadie, and why was she mentioning David?

"This means so much to me," she went on, "and will help more than you can ever know."

At the bottom, it was signed, "All my love, Sadie x"

Chapter Thirty-Nine

Laurie placed the letter in a waterproof evidence bag before leaving the house. Frank must have been reading it before Maurice was killed, and she wondered at its significance. Something about the styling felt odd, especially the mention of David. Maybe she was reading too much into it, but it was possible the letter had some bearing on recent, and past, events.

It felt wrong leaving Maurice's corpse unattended, but there was nothing for it. The storm attacked her from all angles and almost floated her down the hill toward her vehicle. The lieutenant was right: the storm surge had reached the area, and the dirty seawater was halfway up the tires on her car. Laurie forced her way through the deluge, the blood on her trousers mixing with the mud-brown water as she forced the car door open.

Hurricane Heather had arrived, even if this was its outer limits. Billowy clouds hovered in the sky as rain hailed down on her. Her car was being buffeted from side to side, and she'd only moved a hundred yards before the car lost traction. As it momentarily drifted along the road, it reminded Laurie of driving on black ice. She steered as well as she could, fearing she was going to veer off at any second, before the wheels finally made contact with the tarmac beneath the water.

Filmore had been right about being stranded. The storm surge was building relentlessly, and had she stayed any longer she would have been stuck there with Maurice's corpse for the duration. She'd just picked up her phone to call the lieutenant when the radio crackled to life with a call ordering all rescue personnel to return to their respective shelters and to prepare for the worst. Filmore's phone didn't even ring, and she hoped he'd managed to get to safety.

Making slow progress along the back streets, Laurie glanced at the letter on the passenger seat. She recalled the name Sadie Cornish from the initial investigation, but hadn't realized her significance to Frank. The mention of David's name still confused her. It wouldn't have been difficult for Sadie to find out the name of Frank's child, but it still felt a little odd that she had mentioned him by name. Other questions sprang to mind as the car trundled through the deserted streets. Had Frank left the note out on purpose for someone to find, and to what end? Was it somehow an admission of guilt, or a cry for help? Laurie wasn't one to jump to conclusions, but she had to consider what role this Sadie had had in all the events that had plagued David's family.

The water she was moving through must have been a foot deep now, obliterating any wayfinding assistance but stop signs and mailboxes, which kept popping up where she hadn't expected them to. It was hardly a surprise, then, when her car ground to a halt as the front wheels caught on something beneath the murky water. Laurie looked around at the boarded-up houses, feeling at that moment as if she was the only person left on the island. She put the car in reverse, the front wheels spinning and churning up great, splattering boils of mud and water outside her side window, but the vehicle refused to budge.

"Damn," she screamed. She'd just done the worst thing she could've done—gunned the engine like a panicked tourist as though her aim was to sink her as deeply into the mire as she could.

Water was now nearly level with the handle of the car door. Slamming her hands on the dash, she threw the transmission back into drive and willed herself to slowly advance, let off, then rock it forward again. She repeated this three times, until she had to concede she was fooling herself. The car was going nowhere, at least as a result of anything she could do. Further down the street, a line of three parked vehicles appeared to her to be bobbing in the water. She imagined using the car like a boat and navigating back to the shelter, before dismissing the absurd idea and reluctantly switching off the engine.

Abandoning ship was her only option.

Her heart caught in her mouth as she tried to open the door, only for the rushing water to push back against it. The last-resort idea of leaving through the windows was unappealing and she tried again, forcing the door open so the tepid water leaked into the car. It smelled like it had come directly from the sewage treatment plant, and she held her breath as she forced the door open wide and stepped into the brown liquid, which was now up to her thighs.

She forced herself to remain calm as she locked the car and waded away down the street, which was effectively a river. A trio of green recycling bins bobbed along past her like mini unmanned boats. Her radio buzzed, another group announcement ordering all personnel back to the nearest shelter. Laurie called in her position, if only to place herself on the record. She didn't expect, or want, any sort of rescue effort. She was less than half a mile away now from the high school, and just needed to make steady progress and she would be back to relative safety.

Every step along the newly created river felt unreal. It was like being in a new town, a fantasy version of Galveston where the land was being swallowed up. Smells of ammonia and seaweed accompanied the howling pitch of the wind that ripped at her face, making it difficult to see more than a few yards ahead. The warm, brackish water was getting so high now that she had the absurd notion to swim, or to float on her back, and might have done so if the murkiness hadn't contained so many hidden unknowns. Down Bernardo de Galvez Avenue, the sky looked like an encroaching monster, its black tendrils reaching out in all directions as if attempting to snuff out the light.

Willing herself not to panic, she increased her speed through the deluge. If this was what the island was like this early in the storm, it didn't bear thinking about what it would be like once that beast fully covered it. Dismissing her concerns over the chances of surviving the storm even once she'd reached the high school, she'd just ordered herself to put her back into the task of getting there first, then dealing with the next crisis, when a silver metal garbage can lid frisbeed, whistling, past her ear.

She took a staggering step forward, caught her balance and let loose a choked, hysterical laugh. She'd just begun to turn and check where the lid had gone when something else—maybe another lid—cracked her on the back of the head with a force that launched her face-first into the water.

Chapter Forty

Laurie could taste the saltwater in her mouth. It didn't feel quite real, like those semi-lucid moments of dreaming before you fall fully to sleep. All she knew for sure was that her body was utterly devoid of energy, and she wanted to sleep. She'd felt the same way for months after Milly died. She'd barely left her bed in that time and had tried her best to sleep through every second of the day. It had been David who'd rescued her from that fate, insisting she get some fresh air for both their sakes. That had been when she'd started running. She'd walked to the beach and had been freaked out by the number of people there, so had jogged slowly to the shore. So out of shape had she been from the pregnancy and the weeks of inaction that those two hundred yards, at little more than a fast walk, had left her breathless. But it had made her feel something, so she'd repeated it the next day, this time jogging alongside the water for another few hundred yards. And that had been the start of her obsession. Every time she felt something, she would run, and drown out her thoughts by pushing her body to the limits.

David, she thought, opening her eyes and getting her feet under her in the current. She looked about her at the strange new world, the houses being swallowed by water, and tried to get her bearings. A warm wind attacked her after she fought her way to the surface and spluttered out rancid water. Taking in panicked gulps of air, she took a few steps forward on unsteady feet until a feeling of nausea overtook her and she bent over and vomited into the filthy, fast-moving stream. She closed her eyes to try and drown out the pain in her stomach and head, which was now pulsating in an agonizing rhythm, twice as painful as any migraine she could ever remember having. She winced as she touched the soft tissue where the garbage can lid, or whatever it was, had struck her and wondered how many seconds she'd been out.

Her radio was gone, must have come loose as she'd fallen in the water. She still had her phone, but it now appeared drowned out. Something small and dark whipped past her and she turned around to see an array of objects of all shapes and sizes being driven by the wind, each one a potentially lethal weapon—like the one that had nearly killed her. *God, Laurie. Focus.* She needed shelter before it was too late. Placing her hands over her head to protect her against any other airborne projectiles, she waded on down the street, each step sending shivers of pain through her head and down into the rest of her body.

With the streets engulfed by the storm surge, she now had to navigate purely by the road and shop signs, only the tallest mailboxes in view. The water was slowly consuming everything in its path. It was as if she was the only person left in Galveston, and the island wanted to get rid of her too. It was hard to believe that a couple of days ago she'd run across these same streets, sweating as she'd pounded from one block to the next.

Would there even be a shelter waiting for her? The water was so high that it must have flooded the first floor of the high school. She was sure David and Warren would be OK, but was worried that she'd waited too long to get back. Maybe she should not have gone to find Frank, but then they would never have found the body of Maurice Randall. Although that would be the last thing on the minds of most people, it was hard for her to think of anything

242

else—until her numbed, aching mind fastened on the letter. Again, she considered that she was giving it too much significance, but it felt like a turning point in so many ways. Probabilities were still high that Frank was the killer, but what if he wasn't? What if something had been missed, something concerning Sadie that had been overlooked in the initial investigation? Frank had pleaded his innocence to begin with, so it could be true. She was grasping at straws, but just thinking about the effect it could have on David was enough to drive her forward. It would still be difficult, if not impossible, for father and son to reconcile, but even the possibility that David could have an active relationship with his dad again filled her with such hope. Now all she had to do was reach some form of safety, where she could share the information and investigate more.

What had to be the full body of the raging storm was visible now, the monster clouds swirling and throwing sheets of rain down onto her as the wind spun her in all directions, sending her staggering off balance every few steps. Approaching 44th Street, her hope of reaching the high school was diminished as she saw a number of motor vehicles making their way toward her. Each had been caught in the surge of water, and were floating like eerie vehicular corpses in the makeshift river. The first, a two-door hatchback, meandered toward her, Laurie not knowing which way to turn as it veered off to her left and drifted down 44th as if it were being guided by an invisible presence. The other two—a red minivan and a black Camry or Honda coupe—peeled off in the other direction like they'd both just been called home.

There didn't seem to be a sensible place for Laurie to go. She was fighting the artificial tide, each step harder than the next, as the pain raged in her head. At a point where the road narrowed, two more cars passed her by, the second of which cutting close enough to bump against her shoulder as she crouched and braced against the impact. It nearly sucked her underwater in its whirling wake—as it was, Laurie had to sink mostly into the water and use the momentum to kick herself away.

And there she was, swimming now, the absurdity of her situation intensified by the occasional bobbing vehicles providing a shifting obstacle course. Although swimming wasn't her main form of exercise, her strength was good and her running had given her more stamina than she'd ever had in her life, all of which she was utilizing to its fullest now as she stuck her face into the foul water and stroked and kicked, fighting to establish an every-other-stroke breathing rhythm.

Just when she was feeling more than a match for the current, something traveling in the opposite direction grazed her leg, creating a whirlpool effect that screwed up her cadence. As she treaded water to catch her breath, she caught sight of a dolphin darting away from her down a side street. She almost choked, then realized with a jolt that she'd just lost half a block of progress. She threw herself back into her crawl and reclaimed her rhythm.

The situation both above and beneath the water was now so otherworldly that Laurie began to wonder if the blow to the back of her head had been fatal. The water was a swirling, fetid mess where she could hear her own desperate breathing, but it was fast becoming a refuge from the thrashing devastation above the surface, where nothing behaved in the way it should. The wind spun in unfathomable cross patterns that threatened to lift her into the air and away every time she dared to breach the surface, not to mention the flying objects sizzling just over her head.

Laurie adjusted her system to do all she could to keep her below the maelstrom. Now she took a minimum of six front crawl strokes before she dared to take a breath. She felt like she should be making progress, but more and more it was as if she was treading water, the force of the onrushing tide increasing with every stroke.

Something had to change. Working herself into what passed as an eddy near the road's edge, she tried to kick herself far enough above the surface to survey her surroundings. Only yards away, she caught sight of the top half of a lamppost wagging wildly in the wind. Surely her weight would stabilize it, and she'd be out of the water and could at least catch her breath and figure out her next move. She made it her goal and launched herself toward it, thrashing the water with her strokes and kicks.

She thought of David and Milly as she battled through the water. She needed to give meaning to both their lives, and her surviving this would be her last hope for that. She felt as if she were flying over the water then, and when she looked up, there was the lamppost only a couple of strokes away. Her heart soared, then immediately froze at the sight of an unmoored SUV hurtling through the water toward her at a frightening velocity.

Laurie had seen wildlife freeze in the glare of headlights before. That was precisely how she felt now as she stopped, her arms and legs acting on their own volition and keeping her afloat, as the SUV made its way toward her. There seemed little point in moving one way or another. Time was limited and the trajectory of the SUV was unpredictable. The movement of the vehicle was almost balletic as it danced through the surge of water toward her. Laurie took one final thought of Milly and David, and whispered a wish to the universe that she would see them again, as the SUV crashed into the lamppost and veered off to the side, missing her by inches.

She wasted no time, battling through the water and grabbing hold of the now damaged lamppost as, behind her, the SUV careered into the first-floor windows of a shop and was sucked within.

The bent lamppost was battered, but after some struggle afforded Laurie an unsteady perch. She managed to sit atop it, balanced precariously on the bent, bobbing metal, which threatened to give way at any second and throw her into the swirling water already nipping at her heels.

The monster hurricane was everywhere. Laurie watched the crazy patterns of the thundering rain with hypnotized horror as her body convulsed. Everywhere she looked there appeared to be something that would kill her, be it the wind, the swirling water, or the flying objects that kept shooting past her. From her new perch, she could see that the high school was on the next corner, less than a hundred yards away, but her strength was gone, and the surge seemed twice as strong as before. It now carried its own terrifying new soundtrack—an ungodly throbbing rumble that chilled her more than the water had. She tried to dig out her phone again, as if miracles could happen, but it hadn't survived the last few minutes. *How I'd love to take one last look through my photos*, she thought, as the rumble deepened and its volume swelled.

What the hell? Laurie turned her head toward the sound . . .

And found a boat, just yards away. A powerful, rumbling speedboat, bucking the current and bearing three figures within it.

"No time to be hanging around," came the bellowing voice of one of the figures, torn by the wind.

Not for the first time in the last few minutes, Laurie wondered if she was dreaming as she looked down at a speedboat containing two coastguardsmen and Lieutenant Filmore.

"What say we get the hell out of here?" said Filmore, as one of the guardsmen threw a lifesaver overboard and told Laurie to jump.

Chapter Forty-One

Laurie got a glimpse of her reflection, grimacing as she caught sight of the swelling on the side of her head. She'd spent the last thirty minutes in and out of consciousness as she'd taken the improbable boat ride down toward the high school, where she was currently lying in a makeshift emergency ward.

"Follow the light," said the doctor tending her.

Laurie looked away from the mirror, focusing her eyes on the penlight, the pain in her head now a dull ache.

"Any nausea?"

"Not at the moment."

"OK," he said, sitting up straight and swiping his palm wearily over his face. "I want you to stay here for the next few hours. We'll need to monitor you for a possible concussion."

Laurie tried to push herself up but her arms felt insubstantial. "I need to be—"

"What you need to be doing is resting," said the doctor. "Someone will check in on you every twenty minutes, but please, try to get some sleep."

So disoriented had she been that Laurie hadn't even noticed the IV drip in her arm. She couldn't remember leaving the boat once they'd reached the school or what, if anything, she'd told Filmore.

It didn't matter. What she'd tell him now was that a killer was out on the loose somewhere, and she needed to find him.

She tried to get up again, her body feeling like it was floating above the bed. *Maybe he's here*, she thought as her eyelids began to lower. *What would happen then*, she thought, before finally succumbing to sleep.

◆ ◆ ◆

The smell of coffee roused her sometime later. She looked up from her position on the bed to see David holding a cup, his look a mixture of happiness and concern.

"Is that for me?" said Laurie, not recognizing the dry rasp of her own voice as David sat down next to her on the bed.

David placed his coffee down on the side table. "No, *this* is for you," he said, handing her a cup of water.

She winced as she sipped the tepid liquid.

"Umm, good, huh?" he said.

Actually, it was. She felt herself perking up as the liquid passed down her throat. When she'd finished it, she pushed herself up and looked around at the small cubicle. "What time is it?"

"Ten-thirty p.m."

"How long have I been out?"

"You've been sawing logs for about ten hours."

"Jesus, how did you let this happen?" said Laurie, reaching for the tube stuck in her arm.

David lunged for her hand and held it. "Whoa, cowboy. What are you doing?"

"I need to talk to Warren," she said, grabbing hold of David's arm with her free hand.

"OK," he said, "I can get him, but you need to see the doc first. You've had quite a time of it, Laurie."

"I'm fine."

"You always say that."

Laurie matched her husband's smile. "That might be so, but I need to speak to Warren now."

David shook his head. "I don't understand you sometimes."

"This is about your dad, David."

The lightness in David's eyes died at the mention of his father. "I heard what happened to Maurice."

"I'm not sure it was him, David," she said, realizing as she spoke how absurd it sounded.

David frowned. "What? You don't think Frank killed his brother?"

"I don't know," she said. "I'm not . . . I found some . . . evidence." She couldn't get into it all with him right now, certainly didn't want to tell him about the letter just yet. "That's why I need to talk to Warren."

"What's he got to do with it?"

She sighed. "It goes back to the first murder, something I need to know more about," she said, reaching out for David's hand. "It might even prove that Frank didn't kill your mother."

David pulled his hand free and leaned away from her. He squinted sourly at her. "He sure did some job on you, didn't he?"

"David, please. I'll explain everything. I just need to speak to Warren first."

"Fine," said David, who stood up, his head still shaking. "Maybe one day you'll tell me what the hell happened to you," he added, turning away before she had the chance to respond.

◆ ◆ ◆

Laurie looked at the IV drip, contemplating whether it would be safe to remove it. She felt much better, a newfound clarity washing over her following her sleep. Her resolve now was to find Frank. She was still a police detective and her investigation couldn't simply grind to a halt because of a windstorm. She understood David's misgivings, but she had to figure this the hell out. She owed it to so many people, David included, and she was sure he would understand in the long run. It was unfortunate that it had come to this so soon after they'd started talking about Milly again, but that couldn't be helped. The hurt over Rebecca Whitehead was still fresh, even if David's affair was imagined, but she'd managed to put that to the back of her mind. She hoped David would be able to forgive her in a similar vein, for what she had to do now.

When Warren pulled open the curtain of her cubicle, he looked so wiped out it hurt to look at him. He was usually so particular about his appearance that seeing him in mismatched sweatpants and a sweatshirt, his face dotted with silver-gray stubble, made him look frail and vulnerable. Hell, it made him look his age.

At least he could raise a grin. "You wanted to see me, little lady?" he said, doffing an imaginary hat toward her.

"How's David?" she asked as he eased down on the seat next to her bed.

"He was worried sick about you. We both were. Thought we'd lost you."

"And now?"

"Now, he's a little pissed with you, for whatever reason, but he's still worried. It'll work itself out. More to the point, how are you? Filmore told me what happened. Said he caught you clinging to a lamppost like a drunk who'd got stuck up a tree."

"His words?"

"I embellish." In the glow of her table lamp, it was true that he looked every year of his age. His eyes were sunken, and his skin seemed scored with a fresh field of wrinkles. Still, his eyes radiated the same sense of strength she'd always seen in him. Despite those deep crevices in his skin, it was hard to believe he was some twenty years Frank's senior. Put them side by side, and she would have sworn there was little more than five years between them.

"Is he here? Filmore?"

"Resting up. He took a knock too, rescuing some folks before he found you."

"He tell you about Maurice?"

"Sure did."

Laurie racked her brains, trying to remember what she'd told Filmore, but came up blank. She couldn't recall him telling her anything about another rescue mission. "You think Frank did it?"

"Don't you?"

"I found something," said Laurie, retrieving the letter from the plastic evidence bag, which had been placed with her belongings.

Warren took a deep breath, taking out a pair of reading glasses hooked over the collar of his sweatshirt before looking down at the note.

"I see," he said, once he'd finished.

Laurie could tell by the way he refused to make eye contact with her that the note wasn't a surprise. "You knew about this?"

Warren nodded. "They came to me, asking for advice."

"Sadie was trying to extort them?"

"I wouldn't go that far. She was pestering them for money, but as you can see there was no threat."

"There's something you're not telling me, Warren."

Warren held her gaze, but didn't answer.

"Is this in the original investigation? Jim Burnell's report?"

"I wasn't allowed to get involved in that, you know that."

"He spoke to her, though. Sadie?"

"Yes, but she wasn't a suspect."

"Why's that?"

"She was Randall's high school sweetheart," said Warren. "The girl had some sort of bone-wasting disease. Poor thing ended up in a wheelchair."

"That was verified?"

"You can check the case notes, Laurie. What the hell is this about?"

Laurie's head pounded. Frank must have left the letter there for a reason, but it was hard to think straight at the moment. It was as if she was so desperate for him not to have killed his brother, and not to have been at the center of this from the beginning, that she was looking for things that weren't there. "You sure there's nothing else I should know?"

"Laurie, I don't say this lightly. I love you. You and David both. I wouldn't hide anything from you. You must know that?"

Laurie forced her smile.

"Now get some rest," said Warren.

Laurie waited for him to leave before yanking the IV drip from her vein.

Chapter Forty-Two

Laurie was momentarily dizzy as she got to her feet, refreshing her cup of water before pulling open the curtain. She believed Warren, but wasn't finished with the letter and Sadie Cornish's involvement in Annie Randall's murder.

The rest of the building was surprisingly quiet. She hadn't taken much notice before, but her period in bed had been accompanied by a cacophonous noise of people speaking that reminded her of working at the bullpen back at the station. Now that hubbub had died to a general chatter, and the only people she could see were the other patients in the makeshift hospital corridor.

Rounding the corner, she stepped into the large hall and asked a young man in a fluorescent jacket what was going on.

"We're in the eye of the storm," he said, his voice a dull whisper as if his news deserved the greatest of respect.

Everyone else appeared to be in a similar state of hypnosis, straining their ears as if to better hear the eerie silence that had descended outside. That they were in the eye of the hurricane meant only one thing to Laurie: much worse was still to come. Conscious that she was in a gown, she made her way to the bunk where she'd dumped stuff earlier in the day and changed into jeans, sweatshirt, and sneakers. She didn't know where her coat was so she took David's rain jacket, wondering where he was and if Warren had spoken to him.

Changed, she went in search of Filmore and found him outside in the darkness with a group of other volunteers, staring into the abyss of the eye. Water had settled around the high school like a moat. The air was perfectly calm, as above them the moon shone brightly in the clear night sky, the starry blackness circled by walls of cloud. Laurie pictured the monster with its swirling tendrils she'd glimpsed earlier that day. With the clear sky, it was hard to imagine they were effectively in the belly of that particular beast.

"How're you feeling?" said Filmore, not looking away from the sight.

"I'm fine," she said, though in truth she was suffering a relapse. Her head was pounding, and her legs unsteady, as if she were on a boat.

Filmore turned to her. "You don't look so fine, if you don't mind me saying."

"In these circumstances, I'll let that one slide. Have you spoken to Warren?"

"Not since I arrived. Why?"

Laurie wasn't sure how much she'd told Filmore during the rescue, if anything at all, so relayed everything about what she'd found at Frank's house.

"I know all this, Laurie. You've already told me. What has this got to do with Warren?"

"I'm worried something was overlooked during the initial investigation. Warren knew about this letter but I didn't see it in the report," she said, handing him the evidence bag.

If this was old news to the lieutenant, then he was hiding it well. At first it just confounded him, then he stared at her in disbelief, his hand running through his hair. "Who is this woman?"

"Her name is Sadie Cornish. Apparently, she was Randall's high school sweetheart."

"The name looks familiar."

"Her name is on the interview list from the original investigation, but there was no mention of her asking for money."

"It's not a crime."

"No, but it could be significant. Especially as Frank was reading this letter just before he went missing."

Filmore looked away, up to the walls of cloud circling the island. "That's quite a leap."

"Maybe, maybe not. Either way, we need to find Frank before something else happens."

"You're aware we're standing in the eye of a hurricane that could yet kill us all."

"What can I say, Lieutenant? I'm always working."

Filmore laughed at that. It felt like the extremis of gallows humor, but Laurie was serious about finding Frank. "Do what you have to do, Laurie, but first we need to get everyone inside. Only a fool would be outside now," he said, with an ironic smile.

Laurie helped usher everyone back inside the building. It was hard not to feel false hope in the peace of the eye. How easy it was to believe that this was it, that the worst had passed. The only positive she could think of was that the dirty side of the hurricane had passed through the island first, but now they would have to endure the eye wall from the other side and although she was no meteorologist, she knew things could still get worse.

Laurie hadn't noticed before, but water was leaking through the front doors of the high school. Being inside, she had grown accustomed to the smell, but after her blast of fresh air, the interior of the building was cloying. The school must have been at over three times its capacity and didn't have the facilities to safely contain everyone. The toilets had blocked and the building reeked of excrement, urine, and body odor. It was a stark reminder of how quickly things could change. Accustomed to hurricanes as Galveston was, and even though lessons were always learned, the stark truth was that no amount of preparation, beyond abandoning the island city for good, could fully prepare the place for a hurricane's unpredictability. At least the evacuation process had improved since Rita and Ike, and a greater percentage of the population had left the island in time. But already the hurricane felt more substantial than Ike, and, with the eye hovering over the city now, chances were high that the severe damage Heather had already caused would get much worse.

Laurie had meant what she'd said to Filmore. She needed to find Frank. But that wasn't likely to happen anytime soon. What power they had was coming from the backup generator, and although she had bars on her phone, there was no service. As she made her way to the main hall, she wondered where Frank was now and if he'd managed to get out of Galveston while he still had the chance, or if he'd suffered the same fate as his brother and was lying somewhere in the trophy position.

A buzz of frightened excitement filled the high-ceilinged gymnasium as Laurie moved through the people spread across the floor toward her bunk, which had been taken over by a young family, a girl who couldn't have been any older than eight sleeping in the bed. "Excuse me," whispered Laurie to the girl's mother, retrieving her bag and scanning the room, where eventually she found David and Warren, who'd both also given up their beds and were hunkered down in the corner.

"Mind if I join you?" said Laurie, both men smiling silently at her as she sat down next to David. The proximity of death meant there was no room now for recriminations. David placed his arm around her and she moved into his side, his familiar scent calming her.

As the eye of the storm moved on, Laurie imagined the tendrils of the hurricane reaching down for the island city. Yet, despite the screeching howl of the wind as the hurricane picked up, she somehow found her eyelids drooping, and within seconds she was fast asleep.

Chapter Forty-Three

Randall had stopped trying to free himself. It had been hours since the man who had claimed to be his son had departed. He'd been left chained to half a dozen stout metal rings drilled into wall studs, as the house moaned and creaked in time with the buffeting wind outside. Directly in front of him sat the corpse of his high school love, Sadie Cornish. The man had done a fine job securing her chair in place. Each gust of wind set the creaking chains to work, providing Randall with a new perspective on the woman he hadn't seen in nearly four decades.

Could the killer really be his son? Everything felt so off-kilter nowadays that the man's claim had felt like just another surreal twist in Randall's life. But had he seen a glimpse of David in the man that first time he'd met him? A steeliness in his blue eyes that he'd dismissed, but now felt recognizable. Had Maurice seen it in him, too—even perhaps known about it from the beginning?

Randall was trying his best to fight the growing hysteria, but if the madman who had killed Maurice and kidnapped him was his son, he was also the person to have killed Annie. The thought filled him with a mounting dread, as if poison was slowly filtering into his bloodstream. He'd had no idea, but that was irrelevant. His son had killed his true love, and fitted Randall unequivocally with the blame for her death.

He'd tried to do right by Sadie, but not hard enough. When she'd told him about her diagnosis, he'd proposed to her on the spot, but she'd dismissed him. She'd assured him she didn't mind, and that he should get on with his life, but he'd carried the guilt with him ever since. He'd loved Sadie in the infatuated way of first love, and his proposal, however ill-advised, had been genuine. He'd had no idea that, as the killer had suggested, she'd been pregnant at the time, and had never heard from her again until her circumstances at last grew desperate enough to compel her to write that first letter. If only he'd been more persistent . . .

Feeling his thoughts beginning to loop in on themselves, he tried to shut his mind down. All he could hope for was that it would soon be over. The house he and Sadie were lashed to was on stilts, and Randall could hear the water rumbling beneath them. He'd been in prison during Rita and Ike, but he'd read about the damage the hurricanes had caused and knew it was feasible, if not inevitable, that the storm surge could reach where he was sitting now. He didn't like the idea of a slow, drawn-out death, waiting for the water to rise high enough to drown him, but nothing about the present situation was particularly palatable.

Judging by the condition of her body, Sadie's death must have occurred in the last few days. He hoped to God it had been from natural causes.

Randall had thought about her often over the years. Her life had been undeniably tough, and she'd deserved far more than this final horror. He wondered what type of love the boy—if the killer was her son—had had for his mother. It was clearly twisted, but he hoped that the child had shown Sadie love over the years.

Outside the storm raged, causing the house to shake. Vibrations rattled the walls, and Randall felt it shuffle into his bones.

"Beautiful, isn't it?"

The boy had returned and lurked in the shadows behind Sadie. Such was Randall's fragmented grasp on time and reality, he couldn't be sure if he'd been there all along, and that he'd imagined being alone.

"Why didn't you come and see me? I could have helped you," said Randall, his voice all but lost in the storm's rising bedlam.

"I tried that, Dad, didn't I? And where did that get me?"

Dad sounded alien on the man's tongue, and not only from the sarcasm-laden way he used the word. "What do you mean?"

"I wrote to you, Dad. Those letters weren't from Mom, they were from me. We needed help and you didn't provide it."

"I gave you what I had."

"And I took what I had to take."

"I'm sorry this has happened to you," said Randall.

His son recoiled at this, a look of indecision crossing his face in the gloom of the rickety house. "It's a bit late for that, but I appreciate the sentiment."

"I sort of understand why you killed Annie, but why the others? Why that girl, why Maurice?" said Randall, trying to capitalize on the flash of doubt he'd seen.

"I don't think you understand anything, old man, but let's get you out of here. I don't think this place is going to last much longer."

"What about Sadie?" said Randall, as the man unlocked the chain holding him in place.

"She always loved the view from here," said his son, a faraway look in his eyes.

Randall took one final look at Sadie's corpse, which was facing the wall where he'd been held captive, before he was all but dragged outside into the water. He stumbled and fell headfirst into the murkiness. As his lungs began to fill, he wondered if this was it, before he was dragged back up, hacking and puking filthy saltwater.

Once he'd recovered enough to focus on it, the noise was like nothing he'd ever experienced, as if hundreds of storms were occurring all at once. If it wasn't for the man's hands on his shoulders, he was sure the hurricane would have swept him up from the water and consumed him.

It was hard to make out in the gloom, but strange foreign objects appeared to be floating in the water. The man pushed them on through the warm, swirling water regardless, as if impervious to the dangers that surrounded them on all sides.

"Where are you taking me?" said Randall, but the noise was such that even he couldn't hear the words leave his mouth.

The man—his son—placed his arm across his chest, blocking his path, as an immense object fewer than twenty yards from them cruised past. Randall blinked and saw it was a house, almost fully intact, making a slow procession toward the Gulf of Mexico.

The man placed his mouth to Randall's ear. "There's a sight," he said in what sounded like genuine wonder as the house rolled onward. Then a chuckle escaped him. "Yessir, some days you just feel lucky to be alive, eh, Dad?"

Despite the howl of the storm, it seemed to Randall that it must have begun to abate. The gales were strong, but he doubted they were currently strong enough to do such damage to a house, a position supported by the fact that they were both still alive. Had the worst come and gone? He couldn't tell for sure, but it was possible he'd fallen asleep at one stage. Certainly, the water hadn't been this high when he'd arrived.

The man pushed him onward until at some point they reached dry land. "I'm not sure I can go on much longer," said Randall, collapsing to the ground in the shelter of some damaged cedar elms.

A look of pity formed on the man's face. "We can rest here. I need to see where she goes when she arrives," he said, offering

Randall a flask of what turned out to be water. "I wish it wasn't like this," he added, as Randall drank.

"Did Maurice know?" asked Randall.

"About me? No."

"Did you have to kill him?"

"He wanted to die. I know you do, too."

That much was true. "So why not do it?"

"That time will come," said the man, hoisting him up onto his feet.

"Let that time be now."

"I'm afraid I can't do that. I need her to come first, and then I will have taken everything—well, nearly everything—from him."

Randall stared hard at the man. "What are you talking about? Who will you have taken everything from?"

The man smiled. "My brother, of course."

Chapter Forty-Four

The last few days must have taken a greater toll on Laurie than she'd realized. She'd slept for the duration of the second half of the hurricane, only stirring now and then to adjust her position next to David. She'd woken at dawn, to find David and Warren gone, and joined many of the others outside as Heather had dissipated to see what further damage the hurricane had wrought. The wind was still up, but even a gale force wind felt tame in relation to what had come before. The water had retreated but was still a good couple of feet high, its murky surface skin alive with bugs. The air around them was ripe with sourness.

People congregated outside the shelter, some lining up for emergency rations, others for medical attention. Despite her weariness, Laurie was ready to help with the rescue operations when they began. But first she needed to locate Frank Randall. She thanked the young volunteer handing out water and took three bottles, drinking down one in a single series of gulps before heading back to the main hall to find David and Warren.

Warren had returned to their little area in the corner of the hall, and she bent down into a sitting position and handed him a bottle of water. He looked confused as he sipped, the liquid trickling down the fine points of the gray stubble on his chin.

"I don't want to argue, Warren," she said as he took another sip. "I just need you to tell me about Sadie Cornish."

Warren closed his eyes for the length of one breath, then glanced around the hall, as if he didn't want to be overheard. "I've told you all I know. She left town after high school. Her family used to live over on Bolivar, but they moved to Corpus Christi after Sadie graduated from high school."

"You must know something else. Was there a check on Sadie's family during the investigation? Did Burnell meet her?"

"That I don't know. Everything would be in the file. I wasn't allowed to get involved, as you well know."

"You're telling me you didn't look into it?"

Warren offered her a sly grin. "I didn't know much about her," he said. "I looked into her when Annie told me about the letters. She was a runner at the high school. Middle distance. It was how she ended up being diagnosed. She kept getting injured and they were never sure why."

Laurie let out a sigh. "A runner, like Grace Harrington?"

"Yes," said Warren, momentarily confused, as if he'd never before made the connection.

"Her family?"

"The parents died. That was why she was writing to Frank asking for money, I think."

"But you never spoke to her?"

"Annie died, Laurie. I told Jim about the letters, but a woman in a wheelchair wouldn't quite have been in a position to do those things to Annie, now would she? Anyway, Jim surely checked it all out. You know how professional he was."

Warren was probably right, but she couldn't shake the feeling that Frank had left the letter out for a reason. "Drink that," she said, getting to her feet. "You need something to eat as well."

She found Lieutenant Filmore talking to some workmen outside a pair of lavatories being boarded up down the hall from the gym. Laurie pulled her sweater over her nose against the unholy stench coming from the room.

"How are you doing, Laurie?" said Filmore, his face cemented into a grimace against the smell.

"I need some fresh air, but aside from that I'm fine."

"I could use a break, myself," said Filmore. "Come on." He walked her outside, and for a moment the two of them just filled and emptied and refilled their lungs with comparatively pristine oxygen. "Oh Lord, that's sweet," said Filmore.

He'd get no argument from her.

"We need to get people out of here," he said. "We're way over capacity and people are going to start getting sick."

"Any help coming in?"

Filmore nodded. "The hurricane has moved back out over the gulf and seems to be dissipating. Looks like that part of this is over, anyway."

They both understood that was far from the end of it. Even from the snapshot Laurie had seen outside, she knew the damage to the island was catastrophic. The process of rebuilding would start again, but if it was anything like Ike, it could be days before power and facilities were up and running properly.

"I hate to ask it, but do you have a working radio?"

"Limited numbers," he said, holding up a handheld unit. "You'll get one." Filmore understood her priority and directed her to an office inside the building where a team of operatives were in contact with the outside world. "You can get yourself a replacement phone there, too, if you need one."

David was standing in line to get food as she returned to the building. "You're up, then?" he said, as she approached. "Thought we were going to have to drag you out of there."

Despite their strained relationship over the last few months, Laurie always slept best when David was there. They both hated the time they were forced to spend apart when he was away at work. That she could never rest properly when she was alone was a type of dependency she'd never minded, and it worried her that she'd come so close to losing it.

"I'm going to volunteer to go out with the rescue teams," he said, taking a shuffling step forward in the queue, which appeared to be growing by the second.

"Make sure you come see me before you go," said Laurie.

"You still looking for Frank?" he said, his quiet tone suggesting he wasn't looking for a fight.

"We need to find him."

"I get it, Laurie. I do. Sorry if I've been an ass."

Laurie grabbed his hand. "It's an impossible situation for all of us. We'll get through it," she said, doubting her own words as she walked back into the school, where the first thing she did was place her hand over her nose. The smell in the whole building was close to unbearable now. Little wonder everyone was streaming outside. Sweat prickled her back, and she did her best to breathe through her mouth as she climbed the steps to the main office, where the emergency communication room had been established.

Laurie didn't recognize any of the three people working in the cramped room, which, mercifully, had an open window. She introduced herself before asking for access to their radios. "I need to speak to a colleague in Houston," she said to one of the operatives, a man in his sixties with a silver-gray beard and matching ponytail, who sighed and took the details from her before handing her a burner phone. "We need the radio for emergency contacts at the moment. You can use this for now. Pre-charged."

Laurie stepped out and called Remi, who, true to his word, was working from a station in Houston.

"How y'all dealing with it down there?"

"You're not going to recognize the place, Remi, but it is what it is. I need to find Frank Randall. I've got no Internet and I'm surprised I even got through to you," she said, before informing him about the letter. "See what you can find about Sadie Cornish. Jim Burnell interviewed her during the investigation, but that letter has got me thinking. May be nothing, but why was Frank reading the letter just before Maurice was murdered and he himself disappeared?"

"Understood. I'll be back as soon as I can."

"Anything I can do to help?" said Laurie, returning to the radio room as she waited for Remi to get back to her.

Silver Beard didn't miss a beat, handing her a spare headset. Calls were finding their way in by different means. Rescue groups were spread across the region, including the Coast Guard's boat and helicopter teams. Laurie took the calls as best she could. All she could really do was relay the information on, the rescue teams having to make the tough decisions on what to prioritize.

Remi called ten minutes later. Breathless, he said, "I think I've got the information we need, boss. Sadie Cornish did move to Corpus Christi, but that was forty years ago. But there's more. She had a baby boy around seven months after she left Galveston."

It took Laurie some indeterminable time—ten seconds? a full minute?—to process this information.

"It could be Frank's," she said. "That could explain the DNA profile found on Grace's body."

"Exactly," said Remi, his voice an excited rush. "But that's not all."

"Don't leave me in suspense here, Remi."

"Both Sadie's parents died a few years after Sadie left Galveston. They had kept a small property on Bolivar, which they used to rent out. Sadie returned there with her son."

"Who was the son?"

"The son was called Bill Cornish."

"Was? What, he died?"

"Nope. Changed his name when he was eighteen, before he started at Texas State University, following which he went to law school. We know him, boss. Had him at the station the other night."

"You're kidding."

"Sorry, not this time. Maurice Randall's lawyer, Neil Mosley, used to be Bill Cornish, and I guess if the math is right, he could be Frank Randall's son."

Chapter Forty-Five

Had Laurie seen something of David in Neil Mosley, or was she reimagining the past to fit in with the present? In retrospect, they had similar builds and the same strong blue eyes shared with Frank Randall. But David and Mosley had different mothers and if Frank hadn't managed to recognize his son, then how could she have been expected to?

That was presuming Frank hadn't known that Mosley was his son. From the piecemeal information Remi kept sending her way, Neil Mosley had been representing Maurice Randall since not long after Frank was sentenced for Annie's murder. Again, Laurie had to face the possibility that Frank had been playing her all along. He'd never mentioned Sadie in all the time she'd spent with him, and the fact that David could have an older half-brother was still something she was struggling to come to terms with.

If it was true, how and what she was going to tell David was beyond her at that moment. That his father had hid the information of a brother from him was going to be tough to bear, but what if Annie had known as well? Laurie couldn't imagine the betrayal he would feel at finding that out, and wished that she could somehow protect him from the knowledge. But she was getting ahead of herself. Neil Mosley was definitely someone they needed to find, but for now they had no proof he was related to Frank.

"I'm going to try and get back to the island," said Remi, after he'd provided her with the last known address they had for Sadie Cornish and Mosley, both on the Bolivar Peninsula.

"Don't be ridiculous, Remi. They aren't letting anyone back and you have to look after that family of yours. You would never forgive yourself if Ava went into labor and you were stuck here."

Remi sighed. "I don't want to patronize you, boss, but you will look after yourself, won't you?"

"I'll do my best, Remi."

"It's just that . . . I don't think I have the patience to break in a new partner."

"You're lucky you're in Houston, Detective," said Laurie, with a smile. "Radio in if any more information comes to light," she added, before breaking the connection.

She radioed Filmore on her way back to the main hall, where she searched for Warren and David. The place was emptying, everyone avoiding the cloying atmosphere and the stink inside that seemed only to be intensifying. The majority of people had filtered outside, the atmosphere muted as signs of the hurricane's damage reminded them of what they'd endured. The storm surge had retreated, but all power was still off. In the radio room, Laurie had dealt with numerous cases of people who were stranded or had been stuck inside for the last two days with no power. In many ways, those here were the lucky ones, even if it didn't feel like it now.

Filmore answered and she told him about Neil Mosley. "I want to go to Bolivar," she said.

"Are you crazy? We're taking people off that place at the moment, not putting them back."

"I need to find him. I think Frank Randall is in danger, and he might not be the only one."

"And how are you intending on getting there? Swimming?"

"I'm going to go over with one of the rescue teams. I just need your permission, Lieutenant."

The line went quiet and Laurie imagined Filmore cursing her. "I can't authorize this, Laurie, I'm sorry. Not until conditions have improved and we have a better handle on things."

Laurie had expected the response. She waited for a couple of seconds before replying. "Sorry, Lieutenant, can you repeat?" she said, switching the radio off before he could answer.

◆ ◆ ◆

She found David and Warren two blocks away. Each wearing a fluorescent vest, they were helping clear the debris off the roads and storefronts. The water had retreated but dumped the contents of the homes and businesses it had ravaged in its wake, laced with a thick, slimy coat of mud.

"Didn't think we'd have to go through this again," said David, swiping at the buzzing insects close to his face.

Warren had perked up since she'd seen him earlier in the morning. Back in his usual civilian clothes, a trucker's cap on his head, he'd reclaimed some of his former authority. Still, he failed to meet her eyes as he excused himself so Laurie could speak to David alone.

"Everything OK?" said David, pulling her gently to the side.

"Crime doesn't stop, even for this," said Laurie, accepting his offer of a hug.

"You look ready for action."

Laurie wasn't sure how much to tell him but she needed to be honest. "I need to find Frank. I think he's in trouble."

David's lower lip jutted out, a sign that he was thinking. "Trouble how?"

Laurie took a deep breath before telling him everything she knew. She noticed the little twitches his eyes made as he tried to make sense of the information. "This lawyer guy could be my half-brother?" he said when she'd finished, his eyes darting from side to side as he continued to process what she'd told him.

"I believe so."

"And he wants to kill Frank?"

"I don't know for sure. I think if he'd wanted him dead immediately, he would have killed him when he murdered Maurice."

"And you're sure of this? You don't think Frank is responsible for all of this? From what you said, he didn't think much of Uncle Maurice."

"I can't answer that for sure, David. Too many unanswered questions."

"I'm coming with you," said David, speaking without thought, as if his mind was jumping from scenario to scenario. "How are you getting there?"

Laurie placed her arms around him. "They're trying to stop me from going as it is, David. There's no way they'll let you come too." She squeezed him to her. "I know what I'm doing. I'll find them."

"Frank knew all this time, and never told me?"

"Possibly, but he might not have known either."

"Stay. Wait until this is all over," said David, his voice breaking. "I can't lose you, Laurie. You're all I have. You're all I've ever had."

"I'm coming back, David. I promise," she said, pulling herself away from him while she still had the strength to manage it.

Chapter Forty-Six

Laurie caught a lift on the back of a highway patrolman's motor-cycle through the devastated island to the Coast Guard station. It was slow going, as they had to stop more than once to push the bike through thigh-high water or clear debris blocking the road.

The current estimate was that three-quarters of the island had been flooded, and she saw nothing to make her doubt it. Evidence of the storm surge was everywhere. Along the seawall, parts of the road and sidewalk had been torn up, leaving jagged concrete boulders in their wake. Fallen power and phone lines lay in tangles from toppled poles, and even some of the boarded-up store windows were smashed, the businesses' interiors ripped out and scattered in all directions. The insect-strewn sludge that had been left in the aftermath of the surge brought with it an unholy stench that Laurie knew would only worsen over the coming days. The islanders had been here before and would come through it, but she knew firsthand the financial and emotional toll the storm's fallout would exact on them.

A helicopter was being refueled at the Coast Guard station, and Laurie introduced herself to the pilot, Patrick Markham, with whom she'd spoken earlier, back at the high school shelter.

Patrick was no more enthusiastic regarding her scheme than he'd been on the phone. "My priority is going to be working on rescue calls. You understand that?"

"Of course," said Laurie. "And I'll make myself useful however I can, I promise. I just need to get to Bolivar."

"You're going to be putting yourself in danger. It's probably not as bad over there as during Ike, but anyone fool enough to have stayed is now going to be on fire to leave."

The crossing to the Bolivar Peninsula was usually just under a three-mile journey by ferry, but although the water had calmed since Heather had moved out into the gulf, no boats were currently making the journey. When Ike had struck, Bolivar had taken the brunt of the storm, which had all but decimated parts of the island, including the small beachfront community of Gilchrist. Early indications were that the peninsula hadn't suffered as much this time around, but it had flooded, and many homes had been destroyed.

"I understand," Laurie assured him. "All I need you to do is get me over there and I can do the rest."

"We're going to do another swing over there, but I'm not sure there'll be anywhere easy to land. We rescued a few stragglers from there earlier, but had to use the airlift. You prepared for that?"

"I just need to get on land," said Laurie, checking the address she had for Neil Mosley on the map she'd packed with her.

"Old school," said Patrick, nodding to the map.

"I've been told it's the best way, but then, the guy who told me that is old as dirt."

He grinned. "You don't risk losing signal, I'll say that much for them." He nodded toward the back of the bird. "Grab a seat back there. Leaving in five," he said, placing headphones on as he settled into his seat in the cockpit.

Laurie introduced herself to the two coastguardsmen working the back of the helicopter. The machine was an MH-65 Dolphin specifically outfitted for search and rescue. The guardsmen told her they'd already rescued fifteen people in the last few hours from various parts of Galveston, and had taken a flyby of the peninsula.

The wind was already buffeting the helicopter as the pilot started the propellers. The three guardsmen had flown in earlier that day from Corpus Christi, the small city where Sadie Cornish had moved with her family many years previous. As well as rescuing those stranded by the hurricane, their mission was to document the devastation unleashed by Heather, as evidenced by the compact video camera wielded by one of the guardsmen.

"Ready for takeoff," said Patrick over Laurie's headset, followed immediately thereafter by the helicopter's stomach-lurching leap into the still decidedly unsettled air. "Be prepared, Detective Campbell. It's going to be a rough ride, both up here and down below. Ugly down there."

Laurie had already seen her share of devastation on the ground following Hurricane Ike, but the pilot was right. Below her, Galveston looked like some waterlogged foreign country. The majority of the island was still blanketed by water. Great, tangled piles of debris snarled the roads and many of the beachfront properties on the West End were utterly destroyed.

"Estimates just jumped up to eighty percent of the island being flooded," said Patrick, as he swept the rocking, bouncing copter back east toward the Bolivar Peninsula, scanning for signs of life below as he flew. "Thankfully, most folks had the good sense to get out this time. Look there," he added, pointing to a herd of cattle that had somehow congregated near one of the resorts a little inland. "That's a bunch of lucky hamburger."

As they approached Bolivar, it was clear that most of Highway 87 was still underwater. If Frank and Mosley had made it to the peninsula, they would have had to have done so before the hurricane made landfall. Judging by the flooding and the property damage below them, they would have done very well to have survived the last twenty-four hours.

"You have to wonder why folks would rebuild here after last time," said Patrick, flying low over the waterlogged Crystal Beach Road to the bay side, close to the address they had for Sadie Cornish. "This the area?"

"This is it," said Laurie, staring at the flooded land, which held no sign of life.

"I can't in all good conscience put you down here, Detective, even if I could find somewhere to land. I'd likely be dropping you to your death."

Laurie was tempted to agree. It already looked like a fool's errand, and there was also the fact that Filmore had forbidden her to make the trip. Still, she had no option. "I understand what you're saying, but we have an active, highly agitated killer on the loose down there," she said, still unsure who exactly that was. "Just letting him wander around and go off on somebody else isn't an option for me. Surely there must be somewhere to land."

Patrick shook his head slowly as if she were nuts, but he did appear to be scanning for some solid earth. As it happened, though, it was Laurie who spotted some. "What do you think about that, down there?" she said, leaning forward into the cockpit and pointing down at what seemed to be a clear patch of muddy ground.

"Not much," said Patrick. "That's only about a thimbleful of dirt."

"I don't require much. Dainty little me."

He heaved a sigh as they hovered over it. "Last chance to think it over, ma'am. Your lunatic down there won't be going anywhere."

"Only way to be certain of that is if I get down there."

After grumbling something that got lost in static, Patrick said, "All right, ma'am. Fellas, let's get Detective Campbell prepared." He cranked a look back at her. "You'll have to go down the hard way, I'm afraid."

"Story of my life."

A few minutes later, Laurie was in a harness lashed to one of the coastguardsmen, and the two of them were being lowered to the ground. Deprived of her headset, the world was a madness of noise, what with the racket of the helicopter above them and the high winds pushing them to and fro as the machine battled to hold steady over their target. After maybe two minutes that felt like an hour, the pair settled squarely onto it. Laurie had never been more pleased to sink into ankle-deep mud.

"You sure about this, ma'am?" the guardsman said, detaching her from him and helping her free of the harness.

"Oh, not in the least, Guardsman," she said, "but thanks for all your help, anyway." She slapped him on the shoulder and turned away like she had an immediate plan for where in the hell to go. When she looked back, he was already being lifted up to the helicopter, which hovered for another few minutes before moving off.

Laurie watched the helicopter fade away into the distance, the sound of its whirling blades replaced by the rushing wind, which seemed to highlight her remoteness. If anyone had been foolish enough to have stayed on the peninsula for the hurricane, they were nowhere to be seen. It was as if she was the only person left on the narrow strip of land. Less than a hundred yards away was the swirling sand of the beach. As she glanced toward the gulf, she saw the floating remains of a beach house in the distance. Nearer to shore, a number of motor vehicles bobbed along in the water, some upturned. The muddy patch of land she was standing on felt like the safest place for miles around, and she was stoking up the courage to leave it when a message crackled through on the radio.

"Detective Campbell, where the hell are you?" Lieutenant Filmore's voice was surprisingly clear, considering the still stormy conditions. Laurie gave some serious consideration to ignoring before deciding to answer. She explained where she was, and how she'd got there, and waited for an uncomfortable few seconds for Filmore to answer.

"Have you lost your fucking mind? I told you . . . I *ordered* you not to go after Randall or Mosley. You're risking your career, Laurie, not to mention your life."

"The opportunity arose to get over here and I was unable to reach you, Lieutenant," said Laurie, grimacing at her lie.

"Don't bullshit me, Detective. You have willfully and knowingly disobeyed an order. What the hell are you thinking? You're out there on your own?"

"Lieutenant."

"This is negligent behavior, Laurie," said Filmore, though she noticed his tone was easing. "You shouldn't go after someone like this without backup at the best of times, but now . . ."

"I know the risks, but I can't let Mosley get away," said Laurie, omitting her desire to locate Frank Randall, which was perhaps her greatest priority at that moment.

"It's not too late, Laurie, but I can only give you this last chance. Do you understand me?"

Laurie didn't answer, feeling the weight of the radio in her gloved hand as she considered how she was going to respond to Filmore's likely demand that she return to the mainland.

"You come back now, we can forget this . . . anomaly. You should never have been involved in this investigation, and that's on me. Couple that with the hurricane and let's say *communication* issues, and I can let this slide. But it's official now, Laurie. You're putting yourself, and possibly others, in danger, and I can't have that. Return now or you're suspended from duty."

Laurie thought about the damage heaped upon her family because of Mosley. She needed to understand what had truly happened, for David's sake as well as hers. "Sorry, Lieutenant, reception is terrible here, can you repeat?" she said, placing the radio back in its holster before stepping into the warm, muddy water.

Chapter Forty-Seven

Dressed in her all-weather suit, Laurie waded through the bathwa-
ter-warm, debris-choked water. She stepped carefully, trying not to
think about the snakes and God only knew what other desperate
wildlife that might be lurking in the murk. The radio had power
but she ignored the occasional calls. Her decision was made, and
the consequences would have to be faced. It was a liberating position to be in and helped drive her onward, past an area where the
road appeared to have been lifted, shaken, and dumped back in a
mound of debris.

Sadie Cornish's place was situated off Nelson Avenue, close to
Horseshoe Lake. It was a stilted property, which would already have
been in need of some renovation before the hurricane struck. It now
appeared to be balancing on a carpet of water, like the few other
properties in the vicinity, and Laurie approached with caution.
Although she was pretending the radio wasn't working, she made
sure it was switched on as she waded through the dank water. She
wanted her location to be known and the radio had a GPS tracker.
Filmore had been correct in stating that ordinarily she would need
backup, but this was no ordinary situation. As she crept along the
side of the house, edging glances at its blown-out windows, she
withdrew her firearm and checked the chamber before continuing.

For now, she had to work on the principle that Mosley was the killer, and if he was here and paying attention, she would be an easy target for him.

Creeping along the brushy edges of the property, she cleared its perimeter while keeping a keen eye on the gaping holes where the windows had once been.

The water was still a foot high beneath the stilts and had pooled in the sunken ground of the front yard. The place, like the rest of the peninsula, appeared deserted, but Laurie kept her gun in front of her as she climbed the slimy steps toward the black opening where the front door dangled from its hinges.

She could tell something was off even before she finished crossing the porch and cleared the doorway, then completed a hurried scan of the front room. The water hadn't reached the upper level, but the breeze whipping from one set of glass-free windows to another did little to eliminate the god-awful smell permeating the darkened room. As Laurie's eyes adjusted to the gloom, the source of that smell became obvious. She didn't need to check for a pulse. The woman in the wheelchair had been dead for at least some number of days. Insects swirled around her, and fed busily on the various liquids beneath the chair.

"Mosley? Frank? Are you in here?" she called out toward the back rooms of the small house, to silence.

Had this unfortunate creature once been Sadie Cornish? Laurie moved closer, making a cursory survey for signs of homicide while trying not to contaminate the crime scene. Nothing was immediately apparent. Her skin was a pallid gray, her body limp. Laurie was no expert on such things, but the absence of rigor mortis, and the condition of the body, suggested that the woman had been dead for at least a week, long before the hurricane had struck. Had she died alone, her body left to rot as the island was vacated? Laurie glanced at her neck but couldn't see any knife wound. As she lifted her radio to call the situation in, a sudden swell of wind billowed through the gaping holes on either side of the room, for some reason making her lift her gun.

"I would drop that if I were you," came a familiar voice.

Laurie turned around to see Neil Mosley holding a firearm trained not at her, but at the bound figure of Frank Randall, clutched to his chest like a rag doll. Frank was gagged, his frail body being used as a shield. She had the opportunity for a shot to Mosley's head, but in the gloom it was a risk she couldn't take.

"Last chance," said Mosley, pressing the gun into Frank's skull.

"OK," she said, bending down and placing her gun on the floor.

"Kick it over to me, then lie on the floor with your hands laced behind your head."

Laurie kicked the gun and began to ease slowly to the floor. Now might be the only chance she would have—firing off toward him like a sprinter exploding off the blocks—but Mosley was intensely focused on her. There was nothing for her to do but settle to the floor. He pushed Frank to the side, his gun locked on her as he retrieved her firearm, then swept toward her in two long strides and placed one knee squarely into the small of her back.

"You wouldn't believe the trouble I've had getting you here," he said, dragging her arms back with considerable force and pulling a zip tie tight across her wrists.

"People know I'm here," said Laurie, trying not to show Mosley she was in pain.

"I've no doubt of that, but for the moment, you're very much on your own, Laurie. I saw the Coast Guard drop you off. I knew you would come," he added, standing and pulling her roughly upright in one motion. "Didn't I, Dad? Said she would come, didn't I?"

Frank was slumped on the ground. He glanced over at her, then dropped his eyes again.

"Why are you doing this, Neil?" she asked.

"That's a very complex question. We'd need to have a stenographer handy to take it all down. Your husband know you're here?"

"No, why?"

"It's a shame brother dearest won't get to watch this firsthand, but not to worry, I will record it for prosperity. Now, if you don't mind, we must be going. I have an uninvited guest I need to deal with before we get to the main event."

Chapter Forty-Eight

So that was that, Mosley was David's brother and had been responsible all along. This piece of knowledge had so many potential repercussions that it made her head swim as she watched Mosley place the radio on the lap of his departed mother, before kissing the corpse and ushering Laurie and Frank out of the house.

Laurie was still coming to terms with her situation, Filmore's warning not to go alone ringing in her ears. The zip ties were tight around her wrists and were already digging into her skin. Aside from that, she wasn't injured. She could walk freely enough and Mosley had yet to gag her.

"Neil, how about you take the gag from Frank's mouth?" she said, at the sound of Frank's labored breathing as they stumbled through the long grass at the rear of the property. The landscape conspired to shelter them from the wind here—the first time in what felt like weeks that Laurie could recall being outdoors without being buffeted by it. Frank sounded like he was near death.

"Why not?" said Mosley. "It's not as if anyone can hear us. Isn't that right, Dad?" he added, untying the gag and ripping it from his mouth.

"You OK, Frank?" said Laurie.

Frank nodded. "I'm so sorry," he said, stumbling as he was pushed forward.

"That was your mother? In the chair?" Laurie asked Mosley, who was by her side, pushing Frank ahead of him like an errant child.

"I guess that's why you're a detective."

"How did she die, Neil?"

Mosley opened his mouth to speak, then closed it again. He stopped in his tracks, turning to stare at her. "I hope you're not suggesting anything untoward, Detective?"

When she only met his eyes in silence, he grinned and set the three of them in motion again.

At the back edge of the property, the water deepened and Mosley grabbed hold of Frank, allowing Laurie to make her own way, mosquitoes flying off the rancid water in clouds as they made their slow progress through this becalmed landscape.

"She's been dead for some time," Laurie said.

"She has indeed. Natural causes. It was a wonder she lasted as long as she did, considering the way he refused to help her," said Mosley, pushing Frank forward until he fell face-first into the water.

"Help him," Laurie cried out as she stumbled over to Frank, who was writhing in the water like an eel.

A perplexed look came over Mosley as he absorbed her concern. "Don't worry," he said, lifting Frank from the water with one arm as if he weighed less than air. "There will be a time for Daddy to die, and this isn't it."

A thin, even coat of muddy filth lined Frank's face as he coughed and spluttered, desperate for air. Laurie tried to comfort him but Mosley gave them no time to rest, urging them forward.

"Where are we going?" she asked, checking the sky for any sign of the Coast Guard.

"We're getting out of here," he said, his focus firmly on Frank, who was doing his best to stay upright.

The situation was surreal, the three of them stumbling through the half-drowned wilderness as if they were the last people on Earth. Laurie continued with the questions. She risked trying Mosley's patience, but she got the feeling that he wanted to talk, and she hoped to gather some vital piece of information that would work in her favor.

"You're doing all this because of Frank? You're trying to get back at him. For what, abandoning you?"

"Close, but no cigar."

"I didn't know about you," said Frank, the rasp of his voice so dry it sounded as if he hadn't drunk anything in hours.

"Look, I love a bit of family therapy as much as the next person, but there is a time and a place."

"Frank is your father. You must have some compassion for him."

"He's alive, isn't he?"

"It was you that killed Annie, wasn't it?" asked Laurie, glancing at Frank, who kept his head down as he continued through the water.

"If only they'd had you on the force back then, hey, Detective Campbell? Oh wait, they did. Pretty little thing, weren't you? I can see why my brother was interested. Not that you're not attractive now . . ."

"Enough," Frank snapped, surprising Laurie with the clarity of his voice.

"Oops, sorry, Dad."

"This is all one joke for you, isn't it?" said Frank. "You killed my Annie, and now these other monstrous things you have done. Why?"

"That one is simple, isn't it, Dad? He took you away from me, so I took something from him," said Mosley, the humor fading.

"What do you mean?" asked Laurie.

"What I mean, Detective Campbell, is that your husband, my brother, stole my father. Stole my *life*, while my mother was left to rot in a wheelchair. This rankled. Then it occurred to me I could take the one thing from him he most cherished. His mother." He sighed. "And it worked like a charm, I can tell you."

"But this, you . . . none of it has anything to do with David," said Laurie. "He's only just now found out that you exist."

"I am most savage and unnatural, aren't I?" said Mosley, not missing a step.

"Wasn't it enough that I paid for your crime?" said Frank, the passion in his voice fading.

"Thanks for that, Dad. It gave me all the tingly feelings to see you locked up, it's true. But you didn't even know I existed."

Frank didn't respond, his focus ahead as they moved toward a sheltered dock area where a number of boats had survived the hurricane.

"I must admit, I didn't expect my girl to make it," said Mosley, stopping by a small craft chained in multiple places to the dock. "One hopes, but . . . you know. I haven't always had the best luck." He giggled. "Anyhoo. Let's get you both on board, and then we can see what state she's in. If you don't mind taking those off," he added, nodding down to Laurie's water-proofed walking boots.

"You're not serious? You want me to put on my deck shoes or something?" said Laurie, wiggling her tied arms behind her.

Mosley frowned. "Watch your step," he said, lifting Frank over the side of the boat before gripping Laurie's upper arm and pulling her to the edge of the dock.

"It's not too late," she said as she allowed him to help her on. "Leave me and Frank here, and . . ."

"And what? You'll let me sail off into the sunset? I wasn't born yesterday, and I don't care if I don't live until tomorrow. Tough odds to work against, I know."

Mosley's death wish was apparent. He'd been trying his luck ever since he'd abducted Frank in Galveston. If he had a plan, it was probably vague at best, she figured. And had it not been for the hurricane, he wouldn't have gotten this far. What *was* clear was that his gripe was more with David than Frank. That he had been driven to these actions by a brother who hadn't known of his existence until a few hours ago didn't easily compute. Laurie forced herself to examine it, knowing that what slim chance she and her father-in-law might have of surviving these next few hours—or minutes—probably depended upon figuring out what drove him. He obviously felt deprived of a loving family, so he'd taken David's. Tit for tat; clear enough, heinous as it was. She couldn't see anything she could *do* with this insight, though. David's mom was long dead, and his wife seemed pretty sure to join her unless she worked some kind of miracle here.

What else did she know about Mosley? He'd obviously cared for his mother—albeit a little too much—and had made a reasonable success of his life as an attorney. Maybe she was clutching at straws, but she hadn't given up hope that he could be reasoned with.

Mosley made her step down into the boat's cabin first. The only light inside came from the faint rays of sunshine filtering in from outside. The interior was dank and reeked of body odor. In the shadows, Laurie saw discarded cans of food and juice cartons before alighting on a shape cowering in the corner.

"Our little stowaway," said Mosley, easing Frank down the stairs, his flashlight running over the shape that belonged to Tilly Moorfield.

Chapter Forty-Nine

"I'd ask you to put lifejackets on, but you won't need them," said Mosley, placing the flashlight in the middle of the cabin as he retreated up onto the deck of the boat, locking the doors behind him.

"Tilly, are you OK?" said Laurie, struggling against the zip ties that by now had ripped through the skin on her wrists.

"I think so," said Tilly, her voice the same dry rasp as Frank's.

"We need some water," said Laurie, shuffling over to the girl as the boat's engine rumbled to life.

Illuminated only by the flashlight, Tilly appeared physically unharmed. "What are you doing here?" Laurie asked her, kneeling before her so she could see the girl better.

"I've been stupid. I wanted to see him, I couldn't let him get away with it," she said, nodding toward Frank, who had collapsed on the bench seat opposite. "I thought he was going to escape when the hurricane struck. I stayed outside his place all night, trying to get the courage to speak to him, and then that bastard caught me outside and did this to me."

"I thought you and your father were leaving together," said Laurie. "I haven't heard anything from him, saying you'd gone missing."

Tilly began crying. "He made me show him where I live," she said, in between sobs.

Laurie's heart fell, knowing where this was going.

"He left me in the van," said Tilly, "but I think he killed my dad."

If that was true, then any hope of reasoning with Mosley was surely over. In his twisted mind, he could feel justified in killing Annie, Grace, and Maurice, however nonsensical those reasons were. But how could he possibly justify killing Tilly's father?

"We don't know that, Tilly," said Laurie, shuffling down into a sitting position next to her as the boat began moving. "Let me see your hands," she added, peering down at the red, raw strips on Tilly's wrists as the girl leaned forward.

The boat tossed from side to side as it made its way out to open water. Laurie fought against images forming in her mind of being sealed in a tomb, as the water slapped against the hull of the boat. The motion was rhythmic and soothing in its way and Frank appeared to be drifting to sleep. "We need to get these off," said Laurie, using all the strength in her legs to push herself up, a cramp seizing one hamstring, then flashing into her calf muscle.

She was thinking there had to be something sharp enough to break the zip ties, when the cabin was thrown into darkness. Tilly screamed, waking Frank, who asked where they were.

"We're in the hull of the boat, Frank, and the flashlight just went out. Nothing to be worried about."

Leaning up against the small metallic sink, Laurie devoted herself to working the zip tie against the counter, though each movement sent shivers of pain through her. Even if she did manage to get free, the doors were sealed and she was growing increasingly worried that Mosley planned to abandon them in this floating grave, which wouldn't last long against the elements.

"What's that?" said Tilly, as above them the familiar, deep, tight rhythm of churning blades reached them.

"Coast Guard chopper," said Laurie, picturing Patrick and his colleagues hovering above the boat, checking with Mosley that he was safe.

Tilly started screaming and Laurie waited for the sound to ease before telling her she was wasting her breath. They couldn't possibly be heard, and there was nothing to arouse suspicion about Mosley's boat. It wouldn't be the only one out on the gulf on this day after the storm, and even if it was registered to him, she doubted he'd left any identifiable marks on its hull. She hadn't seen a name on the hull, and the color and style of the boat were similar to hundreds of small pleasure craft she'd seen out on the gulf before. Maybe Mosley would arouse the suspicion of the Coast Guard enough for them to send out a boat to check on him, but there was so much going on just now that it felt unlikely.

The sound of the helicopter faded and Tilly began crying as Mosley throttled back on the boat's engine. Laurie worked frantically on her ties, but she couldn't get any purchase on the work surface. Her actions only made the pain that much more acute.

She sat down next to Frank as the door was opened, a blinding shaft of light filling the interior of the cabin as, outside, seagulls squawked and danced in the air.

"I'm afraid your friends are gone," said Mosley, skipping down the steps to the cabin, jumping the last with an elaborate flourish. "But they might be back any time, so we need to get this over with. On your feet. Here, let me help you, old man."

"That's your father," said Laurie, as if somehow in all the chaos of the last weeks Mosley had forgotten.

"I would say in name only, but he didn't even give me that, did he?" said Mosley, lifting Frank once more with considerable ease and guiding him to the deck.

"Follow what I do," said Laurie under her breath as Tilly got to her feet. She didn't know if she said it for her own benefit, or the girl's. She didn't yet have any plan, but she had to remain hopeful that one chance, however small, would present itself.

After the darkness of the cabin, the glare of the sun was blinding as they reached the deck. Squinting against it, Laurie joined Frank, who was standing precariously near the rear gunwale. Mosley was at the other end, his phone pointed at Frank as if he was lining up a photoshoot.

"At least let us have some water," said Laurie, as Tilly struggled through the opening and joined them, her eyes half closed against the sun.

Mosley took three swift strides to reach them, grabbed Frank with lightning speed and cut his bindings. The old man cried out in pain as he lifted his hands in front of him and checked out the red, raw damage to his wrists.

Mosley stepped back. "Won't want to get any saltwater on that," he said, laughing to himself as he took his phone back out and pointed it at them. "There's water in that container by your feet," he added, pointing to a white box next to Laurie.

"Can you reach that, Frank?" said Laurie.

Frank nodded, groaning as he bent down and retrieved a bottle from the box. He unscrewed the cap and offered it to Laurie. "You first, then Tilly," said Laurie, her throat crying out for the liquid.

"Isn't this nice?" said Mosley, as Frank drank heavily before bringing the bottle to Tilly's, then Laurie's, lips. "When you've finished playing happy families," he added, grabbing the now empty bottle from Frank.

This was the opportunity she had been waiting for. Her hands were tied behind her but she had the element of surprise on her side. Bending into a crouch, she ran headfirst into Mosley's midsection, the muscles of her legs groaning with effort as she drove him, staggering backward, toward the edge of the boat.

Mosley had been knocked off balance but managed to grab hold of the gunwale. Both Tilly and Frank joined in the effort, pushing at Laurie's back, but it all proved to be to no avail. Mosley was unnaturally strong, and fought back, springing himself up and forcing the makeshift rugby scrum back until the three of them were in a heap on the floor, panting and defeated, at his feet.

Chapter Fifty

The helicopter was nowhere in sight, the boat alone in the water. They appeared to still be in Galveston Bay, the devastated peninsula visible in the distance.

"Now, that wasn't nice," said Mosley, who'd gone back to recording them on his phone's camera.

"Why are you doing this?" said Laurie, still gasping for breath after the failed attempt to push him overboard.

"We've been through that, Detective, haven't we?" Mosley sounded disappointed in her, as if the line of questioning was tiresome to him. He began speaking into his phone. "Do you hear that, David? Up until the last minute, she wanted to know why. But *you* know why, don't you, David? You stole my life and it's taken me a hell of a long time, let me tell you, but I am about to finally steal yours. The wheel has come full circle. I've taken your mother, and now your father and wife. After that, we will call it even. You can get on with your life and, if I survive this, I will get on with mine."

Their only hope now was a return of the helicopter or a rescue boat. For that to have any chance of succeeding, Laurie had to keep him talking. "I understand that, Neil. You're right, you've been over it. But what about the others—Grace and Maurice?"

"You don't know the half about Uncle Maurice," said Mosley, with a sneer. "I've been representing him for all these years, remember. The man is a pervert. It's been only me and the blind eye of that make-believe sect he's latched on to that's kept him out of prison."

"So he deserved to die?" said Laurie.

"Hell, yes, he did."

"And Grace?"

Something approaching serenity crossed Mosley's face at the mention of Grace. "My, she was a beauty. You like to run, Laurie, don't you? I've watched you. It's not your fault, but you're graceless. You get the job done, but that is what it is to you, isn't it—a job? You stampede your way through to the end. It's the same when you walk. Must be those thick legs of yours. No lightness, no *finesse*."

Laurie had no idea what he was talking about, but willed him to continue. "OK. But what does any of that have to do with killing Grace?"

"I'm getting there. You're in a hurry?" He tittered, then sighed. "Young Grace. Grace was like a gazelle. In the way she ran, and the way she walked. Funny thing is, your wife was like that too," said Mosley, pointing the phone's camera toward Frank, who was shaking next to Laurie. "A beautiful woman. She used to mesmerize me when I would watch her. Grace was the closest I had ever seen to her, and that was why."

"I still don't see why that meant she had to die," Laurie said. "You're not making—"

"My mother was a runner, though I never got the pleasure of seeing her run." Mosley fingered the phone as though zooming in on Frank. "Had a type, huh, Dad? I get that. I do. That's my inheritance from you, maybe, because that's my type, too. Very much my—"

"Your mother used to run?" said Laurie, as she felt a movement behind her. Tilly, struggling to slip something in her back pocket. Mosley had turned the camera on her again and Laurie kept looking intently into it, at Mosley, willing him to focus on her as she accepted Tilly's object.

"I wished I'd been able to see her, just the once," said Mosley dreamily. "But she told me about her races, how she would glide along the track."

"You think she would like what you're doing?"

The look of serenity vanished. "OK," he barked, "all of you up, sit on the side of the boat, facing the water. Do it. Or I'll just start heaving you in the drink, starting with the little crying girl." He chuckled at that, as though it were funny. "You're going to love this, David," said Mosley, as he filmed Frank helping Laurie and Tilly to their feet, and onto the side of the boat.

Laurie was now furthest away from Mosley, her body angled to hide the object she'd retrieved from her pocket. "You don't have to do this," she said, as Mosley stepped toward them, pulling out a hunting knife as he did so, before unceremoniously pushing Frank into the choppy water.

Tilly cried out and the old man's startled yelp was abruptly cut off.

"Hope you're a good swimmer, Dad," Mosley called down to him, filming Frank as he bobbed and spluttered in the brackish, oily-looking surf.

"He won't survive," said Laurie.

"Well, duh. None of you will, and David will get to see it," said Mosley, pocketing the phone then roughly cutting Tilly's zip tie and sending her in after Frank. She disappeared without a sound.

"And now, finally, *you*, Detective." Mosley grinned at her. "I guess you would have been my sister in a way?" he said, wrenching her around and cutting her zip tie.

"Don't," said Laurie, but she was already falling into the water.

Two years ago, she had completed a lifesaving course. The key, she knew, was not to panic. Laurie had managed to jam the object firmly back in her pocket before breaking the surface. A smiling Mosley was waiting for her, camera in hand.

Treading water, she saw that Frank was panicking, thrashing at the surface, while Tilly kept getting sucked beneath the water. "Tilly, move," she said, swimming to Frank. "You must calm down," she said to the man, as he struck out and pushed her beneath the waves.

"On your back," she said to them both when she returned to the surface. "We can float. It's saltwater," she said, ignoring Mosley's grinning face, which was almost close enough to touch.

After a panicked start, Tilly was now on her back, her breathing labored as she tried to keep afloat.

"Who will go first?" said Mosley, as Laurie continued trying to calm Frank, whose teeth were now madly chattering despite the warmth of the water.

"Come on, Frank, get on your back and use small movements to keep yourself afloat. Like this," said Laurie, going onto her back to demonstrate. They couldn't last long this way, but she needed Frank composed before she tried anything. "That's it," she said, as Frank began controlling his breathing and floated onto his back.

"This must be hard, seeing them go out this way," said Mosley as Laurie fought her way into her back pocket and extracted what Tilly had passed along to her. She'd recognized the object the second she held it in her hand: a mini flare launcher. She'd used them on the same training course where she'd learned the lifesaving procedures. Pen-shaped, it was less powerful than a flare gun, but could send a flare a hundred and fifty feet in the air. Now Laurie had to decide whether she should fire the flare into the air or aim it straight at Mosley, still hovering over the edge of the boat, happily recording their last minutes.

The flare would alert Patrick and his colleagues if they happened to spot it, but at what cost? Mosley had a gun, and was close enough to get in three fatal shots before fleeing the area. Even if Mosley decided not to shoot them, any rescue attempt would probably take too long to be successful.

So, then. Decision made.

Weariness spread through Laurie's body. Soon, exhaustion would take all of them down. She fumbled in her pocket, trying not to alert Mosley to her intentions. She would only get one opportunity. It was unlikely the flare would be fatal, but if it hit Mosley in the chest it could give her enough time to try to board the boat.

Arranging the mini flare launcher into the correct position, she found the trigger switch and prepared herself. Mosley had been focused primarily on Frank, no doubt—and probably correctly—figuring he'd be the first to go down.

She needed Mosley fully facing her to give her the broadest possible target.

"Let them back on the boat," she yelled over the sound of the sea and wind. "It's me you want to hurt, isn't it? David doesn't even speak to his father, and he doesn't know Tilly."

"It's too late for that, but do keep fighting."

It had worked: he'd shifted to face her. Laurie understood the rough childhood Mosley must have experienced. She hadn't been able to check, but with Sadie's parents passing away, it was likely that Mosley had been his mother's primary caregiver for much of his childhood. That must have been tough, and she could understand his resentment, but the mind behind the brutal murders of Annie, Grace, and Maurice, and now this, had been twisted beyond comprehension. Not that it mattered. Three lives were at risk and she was justified in her actions. She floated closer to Mosley, smiled for the camera, raised the flare launcher, took aim and fired.

Mosley lifted his camera phone up so he could see her eyes. The flare hadn't activated. "Good try, Laurie. David will be so proud," he said, training the camera on her as if nothing had happened.

Chapter Fifty-One

Laurie's body was shutting down. Ever since her ill-fated attempt to fire the flare at Mosley, her energy had dwindled. She'd spent the last few minutes offering encouragement to Tilly and Frank, but now it all seemed like wasted breath. She didn't have long left and her thoughts turned to David and Milly.

She wasn't religious, and the things she'd seen both personally and professionally meant she was unable to believe in some overseeing deity, at least not a compassionate one, but she still had hope that death would bring her closer in some unfathomable way to Milly.

For now, it was David she worried for. The last year had been hard, and had grown worse these last few weeks—the pressures of Frank returning, the death of Grace Harrington, and Laurie's suspicions about Rebecca Whitehead making things so toxic between them that they almost hadn't been together during the hurricane. She was pleased they'd finally managed to speak about Milly, but Laurie couldn't imagine how David was going to cope going forward. If there was some sort of God, she prayed to him now that David would never get to see the video Mosley was recording. She wasn't sure if watching it would be something he could ever recover from. But even that thought was hard to dwell on as exhaustion made every action a struggle. All she could hope was that David would forgive her for being so distant this last year.

◆ ◆ ◆

Randall looked up at the clouds and wondered if he was dead. Although bone-weary, he could see that his hands and feet were making elaborate patterns in the choppy waters. It seemed like only yesterday he'd been on that Greyhound from Houston, returning to Galveston for the first time without Annie.

A fugue had crept over him in these last few weeks. A memory that had started to fade during his period inside was now warped. It played tricks on him and it was impossible to know what was real. Instinctively, he understood he was fighting for his life in the unforgiving water, but he wasn't sure why. Maurice returning into his life had been a dream, one that had morphed into a nightmare, if his last memories of him were anything to go by. Could it really be that he had been killed in the same gruesome manner as Annie? And was the madman shouting nonsense from the boat really his son?

That last thought brought unwelcome clarity to Randall's thoughts. His mind worked that way sometimes, and had rewarded him now with a perfect snapshot of what he'd done and why he was here.

Annie. Every time he thought of her now, she was walking away from him, gliding toward the gulf on the shore of which she was ultimately killed by his son. If only he could stretch through time, reach out and tell her not to go. But regrets were pointless. He'd made so many mistakes. If that man on the boat was truly his son, then in some ways Randall had to take the blame. He'd tried to help Sadie, and would have done more if he'd known about Mosley. He guessed he'd paid his penance for that particular mistake, whether it was his fault or not, but that was obviously not enough. This man, this monster, he had created hadn't been satisfied with that, and Randall didn't know what would ever appease him.

But no. He thought maybe he did know.

Maybe he deserved to die, but the others didn't.

It was time to go.

Hopefully, watching him die would be enough for his son to show mercy on Laurie and the young woman. His energy was all but spent anyway, and the warm water felt welcoming, as if it were beckoning him toward Annie. He took one last breath and was about to sink beneath the waves when a piercing screeching sound, like metal on metal, stopped him.

Laurie didn't realize until it happened—the violent, shrieking sound of the boat ramming against something lurking just beneath the surface of the water—how peaceful she'd been in those final moments. It was as if her acceptance of what was happening had switched everything off, and for the briefest moment she'd been one with the water.

That had all vanished the second the screeching-metal sound ripped the world in two. It felt like someone had jabbed her with a shot of adrenaline directly into her heart. Had she not been in the water, she would have leaped to her feet. As it was, she rolled onto her front in time to see Mosley launched, pinwheeling, from the boat and vanish under the water.

With no time to consider what had struck the vessel, she began swimming toward Mosley. "Get Frank to the boat," she yelled to Tilly, then left her two companions fighting the water.

She'd marked the point where Mosley had disappeared below the surface and churned toward it.

With any luck, he'd been struck in his head when he'd fallen. Only now did she notice that the boat was tilted precariously, seemingly caught on something. She'd just sent Tilly and Frank toward it. But it didn't appear to be taking on water, and making for it was their best, their only option.

Reaching the spot where Mosley had hit the water, Laurie treaded water in circles next to where he had gone under. Did he just sink to the bottom? Should she join Tilly and Frank at the boat? She fought to raise herself high enough from the water to locate them. There they were, swimming—toward *her*, not the boat—as though in slow motion.

She'd just decided to turn one more full revolution, had just mouthed "Where are you?", when Mosley erupted to the surface right beside her, spluttering and coughing. Laurie wasted no time. It was hard to get any purchase in the water but she began raining blows down on the man. She didn't know if he still had the gun but she didn't care. Mosley had proved his strength before, and most of hers had faded during her time overboard. If she didn't stop the fight before it started, then Mosley would have more than enough power to drown her and probably Frank and Tilly, too.

The blows didn't seem like they were landing. Mosley wasn't reacting. He was still spluttering water, a manic smile on his face as the surrounding area began turning red. Laurie looked beneath the maroon-tinged seawater to see a metal rod protruding from Mosley's gut—the source of the blood. He noticed her looking and reached his arms around her body. His strength was undeniable. Even in the water, with what should be a fatal injury to his body, his grip was still vice-like.

"I've enjoyed this, Laurie." He said this in a conversational, almost intimate tone. "Who knows, under different circumstances, we could have got along," he said, as his weight dragged them beneath the surface.

300

Mosley's eyes were still open underwater as Laurie bucked against him, trying to wriggle free of his grasp. The manic smile was painted on his face and Laurie refused to allow that to be the last thing she ever saw. She tried to relax, breathing out and willing her body to go limp. She thought of the hundreds of runs she'd completed since Milly had died. So many times she'd felt just like this, her lungs fit to burst from the effort of staying in motion, but she'd continued. She could outlast Mosley, she was sure of that, as long as she didn't panic.

As if Mosley recognized her resolve, he held on even tighter, but even so she sensed his strength fading. She wriggled in his arms, trying not to exert herself too much, and found her hand resting on the metal rod. Mosley's eyes opened wide and she pushed down on the bar with all her might, Mosley offering her a silent, bubbling scream as his arms loosened.

He tried to grab on to her as she kicked for the surface—she felt his right hand brushing her ankle—but she was too strong for him. Above her, she could make out the orange circle of the life preserver and she kept going, with that her only focus.

Breaking the surface, she gasped out for the salt-tinged air and used the last of her strength to clamber onto the life preserver. Above her, the Coast Guard helicopter hovered, one of the team already descending toward the weirdly angled boat where, clinging to each other on the edge, waves lapping at them, were Frank and Tilly.

Chapter Fifty-Two

Laurie looked straight ahead, her leg jigging in anticipation. After Mosley's body had been fished from the sea, Frank and Tilly had been flown to Houston, where they were both recovering. Laurie had insisted on returning to Galveston, and was now sitting in the back of a patrol car. Every time she closed her eyes, she felt like she was back on the sea, or worse, within it. She could see Mosley's unworldly grin as he grabbed her under the surface, and it was hard to believe that he was gone; harder still to believe he could ever be related to David.

Galveston was still a ghost town as the car made its way to Tilly's house. The mayor was still only letting emergency personnel back onto the island for the next two days, as rescue and salvage crews ground away at the work that would consume them for weeks to come. The place was still littered with debris. Power was down, the island covered in a thick layer of sludge, a combination of silt and raw sewage that swarmed with great black clouds of mosquitoes.

The number of bodies being discovered in Galveston and the Bolivar Peninsula was so far very low, but Laurie feared that was about to change.

Remi had managed to get back onto the island and was driving, Lieutenant Filmore in the passenger seat, as they approached the Moorfield house, which had not yet been visited by the salvage crews. Filmore had tried to stop her from coming, but after what she'd gone through with Frank and Tilly, she felt she had to be the one to do this.

The storm surge had reached over ten feet in this neighborhood, judging by the tide marks visible on the stone walls. It was hard to see the extent of the damage the water had caused inside the buildings, but Filmore was able to break in the Moorfields' door with a single, easy blow with his boot's heel. Although the corpse of Mosley was secure in the Harris County morgue, the three of them had their firearms out, Remi shining a flashlight as they stepped into the house.

Water had seeped in and had left its mark before retreating, a carpet of insect-patterned mud coating the floor. They moved upstairs, past pictures of Tilly with her father. Twisted as they were, Laurie understood Mosley's motives in his killing of Annie Randall. With Grace and Maurice, the picture was less clear. It seemed that Grace reminded him to some extent of his mother, and that Mosley had some fetish to do with legs, perhaps springing from caring for his chairbound mother for so many years? That was a charitable interpretation. Tilly and her father, though, were surely just collateral damage.

Tilly had been in the wrong place at the wrong time, and Mosley seemed to have just taken her along on a whim, or as a distraction.

It was wishful thinking, but as she opened the door to the master bedroom on the first floor, Laurie still hoped that Tilly's father wouldn't be there.

But she was disappointed.

Steven Moorfield was tied to a chair that had toppled over onto the floor. Laurie lowered her gun and moved toward him.

She honestly couldn't believe it—would never be able to believe it, looking back—when she touched his neck and felt a faint pulse. "He's alive," she shouted, as Tilly's father opened his eyes.

Epilogue

Six Months Later

With the sun gleaming on the Gulf of Mexico, the beaches spotted with sunseekers, it was easy to think that the city island had returned to normality. But, like every time a hurricane hit the area, life would never be the same again.

As had happened following Hurricane Ike, the town had started rebuilding, but many islanders had decided enough was enough and left the place for good. Billions were being spent on assisted funding for building repairs, but sometimes it was hard not to wonder if the money could be best spent elsewhere. The boosters' argument was that the island had endured storms since the great one of 1900, and had always survived and come back stronger, but Laurie wondered if that was really true. Each storm brought with it a destructive legacy all its own, she believed, and every time they built the island back up, they knew that sooner or later it would be knocked down again.

But she wasn't a policymaker and it wasn't as if they could abandon the island and start again somewhere else. With global warming, Galveston would always be at risk, but so were many other places. Safe havens seemed in swiftly diminishing supply, if indeed they'd ever really existed.

"You OK?" she said to David, who was staring out of the passenger window of their car as they made their way along Seawall Boulevard.

The last few months had been rough on him. The revelations about Mosley being his half-brother had hit the national news. He'd struggled to come to terms with the fact that a half-brother he'd never known had killed his mother, uncle, and Grace Harrington, and that the father he'd always thought was guilty had gone to prison for no reason.

Tilly's father had survived, and along with Tilly had left the island for Texas City. Laurie had spoken to Tilly last week. She too was slowly recovering from her ordeal, and was planning to study marine biology in Austin come September. Laurie had also spoken to Sandra Harrington a few times since the hurricane struck. She'd also relocated and was trying to rebuild her life alone on the outskirts of Dallas.

An investigation had been launched into the Annie Randall case, but with Jim Burnell long in his grave it was doubtful there would be any repercussions for Mosley having not been identified as a suspect. Warren had pored over what information they had, but the written case notes from the time had only recorded a one-way conversation between Burnell and Sadie Cornish. If Sadie's son had been mentioned, Burnell hadn't recorded it and had taken that failure to his grave.

Laurie made the turn to Frank's house and paused to check again with David that he was all right. This was the fourth time he'd met up with his estranged father, and things were getting both easier and more difficult. David was beginning to wrap his head around the whole situation, but Frank's condition was such that it wasn't always easy to talk things through. After he'd recovered from his hypothermia scare, Frank had been diagnosed with Alzheimer's. It was believed that he'd probably been suffering from it since his time in prison. He had good days and bad days. Most of the time he was lucid, but every now and then it was as if he disappeared right in front of them.

They parked and Laurie walked with David toward the tree where, just a few months ago, she'd witnessed Warren attack her father-in-law. Frank was waiting for them on the porch, sitting with a coffee in his hand. "Laurie, David, so glad you could make it," he said, getting up before they had a chance to stop him.

On days like these, it was difficult to imagine he had Alzheimer's. He grimaced as he stretched out his bad leg, but he looked well. Laurie had been making sure he was eating properly, and he'd put on a few pounds since the hurricane, giving shape to his once gaunt face. "Come on in," he said, "I have some more coffee going."

Despite its elevation, the house hadn't missed the flooding. Laurie had arranged for a team to clear out the place before Frank's return, but it still retained its place-out-of-time quality. She glanced over at the pictures like she did every time she came here, the photos of Frank, David, and Annie now telling a different, still achingly painful, yet truer story than before.

Frank made them lunch and though she sensed David's reserve—he might always call his dad by his first name—Laurie thought things were nonetheless better than the last time, which had been better than the time before that.

"Here," said Frank, as they were about to leave. Dusk was falling, and the peaceful sound of birdsong rang through the air. "I was going through some of the stuff they salvaged after the storm, and I found this. You remember this, David? I took this of you both. We were so proud of you that day." It was a picture of David's

306

graduation, of David arm in arm with his mother, a few years before Annie's death.

"Thank you," said David, taking the frame from Frank, before giving him the briefest of hugs goodbye.

◆　◆　◆

Laurie marveled at the shape of her legs as she cycled along the seawall. Would she always be such a perpetual work in progress? She'd cut down on the exercise these last few weeks, and already her legs felt slenderer, the muscle still there but no longer dominating as once it had. It was heartbreaking passing the boarded-up shops and restaurants, devastating when those places were missing completely, empty spaces or ruined foundations in their wake. She turned from such thoughts and focused on her momentum, gaining speed until all she could think about was the rush of the cooling breeze she created.

Things were better than ever with David, but she still needed these times of being alone, her only concern the power of her body as she drove herself on.

She pulled up outside their apartment thirty minutes later. They'd been fortunate that the apartment had been above the water level of the surge, but even here, reminders of the hurricane were everywhere. It clung to the building with its restored windows and shiny new gutters, and appeared to hang in the air as if reminding Galveston's citizens that it wasn't over; that for them, it would never truly be over.

Checking her watch as she sprinted up the stairs, she realized she would have to shower quickly. They were due at the meeting in forty minutes. She'd started attending the weekly gatherings once they'd resumed, and had even, red-faced, met Rebecca Whitehead. At first, she'd felt out of place in the group, but hearing the other stories of families who'd endured the pain of child loss had, in its own melancholy way, brought her to a better understanding of what had happened to her and David. So much so that last week she'd spoken for the first time in front of the group. The experience had been so cathartic that it was hard now to imagine what had stopped her in the first place.

"Hey, sweaty," said David, kissing her on the cheek the second she opened the door.

"Hey, yourself."

"Look," he said, thrusting his phone in her face.

"Give me a sec," she said, taking a step back as she focused on the screen.

After a lot of soul searching, they'd decided together that they didn't want to try directly for a baby again. Many in the group had already given birth after their first stillborn experience, but the chance of it happening again was something she wasn't prepared to face. But that hadn't stopped them looking at other avenues.

"Next week?" she said, her vision wavering, then blurring altogether until she backhanded the tear away.

The message on the phone was from an adoption agency who wanted to interview them.

"It's hard not to get too excited," said David, grabbing her. "But dammit, it's too late."

It was just the first step on a long road, but Laurie agreed with her husband. She gave him another hug, giggling as she pulled away in her sweaty clothes, and skipped to the bathroom to shower.

ACKNOWLEDGEMENTS

Huge thanks to everyone who has contributed in some way to *The Running Girls*.

The wonderful team at Thomas & Mercer: the book's editor, Leodora Darlington, for her help in shaping the story, Jenni Davis for the perfect copy-edits, Sadie Mayne for her detailed proofreading, Tom Sanderson for his beautiful cover, Nicole Wagner for all her behind-the-scenes assistance, Dan Griffin and all the marketing team for helping the books reach as wide an audience as possible, and Sammia Hamer for pulling everything together at the end.

My wonderful development editor, David Downing, for his invaluable help in shaping the story. It truly wouldn't be the same book without his input.

Alexia Capsomidis for her early readthrough and feedback.

My Texan family and friends, in particular Beth and Warren Eardley, for their early feedback and notes on Galveston and the surrounding area.

To Herbie for his cameo.

To Alison, Freya, and Hamish for being my inspiration.

And finally, to the wonderful people of Galveston. I hope I did your wonderful island city justice in the writing of *The Running Girls*. The book was written out of love, and I look forward to visiting you again soon.

ABOUT THE AUTHOR

Photo © 2019 Lisa Visser

Following his law degree, where he developed an interest in criminal law, Matt Brolly completed his Masters in Creative Writing at Glasgow University. He is the bestselling author of the DI Louise Blackwell novels, the DCI Lambert crime novels, the Lynch and Rose thriller *The Controller*, and the acclaimed near-future crime novel *Zero*. Matt lives in London with his wife and their two children. You can find out more about him at www.mattbrolly.com or by following him on Twitter: @MattBrollyUK

Follow the Author on Amazon

If you enjoyed this book, follow Matt Brolly on Amazon to be notified when he releases a new book!

To do this, please follow these instructions:

Desktop:

1) Search for the author's name on Amazon or in the Amazon App.
2) Click on the author's name to arrive on their Amazon page.
3) Click the "Follow" button.

Mobile and Tablet:

1) Search for the author's name on Amazon or in the Amazon App.
2) Click on one of the author's books.
3) Click on the author's name to arrive on their Amazon page.
4) Click the "Follow" button.

Kindle eReader and Kindle App:

If you enjoyed this book on a Kindle eReader or in the Kindle App, you will find the author "Follow" button after the last page.